HIS 1–800 WIFE

Jarrod's knuckles touched her sweater's collar. Catherine jerked, as if he'd shocked her. He looked into her eyes. Dark as the African continent, they smoldered. Jarrod grew warm, his body tightening in places that felt good. Cathy made him feel good.

He pulled on her collar and her head moved closer to his. Jarrod felt her breath on his mouth. He smelled the light fragrance she often wore—that underlying scent that made him want to growl—along with the champagne. He saw her eyelids droop, then close. Barely an inch separated them. He moved to eliminate the separation.

"No," Catherine said, turning away from him.

Jarrod took a deep breath and let it out in a whoosh that emptied his lungs. She was in his arms, her head on his shoulder, his arms around her. He could feel her body vibrating. He should let her go, but he didn't want to. This was what she did to him. She'd bring him to the brink and then set a limit.

HIS 1-800 WIFE

Shirley Hailstock

ARABESQUE

BET BOOKS

BET Publications, LLC

ARABESQUE BOOKS are published by

BET Publications, LLC
c/o BET BOOKS
One BET Plaza
1900 W Place NE
Washington, D.C. 20018-1211

All Kensington Titles, Imprints, and Distributed Lines are available at special quantity discounts for bulk purchases for sales promotions, premiums, fund-raising, and educational or institutional use. Special book excerpts or customized printings can also be created to fit specific needs. For details, write or phone the office of the Kensington special sales manager: Kensington Publishing Corp., 850 Third Avenue, New York, NY 10022, attn: Special Sales Department

0-7394-1729-0

Printed in the United States of America

To Jim and Nikoo McGoldrick,
for their friendship

ACKNOWLEDGMENTS

To Jim and Nikoo McGoldrick, who write as May McGoldrick. They lived in Newport, Rhode Island. While on my research trip to this wonderful playground of the rich and the super-rich, they kept in contact with me daily through E-mails, telling me places I must see and restaurants that had the most delicious food on earth. Thank you.

Chapter 1

1–800–WIFE. Catherine listened to her disguised voice on the special line she'd had installed when she came up with the plan. *Are your parents constantly pushing you to get married?* "Of course they are," she said out loud. "I'm not the only one this happens to." She applied mascara to her eyes as she dressed for another of her sister Audrey's parties. Sometimes she thought Audrey only gave these parties to set her up on another blind date. *Does every conversation with them begin and end with examples of the joys of marriage?* "You guessed it, honey." *Well, so do mine. So if you're interested in details about ending that conversation, tell me about yourself. And don't forget to leave your phone number. I'll get back to you.*

She heard the beep. The caller hung up. Catherine went to the machine and pressed the PLAY button. Frankly, it surprised her, the number of calls she received on the newly installed line. The first message started as she returned to her dressing routine. He hung up. The second did the same. The third caller started speaking. "Uh, my name's, uh . . ."

Catherine stared at her reflection in the mirror. It was an afternoon party; more than a picnic, less than a reception. All camouflage, she thought. She picked up the blush brush and added a few strokes to her cheeks, blending the color in an upward sweep.

The message ended, and a beep indicated another. Catherine had become adept at screening calls from the sound of his voice and the message a man left about himself. She'd placed one ad in the PERSONALS section of the newspaper, and the phone rang at all times of the day and night. A few crank calls came across the line, but most of them were genuine, men looking for meaningful relationships. That told her a lot about the state of marriage in America, or at least in Rhode Island, but she wasn't researching a graduate school thesis, and a life mate wasn't on her agenda either. She'd tried that route once. It hadn't worked. Her idea was better.

She'd risked her heart on one undeserving man. She would never do it again. She wanted six months, nothing more, nothing less.

Another male voice stammered for a start, interrupting her thoughts. Catherine usually rejected the stammerers. She wanted a man who was sure of himself; someone she could present to her family and have them believe him and their charade. She listened as he went into his story, which she knew would last longer than the tape allowed.

Catherine stepped into her tight black dress, pulling it up from the floor. The fabric hugged her skin, clinging to it like a thick coat of paint. Stopping six inches above her knees, it would surely surprise her sister. Her married sister, she reminded herself. Flat shoes would be perfect, but Catherine put on her heels anyway. They added height and made the dress look even shorter. Man-hunter, she thought as she smiled into the full-length mirror. She donned the hat that only a character from *Hello, Dolly* should wear and started for the bedroom door when she heard the last beep.

"Catherine Carson." She froze. "It's wonderful to hear your voice, disguised as it is." Someone knew her name. "I thought you said you would never marry?" The voice had a smile in it, a mischievous sound that said he was well acquainted with her. She whipped around and stared at the machine. Who was he? His voice had a slight accent that didn't fit New England. She kept staring at the machine, unable to move, wanting him to continue so she could discover his identity. The final long beep came, signaling that was the last message.

Catherine's throat was as dry as parchment. She wanted more. Who was that? She recognized the voice. Closing her eyes, she tried to place it. Quickly she crossed the room and hit the REWIND button. She stopped the machine at the last message and played it again. This was someone she knew, someone who knew her. Why couldn't she remember? Again she closed her eyes and tried to picture every man she knew with rough, sexy voices that reminded her of sunrise and mist on the summer ocean.

Catherine suddenly shook herself. What was wrong with her? She hadn't had feelings like that since— She stopped. She wasn't going there. The engagement had been years ago. He was married now, and even if he wasn't, Catherine wasn't in the market for a man with no foundation for commitment.

Fifteen minutes later, as she entered what she called her sister's palatial mansion, she was still thinking about that voice.

Audrey, two years younger than Catherine, had married her high school sweetheart, but not right out of school. Not until he'd made a fortune that could keep her in the princess style she wanted. She had it now—a fifteen-room house with a large yard, a pool, a tennis court, a solarium, and an outdoor Jacuzzi. Like their mother, Audrey thought every woman should be married. Catherine felt betrayed by her sibling.

She didn't immediately see Audrey, so she went through the house toward the solarium. The huge open room brought the outdoors inside, especially in winter. The walls were completely made of glass. Panes six feet high and six feet wide extended upward twenty feet, allowing light to nourish the jungle of plants that hung, sat, and decorated the room with many varieties and colors. The wall in front of her was movable, folding open like an accordion. Audrey had insisted they install it when she took the house. Beyond it was the veranda and sprawling yard. Tables with blue cloths and white napkins dotted the yard. Between and around them people stood in ridiculous hats talking and laughing. Catherine scanned the crowd.

"There you are." She turned to find her sister behind her. Audrey looked her up and down. Catherine turned completely around, parading up and down several feet, as if she were a runway model showing off the latest fashion. Audrey shook her head. "Mom's going to have a fit, but the hat's nice." They both made faces. "I've got someone for you to meet."

Catherine groaned. "Not already," she complained. "I just got here. You can't be pushing me toward a man before I've had a drink."

"Catherine, you don't drink."

"Today's a good day to start."

Audrey dragged her along. At the solarium door she stopped. "Look who's here."

Catherine stared across the lawn. The last man she expected to see stood smiling down at Emily Colter, Julianna Stone, Meredith Windsor, and Terry Burditt. Jarrod Greene had been her mortal enemy since she could remember. He'd spent the last five years in England. An architect by profession, he'd grown up next door, often playing practical jokes on Catherine, embarrassing her when she tried to impress someone, especially if that someone was male, and showing up at the most inopportune times. Like now!

"What's *he* doing here?" She frowned.

"He got back three days ago."

"Three whole days, Audrey." Catherine raised an eyebrow and cut her eyes accusingly at her sister. "And he's already at one of your parties. That's got to be a record."

"Catherine." Audrey used their mother's tone. "I know you and Jarrod always fought, but he's a different man now."

Catherine doubted it, judging by the harem surrounding him. He probably couldn't walk down the street without people leaving their houses to have a word with him. Women followed him around like

dogs in heat. Why should she think anything had
changed?

She looked at Julianna Stone. The expression on
her face was priceless, rapture under a flapper's hat.
Terry Burditt fluttered her eyelashes so often, Catherine thought she had something in her eye. Emily
and Meredith had the same ridiculous looks on their
faces. Catherine swore she'd never look at him as if
honey dripped from his lips and she were only there
to lap it up.

"I suppose he's still single?" Catherine crossed her
arms as she turned to her sister, putting Jarrod
Greene's gorgeous body out of her line of sight.

"Isn't that wonderful?" Audrey's surprised expression could rival that of someone discovering the cure
for cancer. "Why don't you go over and reacquaint
yourself?"

"I'd rather eat spiders," Catherine said dryly. She
took a step, intent on returning to the house, when
his voice stopped her.

"Catherine Carson. It's wonderful to hear your
voice again."

It was him! The voice from her answering machine.
The one she'd recognized but couldn't place. Jarrod's
voice, that odd English accent underlying his own,
was unmistakable. Catherine felt frozen to the spot.
He knew. Oh, God! She clenched her teeth. Knowing
Jarrod, he'd never let her live it down. He knew about
her, about her search for a husband. How? He'd only
been back in Rhode Island for three days and already
he'd discovered her secret. She turned back slowly,
her smile fixed, ready for that razor-sharp tongue of
his to announce to all within hearing range that she
was the woman behind 1–800–WIFE.

"Jarrod, what a surprise. It's good to see you again."

"I like the hat."

Catherine couldn't help looking up at the wide brim. She frowned, knowing she could use the hat as an umbrella if it rained. It wasn't her kind of hat. She'd chosen it for that reason, but she wouldn't have if she'd known Jarrod was going to be here. She was sure he'd find something to say to embarrass her. But Audrey had themes to her parties, and today's was the Mad Hatter. The hat was part of her statement, although Audrey seemed to take it as a joke. Standing before Jarrod, she wanted to hide under it.

"Excuse me, Jarrod. Welcome home. I'm sorry I can't stay longer. I have another engagement and I really have to go."

"Catherine, you've just arrived," Audrey said.

"And we haven't had time to fight yet," Jarrod added.

She threw him a look that could freeze water. "Jarrod, I don't want to fight with you."

"Ah," he said, "if we don't fight, marriage would be our only other option."

Her whole body went cold, then immediately afterward blood rushed through her system, generating a furnace of heat. She could hear his voice on her answering machine. He was baiting her.

"That would be a real disaster." Catherine turned and walked away. For some reason Jarrod brought out the worst in her. She needed to escape. She was almost at the door before Jarrod caught her.

"Don't leave on account of me."

Catherine turned back. She raised her eyes slowly and took all of him in. "Still at it, aren't you, Jarrod?"

"Still at what?"

"Still here to bait me, belittle me, embarrass me. Don't you want to trip me as I pass the dessert table so I can fall into the cake?"

"Catherine, that was an accident. I didn't know you were behind me."

"Sure you didn't." It was Amanda Fedders's fourteenth birthday party. Catherine had spent half the day dressing for it. She wanted to impress Gregory Lewis, who had spoken to her only three times the entire school year. Catherine had just arrived. She carried a huge box with Amanda's present inside it, one of the large stuffed bears they were all collecting that year. Jarrod and Billy Fedders came running around the table just as she reached it. His foot caught hers, and into the table she went, pushing it over and going over with it. Her dress flew up, she crushed the box, icing covered her face and hands, and Gregory Lewis stood laughing at her with the rest of the party. She never spoke to him again. And she should never have spoken to Jarrod either.

The memory still made her face burn. She swung around and headed for the door.

Jarrod caught her arm. Catherine stopped, her eyes darting from the place his hand touched her arm to his face. He dropped his hand. It had been warm on her flesh. She felt coldness take the place where he'd touched her. A sudden feeling she couldn't identify washed up her arm. Catherine wanted to put her hand over it. It wasn't unpleasant, as she would have thought. It was the first time Jarrod had touched her and caused something other than pain. She was unsure why this unfamiliar sensation, both prickly and soft, should result from his hand around her arm.

"If you leave, I'll feel I drove you away."

"It's not you, Jarrod. Despite what my sister may have told you . . ." Catherine glanced through the room to where Audrey stood in her version of the Jacqueline Kennedy pillbox hat. "I do have a life."

"Just not the one your family wants you to have."

"Is anybody's?" she mumbled, to herself more than to him. She didn't mistake the opening he was giving her, but she wouldn't take it.

"I guess not," he answered. Catherine threw a look at him that said he couldn't possibly understand. No one was constantly trying to marry him off. Then she went on through the door. Jarrod followed her. "Where are you going?"

"Away from here." She pulled the hat from her head. A full sheath of ebony hair fell to her shoulders. "I've seen what Audrey invited me to see."

"Still hotheaded and impulsive," Jarrod characterized. "I thought in the last five years you'd have grown up."

Catherine stopped. Her arms were at her sides, her entire body stiff. She turned slowly, as if gathering strength. "What would you know about it anyway? I can see you haven't learned any more about being an adult during your absence. You're still the selfish teenager out to make my life miserable."

"That was never my intention," he said.

Catherine looked at him. His eyes were serious. They burned into her as if he could see what she was thinking.

"Don't leave angry."

"Why not? I always have in the past."

He took her arm. "It's time we changed the routine." Jarrod slipped her arm through his and led her around the far side of the yard, away from the party. They walked around the east wing, as Audrey liked to refer to it. It was shady on this side, and devoid of people. A small veranda jutted out from the French doors. Patio furniture with colorful cushions made the arrangement lively and cheerful. Audrey often had breakfast here. Jarrod passed the veranda and headed for the stand-alone swing that gleamed with fresh white paint. Catherine stepped inside. He tightened his grip on her arm to keep her balanced as the apparatus started to sway.

She sat down. Jarrod sat next to her, and the swing moved back and forth. He was close to her, his leg touching hers. She knew why he wanted to talk to her. At least he wasn't doing it in front of the crowd. She was surprised. This was at least a different aspect of Jarrod's character. Then she remembered their past. Jarrod often got her to talk so he could use the information against her later.

He'd probably led her here for the same reason. She stiffened and vowed to keep her secrets to herself, including that her body tingled when his leg brushed hers. She fidgeted with the Dolly Levi confection. Jarrod took it away from her and placed it on the opposite seat of the swaying chair. He wore a black baseball cap bearing the single letter *X* stitched in white above the bill. Now he tossed his cap on the other bench too. It landed, bib tipped up against the gauze and flowers of her straw hat. The two looked ridiculous next to each other. Catherine thought of them as the incongruous romance between the sportswriter Spencer Tracy and the political activist Katharine Hepburn in the black-and-white movie *Woman of the Year*.

Jarrod took her hands and held them. Catherine didn't pull away. His hands were strong, smooth, and tender to hold. She looked into his face. His absence hadn't changed the way he looked. She couldn't deny he was attractive. Not just attractive; he was devastatingly handsome. Catherine remembered seeing him in a tuxedo for the first time. He was taking her cousin from Boston to a Christmas ball. Catherine was only fifteen, Jarrod nineteen. When she opened the door for him, she'd nearly melted in the foyer. He'd squeezed her nose and asked her if she got any dolls for Christmas. She wanted to kill him, but she couldn't deny that he was the most handsome man she'd ever seen.

He looked even better now. His face had more character. There were tiny lines around his eyes and a greater confidence that could be seen. His smile showed even white teeth, except for a tiny chip on his front tooth, the result of a tussling match with her. He was over six feet tall, with smooth brown skin that she'd bet was the same even tone over his entire body. His hair was clipped short. His build had been average when he left for England, but now it was more defined. She could see the strength in his arms and legs even through his clothes. He had broad shoulders proportional to his waist and hips, which were easy to delineate since he wore dark gray slacks and an open-collared white shirt that looked as if they'd been made for him.

His smile fascinated her as much as his light brown eyes that said, "Trust me." She wanted to trust him. She wanted to hold his face in her hands and look into the depths of his eyes and see what he was thinking, just as she wanted to run her hands over his hard body. She'd done it only once. He'd been unconscious, or at least acting unconscious. They were both in a first-aid class, and somehow he had been paired with her. After that incident she'd asked for a different partner. She couldn't keep her thoughts off him despite his constant ridicule. Women vied for his attention and he had many dates when he lived there. No doubt they would resume as soon as word got out that he was back in Newport.

And unattached.

"Tell me what's been happening," Jarrod said, pulling her out of the fog she'd drifted into.

Catherine pulled her hands free. She sat back in the swinging chair.

"We used to be confidants," he reminded her.

"I was ten years old then," she said, "and afraid of a thunderstorm." She wasn't often afraid of storms, but that one had made the sky dark as night, and the wind made the rain sound like fingers on her windows. Her parents and Jarrod's were out together. She'd screamed and screamed, and finally Jarrod had come to her room. She flew into his arms, sobbing her eyes out and clinging so tightly to him that he couldn't have left her if he wanted to. He lifted her and sat down in the rocking chair. Catherine fell asleep there, and when she woke the sky was bright and birds sang cheerfully. Jarrod was still holding her.

"So tell me about the storm that's scaring you now. I'm good at keeping secrets."

Catherine stared at him. He'd played practical jokes on her, pulled her hair, grilled her dates as if he were her father, but he'd never mentioned the night of the storm to anyone, or the questions she'd asked him when she was growing up and afraid to ask her parents.

"I'm twenty-six and unmarried."

"Last time I looked that wasn't a crime."

"It is if you ask Audrey or my mother."

"I take it they've been throwing men at you, telling you about the joys of marriage and children, constantly calling to see if you're dating anyone. And setting up days like today."

"How did you know?" Her eyes opened in surprise.

"It doesn't just happen to women, Catherine."

She smiled. "I know that. I just didn't know you had the same problem."

"I hadn't been home thirty minutes before my mother was asking probing questions about a possible *special* woman. Within twenty-four hours she was parading young women of marriageable age before me."

"So there is no one special?"

He reached over and took a lock of her hair. "You're special."

She grabbed her hair back. "Be serious," she said.

"I am being serious."

Catherine couldn't help laughing. Jarrod laughed too. It felt good to laugh with him again. He could be charming when he chose. She knew Jarrod's mother. She was eccentric and a little transparent, but Catherine couldn't help loving her. She was somehow glad there was no one special in Jarrod's life. She told herself it was because there was no one special in hers either.

"I thought of a plan to get them off my back." She relaxed, leaning forward slightly.

"1–800–WIFE?"

"How did you know about that number?" she asked. "I recognized your voice this morning."

"I didn't try to conceal it."

"As I did," she finished for him. "No one knows about the number, not even Elizabeth." Elizabeth Westfield was Catherine's best friend. The two had bonded in kindergarten and been closer than sisters ever since, but this one thing Catherine had kept to herself. It helped that Elizabeth was busy with her business and had little time for getting together right now. Catherine could reach her by e-mail and cellular phone if she really needed to, but she hadn't mentioned the 1–800 number.

Catherine didn't want to explain the number to anyone, but somehow Jarrod, who'd been able to read her like a book for as long as she could remember, already knew.

"I'm flattered you recognized my voice after so long," Jarrod said. Catherine suddenly thought she'd revealed something she hadn't intended. How could she not know his voice? It was brandy dark, warm, velvet soft, and Catherine knew he could use it to entice and seduce any number of females. Catherine was glad she wasn't one of them, yet she loved to listen to its cadence.

She covered with, "You have a very distinctive voice, but you haven't told me how you knew I owned the phone number. Or were you calling the number for yourself?"

Catherine felt at ease. Jarrod often did that to her, before he got her with one of his jokes. She cautioned herself to be careful.

"I didn't know until the machine picked up and started to speak."

"You couldn't be looking for a wife." Catherine knew if he were, there would be a line outside his mother's house that wrapped the full perimeter of their extensive property.

Jarrod shook his head. "1–800–WIFE. It was too intriguing not to call. That number was the topic of conversation almost as soon as I got off the plane."

"Your mother knows about the number?"

"I don't think so. She didn't pick me up. Robert Wells met me. I wanted to surprise my mother. She didn't know I was coming. Robert had a newspaper in the car and I hadn't seen any news of home in months. He pointed out the ad in the personals section."

If anyone knew about the number it would be Robert Wells. Young, healthy, eligible, never married, Robert was prime husband material. He was a ladies' man, suave and handsome, and had just as many suitors as his best friend, Jarrod. The two of them could have been cast from the same mold. They'd known each other since the cradle. Two practical jokers out to turn the world on its side. Robert owned a string of car dealerships all over the area. He'd taken over his father's one dealership and turned it into ten more in the last three years. This year he'd added a classic car dealership to his list. He was quite successful, as Catherine knew he would be. Selling cars was a game, and no one played it better, since Jarrod had gone to England, than Robert. She wasn't surprised that he had been the messenger in her tournament of hide-and-seek.

"And you just decided to call?" she asked.

"Not until this morning. I wasn't going to say anything. I just wanted to know what the message said. Imagine my surprise when I knew whose voice it was.''

He should know, Catherine thought to herself. He'd taught it to her. During one of their periods of friendship, again when the rain was pouring down and there was nothing else to do, Jarrod had taught her how to conceal her voice. He told her that he often used a different voice to play tricks on his parents and the teachers at school. She knew he'd done it more than once to her. Even though she was appalled at his trick, she learned how to do it anyway. It kept him too busy to play jokes on her.

It was one of the few times she remembered sitting in the same room with him without one of them being angry.

"I suppose I didn't conceal my voice very well."

"It's a very good imitation. Only I would recognize it, Catherine. You learned well. Now, what's the plan?"

Catherine swallowed. He already knew about her owning the number, she might as well tell him the rest of it. "I'm so tired of both my sister and my mother harping on my marital status that I knew I'd either have to leave Rhode Island or get married. So I decided to get married."

"Both drastic measures," Jarrod interjected. "But you shouldn't need a machine to find a husband." His gaze rolled over her from head to foot, taking in the shortness of her dress. Catherine accepted his gaze, although it made her uncomfortable and slightly warm, as if he'd opened an oven and the heat blew over her.

"I don't want a permanent husband. It's not like I can walk up to a man and ask him to marry me."

Catherine's voice trailed off. She sat forward, staring at Jarrod. Suddenly she thought of something. Another plan. And she had Audrey to thank for it. There was a man she could walk up to and ask him to marry her—Jarrod. Her 1-800 plan was good. Marrying Jarrod was even better. She inched to the edge of the bench, her feet stopping the gentle swing. She stared directly at him. They knew each other. They would both understand all the rules going in, and they could each satisfy a parent with the same plan.

It was perfect.

Maybe.

"Catherine, what are you thinking? I don't like that look."

"Jarrod, will you marry me?" She blurted it out, not giving herself time to think it over.

"What!" He sat back suddenly, rocking the swing.

Her hand flashed out to brace herself. Then Catherine leaned forward. "It's a perfect plan."

"No, it's not. I'm not looking to get married, no matter how many women my mother parades in front of me."

"That's what makes it perfect," she countered and inched closer. She lowered her voice. "If we get married, we'll get them off our backs, and in six months, a year at the most, we can get divorced."

"Catherine, I've been gone for five years. No one is going to believe a marriage between us. We've always been at each other's throat. How can we suddenly be in love?"

Catherine smiled. "We've never been at each other's throat. It's all been good, clean fun." She paused. "Isn't that what you told everyone?"

He looked exasperated. Catherine didn't wait for

an answer. "Everyone knows the line between love and hate is no wider than a thread. They'll all pat themselves on the back and say they knew all those fights were just to disguise our being in love."

"Not everyone," Jarrod said almost to himself, but Catherine heard the doubtful words.

"Jarrod, you *can* act as if you're in love with me." She moved closer to him. He inched back.

His hesitation was only slight. "Catherine, it isn't a matter of acting. It's deceit."

"And of course you've never deceived anyone." She lowered her head and raised her eyes, staring at him sarcastically. Then she stood up and caught hold of the support beam. The unit rocked.

"Cathy." He shortened her name. She never let anyone do that, but when Jarrod said it she felt as if he caressed the syllables. "What I did were harmless jokes. This could really hurt someone."

She hadn't thought his jokes were harmless. She'd cried herself to sleep many nights, embarrassed beyond her ability to comprehend.

"No one gets hurt, Jarrod. We get married and six months later happily divorced. No one will know about the deception except us. When it's over we'll both be friends and never have to have our parents bother us again. We'll be free to do whatever we want."

"What happens when we get divorced? What will they say then?"

"They'll say they only gave us six months in the first place." Catherine knew this was a good plan. It would make life so much easier. "Jarrod, we already know each other. We won't have to learn each other's habits or pretend anything except being in love, and that only in front of an audience. When we're alone we can just be friends." She took his hands the way he'd held hers. "We can do this."

Jarrod was hesitating. She had to convince him, before he decided against her.

"Jarrod, I'm sure this will work. It will be much easier with someone I know and trust than with a stranger I meet on the eight-hundred line." She paused. "And it will work for you too. You already told me your mother is just as bad as mine."

"Aren't there any other men you know who'd make you a better husband?" Jarrod asked.

"Sure, but they want to be married forever. With you it'll be six months, then we'll be respectably divorced." She crushed her hands together as if she were finished with something. Jarrod's face changed, and she realized how flippant her voice had been. "I didn't mean that the way it sounded," she apologized.

"Respectably divorced?" he asked. "What does that mean?"

She took his hands again and spoke softly. "It means we'll be free and friendly. No one will try to get us married again. We can say we've been married and it didn't work out. Then we can do whatever we want without anyone pressuring us again."

Jarrod sighed. "Have you thought this all the way through?"

"Of course I have," she stated confidently. "What could possibly go wrong?"

Jarrod shrugged. He tightened his grip on her hands. "Suppose you wake up one morning, say three months from now, and find I'm hopelessly, desperately, unconditionally in love with you?"

Catherine's throat suddenly went dry. Had she

heard a crack in his voice? She wasn't sure. Something pulsed within her. Then she laughed. Tentatively at first. "You?" She pulled her hands free. "You, in love with me?" Her laughter intensified.

Jarrod moved, and the sway made her lose her balance. Catherine sobered, grabbing for something to hold on to. She found his arms reaching for her. "That won't happen," she said, her voice a little breathy. "We've been enemies since the dinosaurs disappeared. It's not likely we'll suddenly change in six months."

Catherine's confidence faded for a moment. She hadn't thought of Jarrod falling in love with her. He wouldn't. And neither would she. They were friends, despite their rivalry. She'd go out of her way for him, and she knew he'd do the same for her, but friends didn't fall in love. She was friendly with many men, but she'd never fall in love with any of them. She and Jarrod could marry and nothing between them would change.

Jarrod frowned and started to speak. "Don't refuse right away." She stalled a response she knew was coming. "Why don't you think about it? Let the idea sink in. You can let me know tomorrow."

"Cathy, I'm not the one who needs to think this over." He stepped directly in front of her. He was so close she could feel his body heat, and she was still holding his arms. It made her warm and a little uncomfortable, even afraid. "You need to think about what you're asking, not just of me, but of any man who'd agree to marry and divorce."

"I have thought it over. It's a perfect scheme. And with you it can really work." Catherine made the mistake of putting her hand farther up his arm. She felt his muscles tense under it. Now she wanted to move it, but it would appear as if she didn't want to touch him. Actually she felt good about touching him. Somehow her mind wanted her hand to move over his arm and up to his shoulder.

Catherine saw something out of the corner of her eye and started to turn to look.

"Don't move," Jarrod said. "Audrey is on her way over."

Catherine smiled. "Why shouldn't I move?"

"Look at me." She returned her attention to him. His eyes were serious. He squinted slightly. "Do you really think this will work, Cathy?" There was almost no distance between them. Jarrod put his hands on her waist.

"Of course I do." She answered confidently, but a finger of fear slid over her, along with a ripple that centered around her heart. She came close to shivering even in the heat of the day and the circle of fire that spread through her from the exact point where Jarrod rested his hands.

"Okay."

"You'll do it?"

He nodded. His hands slid around her waist and pulled her closer. Her body touched his from breasts to thigh.

"Jarrod, what are you doing?"

He leaned closer to her. Heat drenched Catherine. She wanted to move back, but she didn't want to at the same time.

"I'm going to convince your sister this is real."

He kissed her. Catherine froze. Jarrod had never kissed her before. He'd hugged her once or twice, kissed her cheek or her forehead. Once they'd been under the mistletoe and kissed briefly, but he'd never made any move that she could construe as sexual. Yet his mouth felt good. Catherine relaxed. She stepped closer, putting her arms around his neck and angling her mouth to fit his, her body to match his. Jarrod's lips were soft when they touched hers, yet sensation as prickly as electrical shock arrowed through her all the way to her toes. Her breasts grew heavy, her nipples pointed, and she felt herself growing wet. Jarrod lifted his mouth, but only for the second it took to resettle it and deepen the kiss. His arms around her crushed her to him.

Catherine couldn't believe how she felt, how he made her feel. Jarrod's tongue pushed past her teeth, seeking entry to her mouth. Without hesitation she welcomed him inside, welcomed the gentle wave of ecstasy that washed over her like a warm waterfall. Her tongue mated with his. She played the dance with him, feeling the chipped tooth that was to her credit. She felt they were alone in the world, with nothing about them except the deep, dark jungle with all its emerald beauty and the echo of silence.

Jarrod's arms clamped around her, drawing her into intimate contact with the full length of him. She felt every part of his body while his mouth worked magic on hers. Catherine was caught in a downpour of sensation, wanting to move closer to him. Her hands moved over his back, caressing him as they descended lower and lower. When she reached his waist he lifted his head. Catherine's entire body could have been made of rubber. Jarrod folded her into his arms and held her close for a few seconds. He must have known how she felt. Then he stepped back.

He stared down at her. She couldn't move. Looking

up at him, she saw the desire in his eyes. She wondered what hers looked like to him. She'd changed in his arms, lost her sense and her mind, she thought.

Audrey cleared her throat, and Catherine suddenly remembered they weren't alone. Her head snapped toward her sister and she stepped back, out of Jarrod's arms. Catherine's body suffused with heat. She felt like a child caught doing something wrong, and tattle-tale Audrey was there to make sure the world or her parents knew it.

The look on Audrey's face was bathed in wide-eyed surprise. Catherine could see this complication wasn't something Audrey had planned when she haphazardly threw them together.

"I thought you two were just being antisocial," Audrey said, finding her voice, which seemed a little higher than usual. "I came to see if either of you needed a referee, but I guess it was a wasted trip."

Jarrod moved behind Catherine and put his hands on her shoulders. "Not entirely, Audrey," Jarrod said.

Catherine was too tongue-tied to try to speak. Her mind was foggy. Her legs were weak, and she could still feel Jarrod's mouth on her tingling lips. She felt hot, both from Jarrod's assault and with embarrassment that she could feel so intimate with someone she didn't particularly like. And to have a witness. One who would no doubt recount everything to her mother and half the population of Newport. The smile on Audrey's face told her that much.

"We don't need a referee, but we'd like you to be the first to know," Jarrod continued.

"Know what?" Audrey looked to Catherine for an answer.

"I'm talking about a wedding, Audrey." Jarrod

spoke first. Catherine couldn't find her voice, though she hadn't planned to answer her sister. "Cathy and I are getting married."

Five minutes later it was show time. Audrey didn't ask them if they wanted to announce their engagement; she'd called for everyone's attention when Jarrod took control.

"Smile," he whispered as he put his arm around her waist and the two of them faced the gathering crowd. She felt her heart beating faster. She looked about the crowd for someone she could count on for support. Usually she would have sought out Elizabeth Westfield, but she was out of town. Catherine's eyes found her mother. Her father came up behind her. She smiled at her parents and looked away. She definitely couldn't look at them while Jarrod announced their plans to marry. Julianna Stone and Emily Colter offered her sardonic smiles. She found Robert Wells in the crowd. She liked Robert, despite his penchant for joining Jarrod in his jokes. He winked at her and she relaxed a little.

Jarrod slipped his arm around her and pulled her against him. The hand at her waist was cold. He cleared his throat and spoke. "Catherine and I have an announcement to make."

She wondered what he was feeling. Did he think everyone in the crowd knew they were lying? She looked at him and smiled, giving him encouragement, already playing her role.

"We're going to get married."

For a second there was silence. Then her mother clapped her hands together and started for them.

"Don't leave me alone," she muttered so Jarrod could hear her.

"The same goes for you."

"Darling, I am so happy for you," her mother said, trying to hug them both at the same time. "I never thought it would happen." She kissed Catherine on the cheek. Tears gathered in her mother's eyes. A pang of guilt pierced Catherine's heart. She and her mother had a special relationship, but she would never be able to tell her about this. It would break her heart. Her mother loved Jarrod. She'd often said he was just like another member of the family.

Her father shook Jarrod's hand and kissed her. He didn't say anything, but he'd often been the quiet type. Catherine wondered if he kept silent to avoid telling a lie.

After Jarrod's parents congratulated them and Audrey pushed her way to the head of the group, Catherine was surrounded by well-wishers. More times than she could count, people kissed her on the cheek or shook her hand.

"Congratulations," Julianna said to Jarrod. She ignored Catherine. Julianna never deviated from character. "This is certainly a surprise, Jarrod."

"Not really," he told her. Catherine was holding his hand. She squeezed it. "Catherine and I have been . . ." He looked at her with a smile. Catherine didn't know what happened to her insides. She felt them melting. ". . . heading toward this for years," he finished. He dropped a quick kiss on her mouth. Catherine closed her eyes and then opened them with a jerk when she remembered where she was.

"You haven't been home very long. You wouldn't want to rush into anything." She emphasized the word *rush,* giving it both its equal and opposite meaning and making it clear that she disapproved of any union between the two of them.

"Do I get to kiss the bride?" Robert elbowed his way to the front and took Catherine in his arms. He looked at Jarrod.

"Be careful," Jarrod told him. "She's spoken for." Robert kissed her on the mouth and released her. Catherine saw Julianna move away. She relaxed. They'd passed her by for the time being.

"Julianna doesn't believe a word of this engagement," Robert said in a voice designed for specific ears. "And I know a fish story when I hear one."

Chapter 2

"Damn!" Jarrod cursed, slamming the highball glass down on the bar. What had he been thinking? "Damn, damn, damn." Both of them couldn't be crazy. Someone had to be the rational one of a twosome, but when he had her wrapped in his arms rationality didn't just take a vacation, it scattered into separate molecules and dematerialized.

Jarrod stared at himself in the mirror over the bar. He looked like a normal man. He *had* been normal until he saw Catherine in that skin-tight dress and Dolly Levi hat. The hat he could laugh off, but the dress—and the woman inside it—aroused him, made him want to put his hands on her. And he had. Look what that did to him.

Made him an idiot.

Now an engaged idiot.

He couldn't marry Catherine. Not because he

couldn't play her game, but *because* he couldn't play her game. Six months of close contact with her and he'd be a basket case. He had no doubt about it. There was no such thing as a platonic relationship between them. If he found himself alone with her, he couldn't be more than what he was—a man attracted to a woman.

Five years ago he'd asked for the job in England. It was prestigious and would help his career in the long run. It involved restoration instead of the new construction he'd done since finishing his architectural apprenticeship three years earlier.

When it was time for him to leave it seemed everyone had something to do they couldn't get out of. His parents were away, and Catherine agreed to take him to the airport. He remembered their banter in the car during the drive. It was happy and normal for them. Jarrod liked her and she liked him, even if he did embarrass her on occasion. When it was time to board the plane he looked at her and didn't know where the decision to hug her came from. She was the only one he knew there and he was leaving for an indefinite period of time.

He pulled her into his arms and buried his face in her hair. It was a hug, only a friendly gesture from someone who was going away, but Catherine's arms had encircled him, returning the hug. For a moment their differences were wiped away and only the friendship they felt remained. Jarrod remembered the smell of her hair, a flowery, summery kind of scent. For five years that scent remained with him. Today he smelled it again while he had her in his arms.

She was young when he left. He imagined her unchanged, yet when he saw her she'd matured. The lankiness was gone, her tentativeness replaced with confidence. She was beautiful, her dark eyes and hair a haunting reflection of the girl he'd once known. Yet this new image took him back to that hug in the airport, to all the practical jokes he'd played on her, and made him understand how everything had been a cover-up. All the times he'd played jokes on her, he was masking his real feelings. He'd denied them, even to himself, but when he kissed her there was no more denying.

How could he pretend for six months? He'd have to pretend he didn't have feelings for her. Pretending he did would be easy, but it would also tell her everything in his heart.

Taking cold showers and controlling himself were things movie actors did. This was the real world. In life it happened the way it had happened today. He'd wanted to kiss that gorgeous mouth and he'd found a way, but he hadn't been prepared for the consequences. He hadn't expected one kiss to turn his life around, to make him want to marry her, but there was something about Catherine that got under his skin. He'd never known it before. And he wanted to explore whatever it was that made him look at Catherine and see a raving beauty, a desirable woman who pushed his arousal buttons.

He'd had to pull back. While he kissed her, while his hands stroked her soft, sensual curves, while sanity was flying away on a tempest, he'd heard Audrey's approach. At the last minute he remembered he'd initiated the kiss to convince Catherine's sister they were in love. Somewhere during the process Audrey had become an intrusion. Jarrod supposed he should be thankful she was there. The screen actor would.

If she hadn't been there, Jarrod would have dragged
Catherine off somewhere and made love to her.

"Damn, Cathy," he said to the face in the mirror.
"Why couldn't you stay that lanky teenager I played
jokes on?"

Very likely now, the joke would be on him.

Jarrod straightened when he heard a shrill of laughter in the hall. He turned, facing the door, knowing
the woman he'd been thinking of was only steps away.
He could hear his mother's voice muffled through
the thick wood. Then the door opened. Catherine
swept in with a huge smile on her face. His heart
thudded against his chest at the sight of her. She no
longer wore the tight black dress. She had on jeans
and a square-neck T-shirt. Every fiber molded itself
to her, outlining her curves in a practical joke that
could drive him crazy. It was pink, and no color could
have highlighted her skin better. It didn't matter what
she had on. Her presence aroused him.

"Wasn't it wonderful?" she crooned, closing the
door and leaning against it. "I couldn't have done
it better if I'd planned it. Your mother was magnificent."

Esther Greene arrived late for everything. When
she got to the party everyone's initial shock was over.
She rushed them as soon as Catherine's parents told
her the happy news. She hugged them both. Jarrod
had never seen excitement more complete. For the
first time since he could remember, his mother was
speechless. Enthusiasm rushed from her, but she
couldn't say a word. Her voice returned and she bub-

bled over with plans, details, things that needed to be done.

"Did you hear the whispers? People were saying exactly what I told you they would."

"Everyone except Robert. He saw right through this charade."

Pushing herself away from the door, she came toward him. Her smile was still in place. She looked like she had a secret and was bursting with it. His expression must have told her something. She frowned. "What's wrong?" she asked when she was only a step from him.

Everything was wrong. He wasn't supposed to feel like this. Catherine was a lanky teenager from his past. She didn't fit the usual type of woman he went out with. She was the girl next door. But she was also beautiful, gorgeous, and tempting. She felt good in his arms. He liked the way she smelled. He liked kissing her and he wanted more of her. Yet he didn't tell her any of the things he thought. He only said, "Nothing."

"You're drunk." It was an accusation.

"Not yet," he told her, "but I'm on my way." He lifted the empty highball glass and turned it up, letting the last drop of scotch slide onto his tongue. Frustrated, he set it back on the bar stool.

"Why are you drinking?"

"Catherine, this is not going to work."

"Jarrod, you promised. You can't go back on your word now. We've only been engaged six hours."

"Catherine, we don't even know each other."

"That's not true. We've known each other practically from the cradle."

"But we're not kids anymore." His voice was almost

a growl. "We're adults, grown-ups, and we should be able to make our own decisions, despite family pressure."

"Jarrod, just think of it as an elaborate practical joke. In this one nobody gets hurt and we both gain freedom for life."

"Someone could get hurt." He paused. "We'll be deceiving our families. If they find out what we're up to, it will break their hearts." Not to mention if his feelings got any stronger, he'd explode. He never thought anything like this could happen to him, or happen this fast. He didn't even know what to call it.

"Then we'll have to make sure they don't find out." She took his hand. Her warmth permeated his skin. "Remember, we want to live our lives the way *we* want to, not the way our parents think we should."

"You don't have to stay here."

She dropped her eyes and his hand. "I know. I could leave like you did. I could go to England or South America or California, but I don't want to. I want to stay here. I love the ocean in the morning and going to sleep with the sound of it outside my window. I love the clean air and the tourists in the summer. I love going to visit the mansions all decked out for Christmas, the ships on the ocean, the smell of the wood in the building yard, and participating in the annual Charity Ball. And I like the people here. I know they have those things other places, but it isn't home. I just want my family to think of different things when they see me. I want us to be able to talk about things other than the state of my singleness."

"But this might not be the best way. You really need

to give this a thorough understanding before we do anything.''

She smiled then, as if light had just dawned. "I understand your concern."

"You do?"

"That was the initial reason I came." She walked behind the bar and pulled a canned soft drink from the refrigerator. Popping the top, she poured it into his empty glass. Jarrod wondered if her small act was to drive home a point. They had known each other a very long time. She was familiar with his family and he with hers. They'd practically grown up together, but he'd only been sexually attracted to her for a few hours.

Catherine came around and stood at the stool next to him.

"I thought we'd better get our story straight, but I don't think you're sober enough."

"I'm sober enough. What is it?"

She handed him the soft drink. He drank it all. "You've been away for five years. Suddenly you're back and after a witnessed argument, we're engaged. We've got to have a story for that."

"How about we say you were the reason I left in the first place? That I was falling ..." He found it hard to say the word. "I was falling in love with you and I took the job in England because I wasn't ready for a commitment."

"That's good." She smiled. "But now you are?"

"I'm older, no longer playing practical jokes. I'm ready to settle down and start a family."

"You are?" Her eyebrows went up. "I didn't know."

"It's a lie, Catherine. It's what I'll tell them," he said. He moved from the stool. It had to be the alcohol on his brain, he told himself. His mind was playing tricks on him. He couldn't be seeing them, himself and Catherine, as a family. The children, their children. He shook his head to clear the image.

"Oh, of course." She cleared her throat. "Do you want to have kids someday?"

He turned back. She was standing in front of the bar stool. "Yes," he said quietly.

She approached him. "Jarrod." She swallowed. "Maybe you're right. I haven't thought this through. I never even asked if you have someone."

"There is no one else," he answered more sharply than he'd intended.

"It's hard to believe you could still be single. You're an attractive man, and I see how women circle you. Julianna Stone would elope with you tomorrow. Why haven't you ever married?"

How had this conversation turned to him? He didn't want to discuss himself. Not with her. "Let's concentrate on us, what we'll tell everyone. Julianna has her own problems."

She stared at him for a moment. He knew she wanted to continue the conversation on its present course, but he wouldn't go there. Not even in his inebriated state.

"Why did you decide to return now?" she finally asked, adhering to his wishes.

"I couldn't stay away any longer," he answered immediately, continuing to concoct the lie they would tell together. "We've been corresponding by e-mail, and when you went to Paris two summers ago I met you there. I couldn't leave England until after I'd completed my contract, but now I'm back for good."

"Jarrod, that's not true."

"It doesn't matter," he snapped; then, more quietly, he said, "They'll believe it because we'll be convincing."

Catherine stepped back. The implication must have hit her and she was back in the swing with him.

"Jarrod, this is a practical joke. We're getting married, but it's not real."

"You mean no sex."

"No sex." She nodded her head, agreeing with him.

"How long do you think that's going to last?" He walked right up to her. He could tell she wanted to move away, but Catherine always stood her ground. She'd been butting heads with him since their childhood. He knew she wouldn't let him know how much his words could scare her. This was his Catherine, the one who would challenge him, who wouldn't back down when it came to a fight. Suddenly he understood why he'd tormented her all those years ago. He loved the way she rose to the challenge.

"You said we're adults and we can act responsibly."

"Like we were doing in that swing this afternoon?" He took another step. Heat enveloped them. He could smell her perfume. He leaned toward her. It wasn't perfume. What he smelled, what had kept him thinking of her for all those years was her own essence, the scent that defined Catherine. It was under the perfume, part of her makeup, as inseparable a part of her as her eye color and the ebony darkness of her hair. His eyes stared at her mouth. He watched her lick her lips. The gesture made him want to taste them, see if they were as sweet as they had been earlier in the day. He wanted to kiss her again.

Jarrod felt her sway. He could feel the hesitancy in

her. At the last minute she sidestepped him, just as
he'd decided to close the gap between them. Jarrod
had to stop himself from falling.

"We only need to kiss if there is an audience. And
we have none."

"Any more rules?"

She flashed him a pointed look. "What about the
argument?"

"What argument?"

"This afternoon in front of Audrey," she said.

"Lovers' quarrel," he supplied. "We can say you
were angry because I came back and didn't immediately call you, but we patched it up in the gazebo."
He watched her face. Color rose under her skin.

"We'll have to set a date," she recovered. "Afterward, I suppose we'll live in my house. Unless you
have some objection."

"No objection."

"What about a wedding date?"

He shrugged. "You choose it."

"Jarrod, I don't want to feel I'm making you do
something you don't want to."

"You're not." He went back to the bar, but not
for a drink. He didn't want anything to impair his
faculties. He was going to need every bit of his wits
intact to deal with this woman. "Six weeks from
today."

"What?" she asked.

"The wedding," he explained. "Saturday, August
fourth. First Baptist Church."

"Audrey won't think that's enough time."

"Audrey's already married," he told her. "She'll
have to adjust."

Chapter 3

The ocean roared. Catherine hugged her knees to herself as she watched the waves splashing, creating a sudsy play with the shoreline. The sky was bright blue. Soft clouds moved gently overhead. A warm breeze blew loose tendrils of her hair. Gulls sang in the sky, cawing their incessant melody to all who would listen. This bright morning Catherine had the entire show to herself.

She hadn't slept well. She should have. She was getting what she wanted: a husband, her family off her back. Jarrod was really a friend. She couldn't have asked for a better opportunity. Six months after the wedding she'd be divorced and life would go on. So why was her plan giving her second thoughts? It was Jarrod, and that comment about children. He had been drunk. She could blame it on that, but when he answered her question there was no sign of drunkenness in his eyes. What she saw was sorrow. She'd never thought of a family. She'd only thought of solving her immediate problem. What would happen if things got out of hand and she got pregnant?

No! She shook her head to reassure herself. No sex. They'd agreed on that. There was no way she could get pregnant. This was going to be a business deal, not a real marriage. Still, her thoughts suddenly included him.

She remembered him last night in the library of his mother's house. Sober he was charming. He'd wrapped the garden party ladies around his finger. In the swing she'd succumbed to that same charm. Drunk he looked just as good, better than good. She'd turned away from him when he tried to kiss her, but she'd looked into his eyes. Searching for some way to explain her behavior, her feelings, her newfound affection for someone she thought of as brother material. His eyes weren't evenly brown. In their depths was a ring the color of a lion's mane. His skin, the wine dark color of a bay mare, contrasted with her own. He was the perfect combination of noble beast and king of the jungle.

And yesterday. What had happened to them yesterday? How could she feel so different in his arms? Her body had become liquid honey, warm and oozing, and raw with power, blending into his. She'd never felt like that before. In all the years they'd been together, the tricks he'd played on her, the rainstorms he'd seen her through, even the hug at the airport when he left for England, hadn't prepared her for the bevy of sensations that raced through her body when he kissed her.

She couldn't figure it out. Even the roaring ocean

didn't give her answers. She'd come here to ask for help, but she couldn't focus on any one question. There were too many of them crowding in on her, falling over each other in their quest for answers. What would marriage be like, even an in-name-only marriage? The ocean crashed in her ears. Was that it? Did she really want that kind of marriage?

She didn't.

She wanted a real relationship, one based on trust, mutual loving and equal giving, but that never happened. She'd seen it. In every marriage she knew, even her sister's and her mother's, something had been traded in, given up, and mostly the women gave up part of themselves, part or all of their dreams.

She wouldn't do that. Not for anyone.

She had dreams and she would see them through. She would never marry for real.

"I thought I'd find you here."

Catherine squinted, raising her hand to the sun. Jarrod stood a few feet from her perch against the rock wall that ran for miles along the rocky coast below, separating, in some cases, the sand from the grass. The sun was behind him, making a silhouette of his powerful body. She blamed his surprise appearance as the reason her body began to tingle. The rush of blood in her ears rivaled the ocean forces, pumping double time.

He wore shorts and nothing else. No shirt, no shoes. But pecs, abs, and muscle definition that could keep Michelangelo busy for an eternity. A living statue. Catherine swallowed.

Jarrod might have been brother material when he left for England, but the muscle-chested god standing in front of her now brought out no sisterly feelings on her part. She squirmed, feeling she needed to remain on her guard. If he found out she thought of him sexually, he might try to kiss her again, and although Catherine yearned to feel that rush of exhilaration that overtook her when he held her in his arms, she had no defense against him.

Jarrod dropped down to the sand beside her. His arm brushed hers. Quickly she moved away, but not quickly enough to forestall the fire that burned her like a thousand suns.

"What's going on, Catherine?"

"Why should something be going on?"

"Because this is your alone place. You come here when you need to talk to the sea."

"I don't talk to the sea." She tried to laugh, glancing at the blue water. His gaze told her that he knew her well enough to know she came to the water when she needed to sort things out. It was kind of frightening.

"You let it talk to you. So what did it tell you this morning?"

"That you were right last night." She grabbed a handful of sand, watching the granules sift through her fingers, rather than look at Jarrod.

"I was drunk last night."

"You still made sense."

"About what?"

"About the plan needing more thought." Catherine watched him playing with the sand as well.

"Is that what you're doing here?"

"I'm trying."

"I gave it some thought last night—after the booze wore off."

"What did you decide?"

"The decision is no longer ours." He reached in his pocket and pulled out a small blue velvet box. He offered it to her.

"What is that?" She stared at the ring box as if it held some strange potion that would forever alter her if she opened it.

Jarrod pulled the blue top open. Catherine gasped at the ring inside. It was beautiful. A huge, blue, square-cut diamond. It was surrounded by smaller white diamonds in an invisible setting. The stone, which had to be five or six carats, looked as if it were floating on the bed of white that covered the inside of the box.

She didn't even know she'd reached for the box until she had it in the palm of her hand. She cradled it as if it were the most precious thing she'd ever held. "Jarrod, it's the most beautiful ring I've ever seen."

"It belonged to my grandmother."

Catherine was staring at the stone. It took a moment for his words to register.

"What did you say?" She looked at him. "Jarrod, I can't wear your grandmother's ring." She handed the box back to him, but even as she did, she was imagining the ring on her finger.

Jarrod snapped it closed. "I told my mother you'd react this way, but she is so thrilled with the engagement that I couldn't do anything but bring it."

"This is getting out of hand," Catherine said. "Couldn't you tell her we'd buy a ring, that I only want a gold band, no engagement ring?"

"I tried," Jarrod said. "She would have none of it. She said every woman wants an engagement ring."

Catherine stared at the box in his hand. She hadn't

thought about a ring at all. She'd never considered a wedding ring either. Of course she figured she'd wear one, but it would be plain, like their agreement, all business, no embellishments. Nothing like the beautiful blue diamond had ever entered her mind.

"I never thought of anything like this happening," Catherine said, reaching for the box. She opened it and looked at the stone again. Its beauty made her remember all the fairy tales, happily ever after, white gowns, babies and dreams of a perfect life.

"You can't back out now." Jarrod took the ring from the box and reached toward her. She stared at his outstretched hand, then at the box, before bringing her gaze to his. Somehow her hand was in his, and he slipped the white gold ring on the third finger of her left hand.

It was heavy, unfamiliar, foreign, beautiful. Tears filled her eyes. When she raised her gaze to Jarrod's, he was blurred through the mist. She leaned forward and put her cheek next to his. The gesture said thank you. They were two friends sharing a moment in the sun. For a long time she held on to him, knowing this was their final moment as friends. After this nothing would be the same for them again. As Catherine held him she changed. She felt something flowing through her, as incessant and powerful as the distant sea.

Jarrod's head turned, and he pressed a kiss onto her cheek. Catherine met him, and his mouth touched hers. Not with the hunger of yesterday, but with the gentleness of understanding. The kiss was brief, and she slid her head onto his shoulder. She felt him breathing. His heart beat fast, and she knew it matched the rhythm of her own.

They were bound now. What had begun as a practical joke had turned into something else. Had she been foolish to think she could control its course? She touched the ring on her finger. Neither she nor Jarrod could back out now, even if they wanted to. She tightened her arms around him. Did she really want to back out?

Did he?

Catherine had never been more confused. She'd lived next door to Jarrod for most of her life. Robert had lived around the corner. Growing up, they were a thorn in her side—two Abbotts to her Costello. Jarrod had pointed out that they were no longer children and this was no joke.

The ring glistened in the light. She thought of what it meant, should mean, to any couple getting married. The unbroken circle, the stone, a shining light in a storm, a beacon to point the way to the one person who'd vowed to stand by you for all their days on earth.

"Jarrod?" She pulled back and set herself apart from him. "Do you want to call this off?"

"We've only been engaged a day," he said.

Catherine looked down. "I said that last night. We'd only been engaged six hours then." She paused. "It's daylight now, and we should both be able to see things more clearly."

Jarrod looked out at the ocean. Catherine looked there too. The sea rolled in toward the rocky coast. It didn't take her fears away as it often did. It didn't lift the worry from her shoulders that her awareness to him had brought, and it didn't move the man sitting next to her.

"We could set a date for late next year," Catherine suggested. "Or we don't have to set a day at all. In

a little while we could break the engagement alto-
gether."

"Still scheming, aren't you?"

"I don't mean to," she said. "Normally, I'm a very
honest person."

Jarrod looked serious. "Catherine, I know you are.
You must be going through something terrible to go
to this extreme."

"I think it's transference."

"What?"

"Audrey's been married for four years. She should
have at least one child by now or be pregnant. Yet
she seems to have parties instead of babies. I suppose
she's getting pressured from my parents to produce
a grandchild. In retaliation she joins Mother in their
drive to find me a husband."

Jarrod took her hand, the one with the ring on it.
"So you thought you'd take matters into your own
hands?"

"It didn't sound so trivial when I came up with the
idea."

"It isn't trivial. I know the pressure."

Catherine looked at him. He still held her hand.
"You mentioned that yesterday. I thought mothers
never wanted their sons to marry."

"Not my mother. I'm her only son and she wants
grandchildren too."

Catherine leaned her shoulder against him. "Do
you think we'll be like them when we have grown
children?" Realizing what she had just said, she tried
to correct herself. "I didn't mean *we.*" She pulled
her hand free to point it between Jarrod and herself.
"I meant when we've finally married and—"

"I thought you were never going to marry," he interrupted.

"Well, I'm not, but you will. And you said you wanted children. Do you think—"

"Exactly," he said.

"Jarrod, how many children do you want?"

"Are you applying for the job of wife and mother?"

"No!" she said a little too loudly. "I never thought of you as a father, that's all. I guess I still think of you as that tormenting practical joker."

"He's gone, Catherine."

"I know," she said. Some part of her wanted him back. "You might look the same, but you've changed."

"Changed. How?"

"You're older, more confident, there's a greater sureness about your actions. You don't seem to need to hide behind Jarrod, the Jokester." He was also handsome. He'd always been good-looking, even devastatingly attractive, but now there was something about his looks that seemed to come from the inside. "I think you have found your heart," she finished, sneaking a glance at him. "And I love that accent you've developed."

"I don't have an accent."

"You could have waited one more lousy day," Elizabeth Wakefield said by way of greeting. She stood at the edge of the restaurant table at which Catherine sat, one hand resting indignantly on her hip. Her white suit looked crisp and new and highlighted her teak-colored skin. "I go away one weekend"—she held up a finger—"and you get yourself engaged. What's up with that?"

Catherine couldn't help but laugh at the mock
annoyance on her friend's face. Elizabeth suddenly
laughed and opened her arms.

"Congratulations." Catherine stood up and
hugged her. "I knew all those arguments between
the two of you were disguising something else."

Catherine had fooled Elizabeth, and she was no
pushover.

"So tell me the particulars," Elizabeth said, taking
a seat at the table. "When did this all happen? I would
have sworn there was no man in your life, and to
think you snagged Jarrod Greene. This must have
flipped out every single woman in the state." She
placed a hand on her chest and reared her head back
in laughter.

Elizabeth would have gone on talking, but the
waiter came over at that moment to take her drink
order. He left to get her iced tea.

"There were a few woman who expressed . . . surprise."

"A few?" Elizabeth raised her arched eyebrows. "If
he still looks as good as he did five years ago, surprise
is an understatement. I wouldn't be shocked if half
the population of Rhode Island suddenly decided to
move to greener pastures, no pun intended. If I'd
known about this, I'd have blown off that trip to
Washington." She laughed again. "To see Julianna's
face when Jarrod announced your engagement would
have been priceless."

The two women laughed until the waiter brought
Elizabeth's drink and they had to sober to give their
order. The small reprieve allowed Catherine time to
collect herself. She needed to talk to someone. If she
didn't, she was going to burst. She thought she could

contain this, but things were rapidly veering out of control. Catherine twisted the engagement ring on her finger. She held her hands under the table so Elizabeth couldn't see how nervous she was.

Elizabeth, who had been her best friend since grade school, had opened a computer consulting firm about the same time Jarrod had left for England. It had taken off with the lightning movement of technology's bits, bytes and Pentium chips. Elizabeth had contracts that had turned her into a workaholic. Yet she always seemed to find time for Catherine. If there was anyone Catherine could trust with her plight, it was Liz.

She'd trusted her before with the details of her brief engagement while she lived in New York City. No one else knew the particulars, only that Catherine had been engaged to be married and for some reason it had been broken three weeks before the wedding. Shortly afterwards she'd returned to Newport and been there ever since.

"You wouldn't believe the buzz," Elizabeth resumed right after the waiter left. "Jarrod Greene getting married. This news even replaces the hype surrounding that 1–800–WIFE line. It's all anyone has talked about for weeks. Every time I go to a new job, someone is talking about calling. I suppose every man in the state has dialed that number. I guess that comes with living in a small town. There just isn't enough to keep them busy."

"Elizabeth." Catherine stopped her friend before she went on. "Remember when we were young and said we'd be old maids together?"

Elizabeth gave her a serious look. "We were children, Catherine. We couldn't have been more than

fourteen, and angry because we didn't have dates to
the school dance." She laughed. "We weren't serious.
Catherine, you're not having second thoughts
because of something we—"

Catherine put up her hand. "I know we weren't
serious. And that's not it."

"Then what is it? You look as if you're on your way
to a funeral instead of a wedding."

"The pact we made is still intact, unless there's a
man in your life I don't know about?"

Elizabeth reached down and picked her napkin up
from the floor. "There's no one serious," she said.
"But what are you talking about? How is our plan
still intact?"

"I own it." Catherine spoke slowly and quietly.

"Own what?"

"1–800–WIFE."

"What did you say?" Elizabeth leaned across the
table, her mouth gaping.

Catherine looked around to make sure no one
could hear her. Their table was along the windows,
facing the water's edge outside. From where they sat
they could see almost every other table. Elizabeth
hadn't been able to meet her during the height of
the lunch hour, so most of the lunchtime crowd was
gone. No one sat at the tables in front of or behind
them. Catherine whispered, "I own it."

"You're kidding."

Catherine shook her head. "I'm not kidding," she
told her.

Elizabeth picked up her iced tea and sipped it
through the long straw. "I should have ordered a
scotch," she said. "I have the feeling I'm going to

need it." She set the glass down and folded her arms on the table. "Talk," she ordered.

The waiter put two chef's salads and a basket of bread on the table. Each woman sat back, waiting for him to conclude his ministrations with butter and the salad dressings they'd asked for on the side.

As soon as they were alone, Catherine related her story, never raising her voice higher than a whisper. She told Elizabeth about installing the number to get her sister and mother to stop nagging her about getting married. How Jarrod's appearance seemed the perfect solution. Her sudden and rash decision that he would make the best candidate for her plan. She explained everything up to the point on the beach when Jarrod had given her his grandmother's ring.

"So you see, our pact will still work unless you find someone to marry. Mine is a marriage in name only. In six months we'll be divorced. Life will go on." She smiled and took a sip of her drink.

The uplifting tone of her conclusion sounded like something out of a storybook, not part of real life.

"I should have known," Elizabeth said. "I admit when I got your message I thought there was something a little strange about it, but you've always been a little strange, especially where Jarrod is concerned."

Catherine didn't ask her what that meant. She never could explain it, even to herself, why she kept coming back to let Jarrod play another joke on her, or why she'd come to his rescue if he was stranded or if he needed her to do something for him. She always called him when she was in trouble and didn't want her parents to find out. He'd come and help and never mention it again. She attributed it to their special relationship. They were friends even if they were also enemies. It was a combination that had no explanation either of them could put in words. They never tried. They just went on. Eventually Elizabeth gave up trying to understand.

"Let me see it?" Elizabeth shook her fingers in a question.

Catherine twisted the engagement ring around on her finger. She'd purposely turned it toward her palm to hide the huge stone. Catherine extended her hand toward Elizabeth. The large blue diamond twinkled in the light coming through the windows. Elizabeth gasped just as Catherine had done when she first saw it.

"Catherine, you've come up with some hairbrained schemes in your life, but this? How could you possibly think this was a good idea?"

Catherine shifted in her seat. She didn't really want to think that her calm, rational and logical friend was making her squirm. "It seemed like a good plan at the time. There are dating services all over the place. People meet through newspaper ads, on the Internet in chat rooms, any number of ways, and marry."

"But you didn't use those methods. Those people date and get to know each other. They fall in love and decide to marry."

Catherine agreed. "I don't want a long-term commitment. I wanted someone who would be willing to comply with my plan, no entanglements, no emotional attachment."

"So what is the problem? Don't you have what you want?"

Catherine leaned back in her chair. Did she? She wasn't sure. She looked at her hand as she moved it back to the side of her plate. Jarrod put that ring on her finger and something happened inside her. Something she couldn't explain to herself, let alone Elizabeth, and certainly not Jarrod. She was alone in this and she'd never been alone before. There was always someone she could rely on to listen, share her stories, understand her problems. Her grandmother had been her confidant, but her grandmother had passed away four years ago, and Catherine wasn't ready to confide in Elizabeth. With this problem she had no one.

"This always happens to you," Elizabeth said.

"What?"

"You start some scheme and then you think better of it, but you're in too deep to get out."

Catherine knew Elizabeth was telling the truth. She had come up with the idea of stowing away on a small cruiser to hitch a ride to Long Island. Elizabeth got seasick the moment the eight-sleeper reached rocky water. They were discovered and told the boat wasn't headed for Long Island and returned to Newport. Luckily Jarrod came to get them instead of their parents.

"Elizabeth, I have done some things that only the young and stupid would think of, but I haven't done anything irresponsible in years."

Elizabeth nodded, agreeing with her. "The last time was before Jarrod left, and now he's back."

"I didn't do it because Jarrod was coming home."

"Didn't you?" Elizabeth's eyebrows rose in question.

"No!" Catherine felt anger growing inside her. "I did it to get my mother and sister—"

"Then why are you having second thoughts?" Elizabeth interrupted her.

"I'm not having second thoughts. Not exactly," she whispered.

"This isn't about that jerk you were engaged to in New York, is it?"

"I can't help it. I know my engagement to Jarrod isn't real, but I was so humiliated by Jeff's defection. He had all these plans for what our marriage was going to be like, and he didn't even discuss them with me. He just assumed he could take over my life, that I would fall into line and be the obedient wife. I admit I was enamored by him. He had a charisma that blinded me to reality. I'm glad I had my eyes opened before we got married."

"Catherine, he was the wrong man. If you'd married Jeff Sherman, you'd be divorced by now, and much worse for wear."

"I know that."

"But I don't think you should cut yourself off from every man because of that experience."

"I'm not doing that." Catherine avoided Elizabeth's eyes.

"What you're doing with Jarrod involves none of the emotions that were in play when you were engaged to Jeff." She stopped, suddenly realizing what she hadn't said. "Or does it?" She put her glass down. "Catherine, are you falling for Jarrod?"

"Don't be ridiculous." Catherine wasn't having second thoughts about Jarrod. Her problem was dreams, daydreams and night dreams. She'd seen herself more than once in situations with Jarrod that she'd have vehemently denied a month ago, but now they were wearing on her. She was getting used to the idea of being engaged to him, having him around, laughing with him and just being quiet in his presence. She actually liked it. "My problem is I might . . ." She stopped. She remembered the beach and Jarrod putting the ring on her finger. The feelings that went through her when he held her. What was she reading into them? Was it all her? Did Jarrod feel any of it?

"You might what?"

She stared at Elizabeth. She didn't know how to finish that sentence or if she should tell the unvarnished truth, even to her best friend. She might be falling for Jarrod. Is that what was happening to her? It had only been a couple of days since they had seen each other again. It took longer to fall in love than that, no matter what happened in movies and on TV. This was real life, and she had more reasons for not falling for him than the opposite, yet she was almost sure this was the case. "I might have more to pay for when this is over than I thought."

The concert hall was small by standards set in larger cities, but for Newport it was a staple of the community. The building was old, had been used continuously for nearly a century. It had been renovated several times, the seats redone and the curtains changed, but the sound of the music still reverberated off the rafters as if the designers understood both architecture and opera.

Catherine sat in the darkness listening to the orchestra play Debussy. She loved his music, having discovered it when she was twelve years old and taking piano lessons. It usually soothed her senses, and often when she was upset or had had a particularly grueling day, she would pop a CD into the machine and let the music restore the natural order of her world. Tonight in the darkened hall, with Jarrod sitting next to her, it wasn't doing its job. In fact, the opposite was occurring. She was thinking of Jarrod, how good he looked in his suit, how white his teeth were when he smiled at her, how attentive he had been since they became engaged. He'd gallantly accompanied her shopping to pick out patterns for silverware and china—something she saw no need to do, but Audrey had insisted on, and Jarrod had backed her up. Nightly they attended the theater or dinner or some event at one of their friends' homes. She could find no fault in his actions.

Catherine suddenly looked up, not at the orchestra, but at her inner thoughts. Had she been looking for fault in Jarrod? Her lunch with Elizabeth two days earlier had been disturbing, but was this the result? Had she been unconsciously trying to find something wrong with Jarrod? Some reason to end the charade?

"You're not listening," Jarrod leaned over and whispered in her ear. Catherine felt his warm breath, and goose bumps skittered down her neck. He took her hand and held it in his. Catherine looked at him and smiled in the darkness. She turned back to the orchestra. The conductor was waving his baton and the violinists were pumping their bows like humming-bird wings. Abruptly the song ended. The audience thundered its applause. Catherine was relieved to drop her pretense at listening.

After a standing ovation and two encores, she and Jarrod made their way up the crowded aisle toward the exit. Both of them nodded and smiled, shook hands and accepted kisses of congratulation from

friends who had heard of their engagement but
hadn't seen them since the announcement. It was
impossible to go anywhere in Newport without seeing
someone they knew.

They finally made it out of the concert hall. Jarrod
helped her into the car, but he didn't drive them
home. Catherine didn't notice until she heard the
roar of the ocean. They had parked on a deserted
beach. She opened her door and got out. The wind
was cold. She turned her face into it instead of away.
She needed something lashing against her skin, something to keep her grounded. There was a mist tonight,
and Catherine pulled the shawl covering her shoulders closer around her. Jarrod came up behind her.
She could feel his strength. She needed it.

Seeming to understand, Jarrod put his arms around
her shoulders and pulled her back against him. She
leaned into him. He put his chin on her head and
together they stood there, looking at the dark water,
watching it roll in from the west. Catherine let him
hold her. She ran her hands along Jarrod's arms,
forgetting everything except how good he felt behind
her. She closed her eyes and listened to the waves
crashing against the rocks in the distance.

"Where were you tonight?" Jarrod whispered, his
voice as deep as the ocean.

"Lost," she said.

He tightened his arms but did not try to turn her
around.

"It was the beach, your grandmother's ring, all
the phone calls that have been coming in, wedding
preparations from Audrey. I suppose I'm feeling the
effects of my own deception."

He took her hand and looked at the ring. Then

he turned her body. "She would want you to have it," he said.

"Jarrod, it's a farce. It's not real."

He didn't answer her immediately. "It's as real as we make it."

Catherine's head came up and she stared into his eyes. He looked down at her. Even in the dark she could see the flash of raw desire burning there. Catherine waited. She held her breath, wondering if he'd lower his head. She'd make no move to stop him. If he tried to kiss her, she'd let him. She wanted him to. He'd kissed her once, and she couldn't keep thoughts of it out of her mind. Eternity seemed to pass and neither of them changed the distance between them by a fraction of an inch.

Catherine dropped her eyes, then rested her head on his chest. Sanity returned in time. What was she thinking? She needed to remember Audrey and her mother and the dreams they had given up after they married. She needed to remember Jeff Sherman and his thoughts on marriage. She was doing the right thing. She was protecting herself from the kind of life where she could lose herself, where being a Mrs. meant not having dreams of your own, only living her husband's dreams.

The taboos and rituals of the Victorian Age were gone. This was a new century, with greater decisions and more rights. She didn't have to have a husband to support and protect her. She didn't have to give up what she wanted to do for a man's dreams. She could be her own person, respectable and *single*.

Chapter 4

Catherine was sure she was losing her mind. She found it hard to concentrate. When she wasn't twisting the ring on her finger, she was thinking about Jarrod. She sat at her desk. She was the Public Relations Director for Butler Boating, Inc., and she had brochures to approve, boat presentations and press releases to write, yet all she could do was look at her finger and think of Jarrod placing his grandmother's ring there. She could feel his hand holding hers, smell the fragrant elixir that couldn't be bottled but came from the essence of his core and stirred her senses.

She'd been confused, disoriented since she put this plan in motion. She felt as though something was wrong with her, that she no longer had control of her own mind. But she did, she told herself. She took a deep breath and picked up the brochure board. It was for their new sailboat, sleek and sure, fast and easy to handle. She'd had a demonstration on one of the prototypes. It was one of the things she liked about working here, the practice demonstrations. When she wrote something or approved the publicity for a boat she believed in her words. The boat in the photo angled toward the horizon. Its sails were full of wind, its body made of dark wood that reminded her of Jarrod—even brown with red tones. The boat sailed into the sun and Jarrod's skin looked as if it had been drenched in the red color of the winter's sunset, then covered with an even veneer that begged her hands to reach out and touch him.

He was back in her mind, but she pushed thoughts of his body aside with a shrug of her shoulders. She would return to her original plan. With them it was a job, a six-month project that they would begin with a lightness of heart, and at the end they would part friends. That's what she needed to remember. Keep it light. Don't let family heirlooms, daydreams, and china patterns get in the way. They would only complicate things and keep her from her goal.

Catherine felt much better after making that decision. She jumped into her work with the zeal of a new employee, excited about accomplishing something. By the time she left for the day, she'd made serious inroads in the stacks of paper on her desk, not to mention the large amount of e-mail that she'd read and responded to.

She went home to shower and dress. Jarrod was picking her up later. They had a date.

* * *

"Wedding invitations should be in the mail six weeks before the ceremony," Audrey insisted as Catherine and Jarrod addressed envelopes. "I'm amazed Mr. O'Neill could drop everything and do this favor for me."

Catherine pushed her hair over her shoulder and smiled widely at Jarrod. Audrey liked to rant. She liked people to think she'd gone to vast lengths to do the impossible. The truth was, it was a standard invitation. All it needed was the names, place, and time inserted into the already typeset spaces. The paper was a standard card stock in silver with black printing. The most Audrey had to do was ask the printer for a rush job. And Mr. O'Neill hadn't survived in this small community by refusing the sudden and unexpected jobs that came his way.

"Audrey, I can plan my own wedding," Catherine insisted.

Audrey stopped what she was doing and turned to look at her sister. "When would you have time?" she asked. "You and Jarrod are out every night at a party or going to the theater. Since Jarrod's return you two have been joined at the hip."

"Isn't that how married people are supposed to be joined?" Jarrod dropped an envelope onto the growing pile in front of them. He winked at Catherine.

"Of course," Audrey answered. "They also need to attend to the necessities of life, and you two have no time for that."

"Aren't we lucky we have you?" Catherine leaned back in her chair, stretching her arms. She pulled her hair into a finger ponytail and gave her sister a smile so sugar sweet it could cause diabetes. Audrey didn't seem to notice it.

"Don't forget Mom. She's doing a lot of the work too."

"I think we should have the people who do all the work stand up at the ceremony and the bride and groom stay home," she whispered so only Jarrod could hear her. He laughed that deep belly laugh, and Audrey switched her attention to him.

"What's funny?" she asked.

Jarrod reached for another envelope. Catherine dropped her gaze so Audrey couldn't see her struggling to keep from laughing.

"Your sister," Jarrod answered. "She has got the dirtiest mind. She says things in my ear that make me blush or laugh."

"Jarrod!"

"Deny it," he said, challenging her.

"I have things to do," Audrey announced, not waiting for Catherine to confirm or deny Jarrod's accusation. "Please finish the envelopes, and remember, Jarrod, you have fittings tomorrow morning. So don't stay out all night."

"Yes, Mommie," Jarrod said in a little-boy voice.

Audrey left them. "How could you say that?" Catherine asked the moment her sister was out of earshot.

"Which part?"

"You know which part."

"Did you really want me to tell her why I was laughing?"

Catherine pulled another envelope. She checked off the last address she'd written and started the next one. "I didn't even know we knew this many people."

"I didn't even know this many people lived in the entire state."

Catherine laughed. She laughed a lot with Jarrod. It was a wonder that she did. She wouldn't have thought she could be this comfortable with him. Yet they seemed to fit together so well. She finished her envelope and reached for another. Jarrod reached at the same time. Their hands collided. Catherine glanced at him and grabbed for the envelope. Jarrod grabbed at the same time. She tried to take it. He stopped her.

"Stop," she said. He continued to hold on to the envelope she wanted in a game of tug-of-war.

Catherine took one of the addressed ones and threw it at him. He ducked but didn't release his hold. Then he took one of the other addressed ones and tossed it at her. She parried left so it missed her.

"This is childish," she told him.

"Yes," he agreed. "You let go."

"I saw it first," she said, trying not to laugh and losing the attempt.

They each continued trying to get the next envelope and throwing the already addressed ones. Smiling turned to laughter as both of them shifted and ducked the oncoming missiles. Jarrod reached for another envelope. He tossed it. Catherine pushed herself back. She overbalanced and started to fall. Letting go of the envelope, she grabbed for Jarrod. He let go too. The fragile hold she had on staying upright fell away. The two of them crashed to the floor into the pool of envelopes they'd thrown at each other.

Jarrod picked up envelopes and again tossed them

playfully at her. Catherine whipped her head from side to side, warding off any impact.

"Stop it," she cried, fighting the missiles. "Audrey will kill us if we don't finish."

"No she won't," Jarrod said. "I'm bigger than she is."

"It isn't strength she'll need."

Jarrod stopped his banter. She looked up at him. The smile on his face disappeared. Catherine swallowed, feeling her heart race and her throat go dry. Jarrod reached down and brushed her hair from her forehead.

"What are you doing?"

"Playing with your hair."

Catherine froze. She felt the warmth of his touch traveling through her.

Jarrod was staring at her. Catherine couldn't move. For some reason his gaze kept her still. His hand caressed her hair near her shoulder. She felt his fingers tugging the lock he held but didn't move, letting him rub the strands back and forth between his fingers.

"I like your hair," he said in a whisper. "I like the feel of it."

"Most . . . most men like women's hair," she got out. What was he doing to her? Why was her body reacting this way? As if she were in some huge cosmic tingling machine. The feeling was pleasant, calming, enjoyable, but she could feel the underlying strength beneath it. She knew the pleasure could change to rapture, the calm to excitement and the enjoyable to inevitable. She needed to stop this. She needed to break the veil that had been knitted around them. She needed to reach for something solid, something that would restore her world to the normality she knew existed but couldn't seem to make herself want to find.

"I like the feel of *your* hair," he murmured. "It's soft like the night."

Catherine had never heard him speak like that before. She'd tried to make his comment general, but he'd refined it to specific. His words enwrapped her. His hand advanced from her hair to her cheek. Somewhere in Catherine's mind she knew this was outside the rules, but she couldn't for the life of her remember what the rules were.

"Jarrod." Her voice was unrecognizable as her own. It was dark, low and . . . *offering* was the only word she could think of to describe it. She was offering herself to Jarrod. Asking him to take the next step, a step she, in her rational mind, had already decided wasn't to be taken. But there was nothing rational going on in her mind.

Jarrod seemed to hear her silent plea. He leaned forward. Catherine's eyelids lowered. She saw his mouth coming toward her. It was a sensual, kissable mouth. She could feel desire building within her. She wanted it, wanted to feel his kiss again. She wanted to know the same sensations she'd experienced in the swing at Audrey's could be repeated.

Catherine reached up and cupped Jarrod's face. She held it for a second, feeling the smoothness of his shaven skin. Then her head lifted the tiny distance that separated them.

His mouth was soft and warm against hers. Emotion replaced logic in her mind. Feelings took control of her. Sensation snaked around, over and under her. Jarrod's body lay partially across hers. He scooped his fingers under her neck and pulled her into his embrace as he deepened the kiss. Catherine's arms slid around his neck, drawing him close to her.

Jarrod covered her with his body. A moan as pure as a first light after an Alaskan winter escaped her throat. Jarrod raised his head for a moment. Catherine saw raw need in his eyes. His mouth took hers again. His tongue dipped into her mouth, then aggressively took control. She welcomed it, welcomed the feelings that climbed over each other as they raced through her system. Her entire being melted in the white-hot explosion that took hold of her. The air was sucked from the room. She could feel it liquefying before it evaporated, leaving them in a vacuum of sensation, a sizzle of emotion. Erotic soldiers charged inside her, carrying out commands Jarrod's mouth issued. She heard him groan and felt herself lifted as if her body merged with his.

Incapable of thinking clearly, Catherine wrapped herself in Jarrod. Feeling the tilt and whirl of a carnival ride, she was dizzy with wonder, drunk with the effect of his mouth devouring hers. She didn't know how long she could go on. She didn't want it to stop, never wanted him to release her, but she was sure she'd die in this magical world of sensual pleasure.

No one was meant to know this. No one was meant to understand the depths one man could carry a woman to. They'd crossed over the threshold somehow, moved beyond the realm of reality and entered a fantastical world of uncharted seas and panoramic idealism, where light was pure, blinding and indescribably magnificent.

Catherine didn't know when Jarrod ended the kiss. She only knew he was holding her against his chest, her head on his shoulder, her heart hammering like an electric drill, and she was panting for breath. Her body was flushed and hot and she felt as if he'd made love to her. Through her clothes, he'd taken her, shown her what life with him could be like, what she would miss in her sham of a marriage. What deception really meant. They weren't deceiving everyone else. The deceit was all internal.

And she was going to have to live with it.

Concentration was out of the question today. Jarrod had a desk full of work to get done. Blue prints spilled from his drafting board onto the floor. Designs for buildings in various stages of completeness could not keep his attention. His return to Rhode Island brought him back to the firm that had sent him to England, but it took only days to become routine and full. Yet Jarrod couldn't think of work. His mind was elsewhere, lost on a dining-room floor in a small house only a few miles from where he sat. He'd relived that kiss a hundred times in the past three days. It and Catherine were taking over his entire life.

The problem was, he hadn't intended to kiss her. He hadn't expected their light banter to land them on the floor, but instinctively his hands had reached for her when she started to fall. Then everything took on a life of its own.

You'd think he'd have learned by now. He was twenty-nine, not nineteen. Men and women didn't play together unless they were both prepared for the consequences. Catherine had explained the rules. And kissing her wasn't allowed, not unless it was necessary, prompted by an audience, expected by a crowd, not when they were alone. Yet her hair had intrigued him, especially the way she kept flipping it over her shoulder.

He should have known better than to start playing with her. He had plenty of history that told him nothing ever went as planned with Catherine. When he'd intentionally hit the tennis ball onto the lawn and she ran to get it moments before the sprinklers came on, she slipped and hit her head. He spent half the day in the emergency room, then the other half keeping her awake all night to make sure she was all right. When she was sixteen, he hired an ice cream truck to come to her birthday party, but instead the male strippers he'd hired for another party showed up. He never thought her mother would get over that, especially when Catherine wanted to date one of them.

He ran his tongue over his tooth, physical evidence of another prank gone wrong. This time he'd been the one in the emergency room when their sailboat had cracked up on the rocks near Benton Point and he'd been thrown head first onto a rock.

And now he was in a quandary. What was he to do about Catherine? He could back out of this, claiming they didn't know each other well enough. But weren't engagements a time for people to get to know each other? Couldn't they say they'd discovered their marriage just wasn't going to work out and they found out before any real harm was done?

Jarrod stared blankly at the blueprint in front of him. He'd been looking at it for nearly an hour and felt as if he'd never seen it before. Everything about the blue and white lines was like a foreign language to his brain. He'd worked with men who had one-track minds. He always prided himself on being able to juggle several things at one time, but he was no longer earning his keep. Catherine consumed his thoughts like a jealous goddess, demanding his full and undivided attention.

He thought more about breaking their engagement. For both their sanity it was the right thing to do. But would Catherine understand? She was convinced Audrey and her mother were out to find her a man, any man; they just wanted her married. Jarrod understood. He'd seen Audrey in action more than once, and when she combined forces with her mother there was no stopping them. But Catherine had managed to elude any unwanted proposals up to this point. She could continue doing it. Or . . . he stopped. He could find her someone else to marry. That would get him off the hook.

Jarrod forgot the plans on his desk and started thinking of the men they both knew, someone who was compatible with Catherine—just enough to make her family believe she could fall in love with him. Half an hour later he'd rejected every male in the area over twenty and under fifty. They were too young, too old, too silly, too starchy, too tight, too loose, too everything . . . Jarrod wouldn't admit he didn't want her marrying anyone else. He couldn't see her lying on that floor in her dining room, throwing invitations and laughing or playing bride-and-groom with anyone other than him. If this engagement was a test of his will, he'd already lost the battle.

The bridal shop was busy with happy brides, bridesmaids and mothers. Catherine turned in circles at the direction of the seamstress, who put pins everywhere. The clerks moved through the aisles, carrying dresses in and out of fitting rooms. Every now and then there was a burst of laughter or a cry of surprise as a bride, completely dressed in wedding regalia, stepped out and awed her friends and family. Catherine turned to look every time she heard the sound. She found it hard not to get caught up in the moment. To remember that she was here to go through the motions. That her wedding was a friendly arrangement and not a real marriage.

"Stand up straight." Catherine forgot the seamstress's instructions. "We're nearly finished." Quickly she obeyed the small woman's command and looked over the brightly lighted room. Audrey was the only person with her. Elizabeth would be her maid of honor, Audrey and two other close friends her brides-maids. Their dresses would be in next week and they would come for their own alterations.

"Okay," the woman said with a satisfied smile. She stood back. She wore a short blue smock over her dress. A tape measure hung around her neck, a wrist pincushion on her arm.

Tears sprang to Catherine's eyes as she turned on the fifteen-inch pedestal and saw herself reflected in the three-way mirror. Pain pierced her heart at the reflection of a bride, a beautiful, lace-covered bride, ready to take her vows and join the man she loved. She couldn't help it. The tears spilled down her cheeks, hot and salty.

"That's a common reaction," the seamstress said to Audrey. "Most brides don't know what emotions will come out when they put on their gown. Then everything is beautiful—blurred, but extremely beautiful."

"Catherine, you're so lucky," Audrey said. "Most brides don't find gowns that need practically no alteration."

Catherine stood on the pedestal, above her sister and the dresser, oblivious of anyone else in the room. She stared at the woman in the mirror. Inside the white lace and beads was her, Catherine Carson, impetuous, capricious, spontaneous, unpredictable, Catherine Carson. But who stared at her from the mirror? Who was this woman, dressed in white? She'd never thought of herself as a bride, never really expected to marry, especially after her breakup with Jeff Sherman. There was too much to lose in marriage, but with this dress on she could see all the promise, all the expectations of the bride and groom. She could hear the music playing, see the church aisle, imagine herself as she floated on her father's arm. She could see the bridesmaids and the groomsmen waiting.

It was surreal, cloaked with streaming rays of light, refracted through stained-glass windows. And at the end of the aisle . . . she gasped.

Jarrod!

He stepped out of the rays with his arms outstretched, waiting, inviting, beckoning. Catherine shook her head, dislodging the image. She had to get out of this dress.

"Unzip me," she said, moving off the pedestal and heading for the dressing room.

"Wait, Catherine," Audrey called. "You'll stick yourself with the pins. The dress doesn't need much, but there are still pins in it."

"Unzip me," she said through clenched teeth.

"Is anything wrong?" A saleslady rushed over, looking distressed. Catherine couldn't explain what had come over her. She didn't know it would happen. She needed to talk to Jarrod. He was right. This was not the right thing to do. Her plan was good, but she should have insisted they elope. A wedding with white gown and orange blossoms was the stuff of couples truly in love. They only needed a justice of the peace. The gown was too much. She couldn't marry him in a gown, walk down that aisle, stand up in front of all their friends and swear to love, honor and cherish.

She just couldn't do it.

"Catherine," Audrey called her name again. Catherine didn't answer. She tore at the sleeves to get out of the dress, uncaring of the delicacy of the fabric. Audrey looked at the clerk. "She's just nervous," Audrey explained.

"I'll get her something to drink," the clerk said, leaving them.

"Catherine, are you all right?" Audrey asked as soon as the woman left.

"I'm fine. I just didn't know I'd feel like this."

Audrey smiled. "That's all right, Catherine. All brides feel like this the first time they see themselves in a wedding gown. Suddenly they understand what everything is all about."

No, they don't, she wanted to shout. If Catherine told her sister what was really going on, she'd be appalled that she would even think of a fake engagement, let alone a wedding.

And after the wedding—what then? She was going to live with Jarrod. They were friends, but not lovers. *Not yet!* Her mouth opened in surprise. Where had that come from? *Stop it, Catherine.* She shook herself mentally. She knew where it came from. It came from the kiss she and Jarrod had shared. While he kissed her, she didn't want him to stop. She wanted him to go on and she wanted more. She wanted him to make love to her. Jarrod, of all people. She hadn't seen him in years, and when he had been there, he was always playing some joke on her or embarrassing her. Yet her mind was full of him. He was the only man she thought of when she thought of marriage. But this wasn't a marriage, she screamed silently. This was an arrangement for six months. Only six months.

Catherine reached down to pick up the dress and hand it to her sister. She stopped in mid-reach. Suppose Jarrod played another joke on her. Suppose he didn't show up for the ceremony?

A fresh batch of tears rushed to her eyes. She couldn't stop them. What was wrong with her? Catherine grabbed her jeans and shirt and quickly pulled them on. The clerk brought her a bottle of water and a glass. Catherine pulled the top off and drank from the bottle, tipping it up and draining the contents.

"Audrey, I have to go."

"But . . ."

"I know we agreed to do some shopping." Catherine couldn't remember what they were supposed to shop for—place settings, silverware, bed sheets, she didn't care. "I need to see Jarrod. We have to talk."

She slipped her purse strap over her shoulder.

Audrey stopped her exit. "There isn't anything wrong, is there?" Catherine's expression must have said something, for Audrey continued, "Most brides get nervous, Catherine. You and Jarrod didn't have a fight, did you? Dwayne and I fought over everything:

the silver, the tuxedos, the number of bridesmaids and groomsmen. You name it, we fought over it.''

"We didn't have a fight." Catherine pushed past her sister.

If only it had been a fight, she thought, pulling the door of her car open a moment later and getting inside. Fights were easy. She wouldn't have these feelings if they'd had a fight. What they had was a kiss, a devastating kiss, a wedding kiss, a forever kiss. Catherine didn't want that. She was getting married to get divorced. So why did she have a daytime dream? Why did she see herself in that dress with Jarrod waiting for her? Why did his expression say happily ever after?

Catherine put the car in reverse and backed out of the parking space. She drove to Jarrod's office. He would be there now. She pulled her car into the spot next to his Jeep. Something wouldn't let her get out. She couldn't see Jarrod right now. Her emotions were too close to the surface. If he looked at her the way he had before he kissed her, she'd dissolve. She couldn't do that. She wasn't in love. She needed time.

Reversing again, she backed out of the space and headed for the exit. She looked both ways but not in the rearview mirror. Pulling out onto the road, she never saw Jarrod come out of the building and stare at her retreating taillights.

Jarrod pulled into Catherine's driveway moments after she stopped her sporty Intrepid. He parked next to her car and jumped down from the Jeep. By the time she cut her engine he was standing at her door. He pulled it open, bent down and put the teddy bear he had in his hand in front of his face.

"I hear chocolates make you feel good."

Catherine got out of her car but didn't say anything. He peeked around the brown-and-white bear. He offered her the box of chocolates he held in his free hand.

"What's the matter? Is my information wrong?" He went behind the bear again. "It's not chocolates. It's Cracker Jack's." He peeked at her, this time producing a single box of Cracker Jack's from behind the bear. "I always did get my *C*s mixed up. You aren't Catherine at all. You're Crystal. Or is it Chantel?"

She crossed her arms and smiled. Jarrod lowered the bear.

"That's it," he encouraged. "Smile some more."

Catherine burst into laughter.

"I'd nearly forgotten the side of you that's silly, impractical and always ready to make a person smile."

Jarrod stepped forward, dropped the bear on the roof of the car and hugged her. He was silly over her. When Audrey called and said she left upset he was concerned. Then she arrived and left his office without coming inside. He rushed after her, remembering her love for Cracker Jack's and chocolate.

"How did you know I needed cheering up?"

"Radar," he said, closing the car door. He handed her the teddy bear and chocolates, and together they went inside her house. "Audrey called me at the

office. I saw you come and leave. Anything happen
you want to tell me about?''

Catherine dropped the bear on the coffee table in
her living room but opened the candy. She took out
a piece and popped it into her mouth. "Nothing
happened, really. I feel silly thinking about it."

"Tell me," he said.

"I don't want to tell you. That's why I couldn't
come into the office."

Catherine dropped down on the sofa, slipping her
shoes off and tucking her feet under her. Jarrod sat
down, leaving enough room between them to keep
from crowding her.

"I'm probably the only one you can tell." He
paused. "Just pretend it's raining outside, that there's
a raging thunderstorm taking place and we're alone."

That was the scenario they had from the past. They
talked to each other, and Jarrod knew the boundaries.
He knew when to kid her and when to take her seriously. He knew how to keep her secrets, and she
would keep his. If they'd started this engagement
differently, they would be a compatible couple.

"It isn't raining," she said.

"You're hedging."

Catherine took a deep breath and exhaled. "Audrey
and I were in the bridal shop. I put the dress on."

"Your wedding dress?"

She nodded. "I never expected to feel . . ." She
stopped. "It was all so surprising." She got up and
paced, as if she needed to collect her thoughts. "The
salesclerk and seamstress kept turning me around,
adjusting this and that. Audrey hovered like a mother
hen and I never really got a look at myself. Then they

all moved away, almost as a group, and I was alone, standing on that pedestal, staring at a stranger."

"A bride."

"A wife," she corrected him.

Almost a wife, he thought. That frightened her. Jarrod knew something about marriage frightened her. She hadn't completely told him what it was, but he could tell something had driven her to using a 1-800 phone number to find a man willing to marry and divorce her. Suddenly seeing herself in the role of wife must have scared her. She'd fight it, run away from it. Yet she'd come to him. Why? Because he represented the other half of her equation?

"I'm sure you looked beautiful," he told her.

"It wasn't me. It was a stranger."

Jarrod suddenly laughed. "Catherine, don't tell me after all these years, you don't know how beautiful you are? That was no stranger in the mirror. It was you."

She looked at him curiously. She was beautiful, breathtaking. Jarrod didn't know how he'd missed it. All the years they lived side by side and he'd played joke after joke on her, while all this beauty had slept in the house next door.

Jarrod went to her and took her hand. He led her into the hall by the door and stood her in front of the mirror. "Cathy, look at yourself," he said. He put his hands on her shoulders and stood behind her. "You're a beautiful woman. In a wedding gown, a nightgown, swathed in a towel or wearing nothing at all, you couldn't be anything else."

* * *

The salt air smelled sweet to Catherine. She took a deep breath and relaxed as Jarrod sped along the beach road with the top open. The wind pulled all the curl out of her hair, but she didn't care. She needed to get out of the house, needed Jarrod to take his hands off her shoulders or she'd turn around in his arms and break her own rule.

His voice had that rough, sexy quality to it. She could feel it undoing her defenses. Warmth burned up her face, into her ears; she even felt the strands of her hair grow warm. She faced him in the mirror, searching his eyes for a sign that he was teasing, that this was another of his jokes. What she expected to see there was a phantom of deception to complement his comment. She found none. What she saw made her heart pound. Did he really think she was beautiful?

Here was a different facet to Jarrod's character. Every time she turned around he surprised her. She was engaged to someone she'd known most of her life, but he was still a stranger. Jarrod had always been the joker, her enemy, a thorn in her side. Infrequently he'd been her savior, but now who was he? And why was it every time she found herself near him, her heart did flip-flops and her knees turned to water? She didn't even want to think about what happened to the rest of her body.

Jarrod had suggested they go to the beach, and she grabbed at the opportunity to move away from him and get her beach bag. He took her to *her* beach, the one where he'd put the ring on her finger, where the rock wall that was so prevalent in the state ran as far as she could see, where she liked to talk to the sea.

Today there were more people enjoying the sun. Jarrod held her hand as he led her to a secluded place in the shadow of a craggy hill.

"Do you want to go in the water?" he asked.

"Not just yet. I love to hear the sound the waves make. I think I'll just sit here for a while, but you can go in."

Catherine dropped down on the blanket Jarrod spread on the sand. She wore shorts and a sleeveless top over her swim suit. Jarrod stripped off his shorts, which came to his knees, and pulled the T-shirt over his head. Catherine struggled not to gasp when she saw him. Through clothes she knew he had a powerful body. Without clothes he was magnificent. His skin was evenly colored, almost mahogany, with rich, red undertones. She couldn't help staring at the tight muscles of his legs and arms. Jarrod looked as if his job entailed manual labor on a daily basis. Everything about him was hard, and Catherine found her hands itching to reach out and touch him, run her palms over his dark physique. Her mouth went dry and definite signs of arousal stirred within her.

"I'm glad you like what you see." Jarrod smiled and ran toward the water.

Catherine couldn't deny his comment. Shame at being caught with her hand in the cookie jar washed over her. Between the sun and Jarrod's affect on her, she should be nothing more than a mass of melted chocolate on the blanket. Yet her skin held her intact. She watched Jarrod run down the beach, unable to tear her gaze away from him. He was beautiful. She'd never seen a man more perfect. He'd stood her in front of a mirror today and forced her to look at herself. Now she looked at him, stared at him. He knew the effect he'd had on her. When had this happened?

She should get in the water. The Atlantic was often cold and refreshing; however, today she feared that if she walked into the water, her body would sizzle.

Chapter 5

It was her wedding day. Catherine couldn't believe how fast the last six weeks had passed. She also couldn't believe this room. Masquerading as a guest room, it now looked like the aftermath of a war zone, a war of roses, baby's breath, netting, gloves, tissue paper and discarded clothes. Bridesmaids crowded the mirrors, applying makeup and adjusting their hair. Catherine's mother bustled about as if she'd lost her way. Audrey muttered to herself about caterers, the band, the photographer, any number of details that needed her personal attention or the world would fall apart. Everyone was talking, raising the noise level to decibels high enough to repel dogs.

Bouquets, shoes, purses and spilled magazines were scattered on the bed, the floor, the dresser and draped across the sides of the antique mirror. The room looked like an explosion of white cotton mixed with clusters of pink and rose.

Catherine was the only one not moving or talking. People skittered about her as if she were an apparition. She looked at her white gown, seeing the irony of her ghostlike appearance. Yet she wasn't a ghost, and the man she was marrying wasn't a ghost either. She wished she were; then she wouldn't be the only scared person in this room; that is, if she discounted Audrey, who was probably afraid something would go wrong, like mayonnaise jelling in shrimp salad or the petals in the pool withering before the reception started.

She wondered what Jarrod was feeling at that moment. Was he as uptight as she was? Catherine looked around her. She wanted to scream, force them all to leave, give her some breathing space, but she was too frightened she'd come undone. Whatever was holding her together, she needed to cling to it or she'd be worse off than the other women around her.

A knock on the door arrested everyone's attention. They all stopped at once, as if some choir director had cut the last note with a quick snap of his thumb and forefinger. Everyone turned and looked at the white-with-gold-accented door as if they expected the horror from 20,000 leagues to enter.

It wasn't a monster, but one of Audrey's maids who came inside. She looked at Catherine and offered her a smile.

"The photographers are here," she said to Audrey.

Moments later, Catherine allowed the platoon of photographers to place Catherine and the bridesmaids in position. Thank God they lived in a small state. It seemed Audrey had hired every photographer available. Video crews and portrait photographers swarmed over the group, separating them and putting them together like marionettes. She smiled for the cameras, doing everything expected of a blushing bride, but her flush was due more to her deceptive plan than the love she should be feeling today.

She wished this whole affair was behind her. If she had it to do over, she would never agree to a wedding. An elopement would be quick and simple. Allowing Audrey to plan this circus had been her second mistake, but there was nothing to be done about it now. In a few hours it would be over. She and Jarrod would have the wedding and reception behind them. They'd be on a plane to Montana, away from everyone and able to relax.

She looked forward to the honeymoon. It would be a time she could literally let her hair down. There would be no one around they needed to pretend for. They'd be free to do as they pleased for a week. By the time they returned home, she'd be in a better frame of mind and could develop the routine she and Jarrod would play for the next six months.

Catherine plastered a smile on her face for the camera and that was how she remained until she stood at the back of the First Baptist Church. The music began and the bridesmaids went down the aisle. It was her turn now. The doors opened and the dream began. Catherine gripped her father's arm hard enough for him to look at her with concern. She released her hold and smiled as best she could. Sunlight streamed into the sanctuary, filtering through the stained-glass windows, giving the room the dreamlike quality she'd imagined nearly a month earlier. She stared at the figures waiting: her sister, her bridesmaids, Elizabeth. Then Jarrod stepped forward and smiled at her. She could see through the veil covering her face a smile that warmed her heart.

The wedding march began.

Catherine took the first step.

In New York City in the 1870s it was fashionable for married couples to accept the loan of a house in the country. The rich, who spent their summers in cottages by the ocean in Newport, set the standards of that closed society.

Jarrod and Catherine had been born in Newport, but neither would fit into the stringent rules of old New York society or even their own. If they did, they wouldn't be in the Montana mountains on a pretend honeymoon. Jarrod hadn't thought of tradition when he accepted the loan of this cabin from his friend. He'd thought of it as a perfect setting for Catherine. He'd been with Rafe, a buddy from architectural school, when he presented the design for the cabin. Jarrod had even seen several photos of the construction as Rafe built it. This place, however, was a cabin in the same way The Breakers was a cottage.

The great room was the heart of the house, a huge central area that ascended to the stained-glass roof. The walls were dark paneling, giving the place a subtle smell of oil soap. A wide staircase sat to the side, angling upward past a sweep of window that covered the entire wall. Uncarpeted steps veered onto a veranda that squared off the room like a Shakespearean balcony.

Jarrod pictured Catherine in this room. The fireplace was stone and enormous. Rustic enough to roast a cow on a spit in it, it dwarfed his six-foot frame. Jarrod hadn't expected it to be this cold in Montana in August. Apparently they were having an unusual cold spell. He'd built a fire as soon as he and Catherine arrived. The central heating was on, but the fire made it much more relaxing. The soft sounds of Wynton Marsalis played in the background.

After the wedding this morning, and the reception and flight, Catherine probably needed sleep more than anything else. Jarrod had brought champagne and set it on the coffee table in front of the sofa, near the fire.

He hadn't thought that being married had a feeling, but it did. He knew he would never allow anything to happen to Catherine if he could prevent it, but now he felt responsible for her, protective of her, that he was linked to her with a strong bond, even if it was for a finite period of time. During that time he'd follow the vows he had uttered this morning.

Catherine came out of her bedroom. Her footsteps echoed on the floor above. He waited for her to appear. She'd looked so beautiful that morning. His breath had literally been taken away when he saw her standing at the back of the church, poised, ready to join hands with him and swear before God and the entire congregation to be his wife. For the length of the aisle, he wished the fairy tale was real.

She came down the stairs dressed in a long white sweater and black slacks. The sweater reached her knees. It had a huge collar that stretched to her shoulders. It stood up and folded over, extending across her body and coming to a stop at the teasing swell of her breasts. The body of the garment hugged her curves, moving as she moved, with the flow of her steps, like those of an African queen, taking her from her private chamber to the cavernous throne room below.

She paused at the turn, her hand on the banister. During daylight the sky and mountains could make the scene look as if she floated on air. Her hair was still in the style she'd worn for the ceremony, pulled up on top of her head in curls that were too numerous to count. A single ringlet coursed down the side of her face, drawing attention to her high cheekbones and soft complexion. Jarrod swallowed.

"You ought to be tired," he said.

Catherine smiled, her eyes shining and bright. "I'm so glad it's over." She came forward. "You brought champagne. Wonderful. I love champagne."

Jarrod led her to the sofa, and when she was seated he poured the wine and handed her a glass flute.

"What shall we drink to?"

"Long life, love." She raised her glass and looked him straight in the eye. "And to the best friend a woman could ever have."

"Long life . . . love," he repeated. They clinked glasses and drank. Jarrod put his glass on the table. "I ordered some food. I thought you might not want to go out."

Catherine turned and looked at him. "From where? It's an hour's drive through nothing but trees and hills to the airport. Or are you hiding a Taco Bell on the other side of that mountain?" Her smile was wide and happy as she glanced toward the window, where all that could be seen was the reflection of the room within.

"Rafe's caretakers provided the food. All we have to do is microwave it."

Catherine sipped the champagne. "I'm not very hungry, but I love the attention. Are you going to be this attentive for the next six months?"

"Absolutely," he responded, hoping she didn't hear the catch in his voice.

Six months, Jarrod thought. Inside him something tightened around his heart. This was temporary. He had to remember that. Catherine was making this light. She was probably trying to put him at ease. It was their wedding night. But he wasn't at ease. He was tense. The last few weeks he'd become used to being with her, talking to her, explaining things, learning things. They were compatible. Jarrod kept to his promise. He hadn't touched her unless there was a reason. He admitted he wanted to, but she had an air that set limits.

He turned and stared into the fire. The flames licked the firewall and leapt toward the dark sky outside. Jarrod linked and unlinked his hands.

"Jarrod, are you nervous?" Catherine asked.

He turned back to her. His instinct was to say no. He found it difficult to be anything else when she was around except nervous. And he found it impossible to lie to someone who looked like a queen. "Yes," he whispered.

"Sit down, Jarrod." She smiled.

He walked to the sofa and sank down next to her. "If I knew it was going to make you happy, I wouldn't have told you."

"Happy doesn't mean power, Jarrod. I'm not planning to use the way you feel. I want you to be comfortable around me."

"Are you nervous around me?" he asked.

She waited a moment, then said, "Yes." Jarrod watched her eyes turn to the fireplace.

"Why?"

She shrugged. "I don't know."

Jarrod took her face and pulled it around so she had to look at him. "Want me to tell you?"

He saw arousal in her eyes. She said nothing, but he noticed the slight movement of the springy ringlet of hair that dripped inside the sweater and onto her neck. Jarrod clenched his hand so he wouldn't reach out and touch it. He watched it, his eyes glued to its movement, as if it were a talisman holding him with its power.

Then his hand moved. Slowly he grasped the hair lightly between his fingers. Catherine's breath caught. If he hadn't moved so close to her he wouldn't have heard it.

His knuckles touched the sweater's collar. She jerked, as if he'd shocked her. He looked into her eyes. Dark as the African continent they smoldered, Jarrod grew warm, his body tightening in places that felt good. Cathy made him feel good.

Pulling on the free strand, her head moved closer to his. Jarrod felt her breath on his mouth. He smelled the light fragrance she often wore, and that underlying scent that made him want to growl, along with the champagne. He saw her eyelids droop, then close. Barely an inch separated them. Jarrod moved to eliminate the separation.

"No," Catherine said, turning away from him.

He took a deep breath and let it out in a whoosh that emptied his lungs. She was in his arms, her head on his shoulder, his arms around her. Her arms were at her sides. Jarrod could feel her body vibrating. He should let her go, but he didn't want to. This was what she did to him. She'd bring him to the brink and set a limit.

He'd reached it.

"Catherine," he whispered.

"Yes?"

"What is the real reason you're afraid of marriage?"

"I'm not afraid."

"You're terrified." Jarrod remembered the times he'd held her before. He knew she was attracted to him, aroused by him. All he had to do was push her back to stare into her eyes to see the truth; the dark phantomless depths dilated her pupils and let him see the fire inside, the smoldering depths that he could bring to the surface and the flare of heat that would ignite if his mouth touched hers. He was sure his kisses set her on fire as much as they did him, but she hid behind her conviction that she only wanted to marry to divorce. There had to be more to it than family pressure.

Pushing herself away from him, Catherine poured more champagne into her glass and got up. She walked to the fireplace and looked into the grate. She was small next to the gigantic hearth. Then she turned to him and took a drink. Jarrod sat back and waited.

"What did your mother do before she married your father?"

"What?" Catherine didn't often evade a direct question.

"What did she do?"

"You know what she did. She was a sales rep for a computer corporation."

"What about your Aunt Marjorie?"

"Catherine, what does my Aunt Marjorie have to do with anything?"

"Do you remember what Audrey's dream was?" Jarrod didn't answer. Catherine seemed to be ready to tell him. "She was going to open her own business. Look at Wendy Miller."

"Wendy had her own business."

"Yes, *had* being the operative word. Wendy got married and gave up her dream."

"So this is why you're afraid? Because Wendy Miller gave up her business?"

Catherine came and sat on the table in front of him. She leaned forward, her arms on her thighs, her fingers linked around the glass. "It's not Wendy or Audrey or any of them. It's all of them. They had dreams and then they married. Somewhere their dreams got lost, but never their husbands' dreams. Look at your father and Wendy's husband and Audrey's. Audrey is too busy running everyone else's life to realize *she* doesn't have one."

"You don't have to be like any of those women. And if you find the right man, you don't have to worry that he'll take your dreams away."

"That kind of man doesn't exist."

"Maybe you just haven't looked hard enough," Jarrod said. "Or maybe you won't let yourself look." His mother had mentioned many times how much she enjoyed selling and meeting new people before she married. Jarrod always thought her statements were tinged with humor. Could she have been hiding a serious statement under pretended merriment?

When Jarrod looked back at Catherine she was staring at him. His statement had been suggestive. He didn't know if she could read his thoughts, but he would never want her to give up her dreams.

"Define marriage," he asked her seriously.

"What?"

"You heard me."

"Which definition would you like—the idealistic definition or the real one?"

"I can handle it, give me both."

She poured another glass of champagne. This time she filled his and handed it to him. He let his hand touch hers for a moment before taking the wine and sipping it.

"Idealistically, marriage is a partnership. Two people fall in love, get married and work *equally* at building a life together. Each half of the partnership is as important as the other. Instead of one partner's job becoming more important than the other. They each are equally important. Instead of one partner making unilateral decisions as to what is the best course, they discuss it and make a decision that benefits the marriage."

Jarrod nodded. "And the real world?"

"In the real marriage, the wife gives up her dream for her husband's. The world pays him more as a rule, society looks at him as the breadwinner, the provider, the protector of the weak and meek. So wives fall in line."

"Even in this day of feminism."

She smiled and drank from her glass. "I'm afraid so."

"So your system to avoid the *real* marriage is the planned divorce method?"

"Works for me." She shrugged.

"Somehow it seems like cheating."

"How?"

"Not taking the chance, you opt out without even trying. Suppose there is a man out there who thinks like you do? You've already decided he isn't worth the effort. And by your own definition, it's a partnership."

"Oh, so you're the exception to the rule."

"I didn't say that."

"You didn't *not* say it either. I understand that going in we all think it's a partnership, but then life takes over. We must eat, so we go the way of the most money. Then it becomes his job, but it doesn't matter about the amount of money. It happens in marriages where money isn't an issue. Then it becomes travel and entertaining. And it's always the female who gives up for the good of the marriage."

"What about love?"

"What about it?"

"Don't you think the fact that these couples are in love with each other and the changes happen for love is a good thing?"

"Of course they happen for love. Most of them don't even realize they've done it. Suddenly they're middle-aged or old and feel like failures because they never did anything they really wanted to do."

"Catherine, that isn't it."

"Excuse me?"

"There's another issue here. One you haven't mentioned. I might believe you if you came from a low-income family and your parents never had enough money to make ends meet, but all the people you cited are wealthy. They have the means to do what they want. If my mother gave up working for her family, it was her choice or because her priorities changed, not because she thought my father's goals were more important than hers. Audrey's life is giving parties and making her house a showplace. She's doing what she wants to do, and Wendy Miller closed her business because it wasn't making enough money. She made a fiscally sound decision." Jarrod took a breath. "What is the real reason?" She stared at him for a long time. Jarrod didn't think she was going to answer. "Catherine," he called her name.

"I've told you the real reason," she said, but she was lying and he knew it.

Jarrod took the glass out of Catherine's hand and set it on the table. "Tell me about him."

"Him?"

Jarrod nodded. "The man you were engaged to."

Catherine recoiled visibly. "He has nothing to do with this."

"I think he does. He obviously put you through a traumatic experience and you've adopted this attitude that you'll never marry because of him."

"I'm already married." She got up and walked away from him.

"No, you're not."

She turned back and stared at him.

"I don't mean sex, Catherine," he said, then paused. "Although I don't rule it out." She dropped her hands. "Marriage is a decision. It's when two people come together and decide to share their lives. A ceremony doesn't make you married. You're only married when your minds meld." He took a step toward her. "Now, tell me about the engagement."

"I thought I was in love," she began. "I know better now. I know that Jeff and I never thought along the same lines. We never would have made it as a couple." She sat down in a chair. Jarrod stretched out on the floor, his back against the sofa. He listened while she related details of living in New York, meeting Jeff Sherman and how he wanted to manipulate her life. Jarrod listened without comment until she finished.

He was irrationally angry at a man he'd never met. He was sorry she'd been hurt, sorry he hadn't been there to help her through it, but now he understood a lot more about Catherine.

"Some guy screws with your head, convinces you to marry him, not against your will, and when you find out his plans don't coincide with your own, you vow to never allow it to happen again." He leaned forward. "You resign from a job that had solid potential, one that you were good at, to run to the sanctuary of home, where you write shipping brochures and discover that all the females in your world have, in your eyes, compromised their ideals for the men they love."

"I did no such thing."

"And you'll never be one of them. It'll never happen to you, because you won't let it," he continued, ignoring her interruption. "You'll pretend to conform to society, because both of us know you've never been a conformist, and you'll bow to their mores for a short time, but you'll cheat everyone in the process. And at the top of the cheat list is you, Catherine."

He got up from the floor.

And me.

The clock read four A.M. Catherine groaned as she turned over. With the time difference it was six o'clock in the morning. She'd been up all night.

She hadn't imagined her wedding night would be

like this; but then, she'd never intended to have a wedding night. Wasn't that what she'd essentially told Jarrod earlier? She hadn't intended to argue with him either. If it hadn't been for her mother and Audrey, Catherine wouldn't even be here. And Jarrod wouldn't be on the other side of the wall, angry with her. She could remember being angry with him, but never had he been angry with her.

She threw back the covers and swung her feet over the side. She couldn't stay in bed any longer. She wasn't going to sleep. She might as well go downstairs and riffle through the books in the great room's cases. She stood, wondering how many people actually read on their honeymoon.

Slipping her feet into shoes with small clear plastic heels, compliments of a misguided Audrey, she pulled the robe that went with the wedding night ensemble, this one from her mother, around her.

Downstairs the fire was almost out. Catherine put more logs on it. Red sparks shot up as the heavy logs fell. Soon the fire roared, lighting the room with a glow that turned her skin richer and darker. She sat down on the sofa where Jarrod had been earlier and pulled the knitted afghan someone had left over her.

The conversation she and Jarrod had had earlier came back to her. What did she want to do that couldn't be done if she were in love and married? Did she want to be in love? She'd tried love. Jeff Sherman had been the man she was engaged to marry, but that had led to disaster. She couldn't face that kind of disaster again. Would she have that with another man, with Jarrod?

Looking up, she stared at the door of the room where Jarrod slept. It concerned her that they'd argued. They had always been friends. She never thought of their relationship changing. She knew they would grow up, and eventually their lives would be different. He wouldn't pull her braids because she wouldn't have braids. When he married, his wife would be her friend too, although she couldn't imagine any of Jarrod's dates as his wife.

She snuggled into the afghan, shrugging off thoughts of their argument. She liked Jarrod more than she'd thought she ever would. Most of the time they were on the same level. Since they'd become engaged his kisses sent her senses rocketing and she missed his touch, even though she set the boundary. At the wedding, when the minister pronounced them husband and wife, Jarrod had lifted her veil and bowed his head toward her. She looked in his eyes and glimpsed something she'd never seen before. Then his arms were around her and his mouth was on hers and she was lost in the sensations that invaded her body. Jarrod could take her to a world she'd only envisioned in fantasies. In his arms she let her fantasies have freedom, something she'd never done with anyone else.

Catherine looked down at her hands. She stared at the two rings resting there. She was married. To Jarrod. The engagement ring was Jarrod's grandmother's, but the wedding band was totally his. He'd shown her their names on the inside of the ring while they were on the plane. They were beautiful. The most beautiful rings she'd ever seen. Though the wedding gown had affected her, Catherine didn't think she'd have these feelings of emotion choking her when she thought of the rings. They didn't represent love or eternity, the endless or unbroken circle of a world without end. They stood for an arrangement, a temporary agreement between two people for a mutual purpose. Yet something moved inside Catherine when she looked at them. Emotion clogged her mind when she thought of her . . . husband. The rings had no power. Their promise held no preeminence, no sovereignty, yet the bond they represented was definite.

"Cathy?"

Catherine's head wrenched upward. She leaned back. Jarrod stood at the railing above her head. She'd been so intent on the rings, she hadn't heard him open his door.

"What are you doing down there?"

"I couldn't sleep."

Jarrod started for the stairs. Catherine watched his progress as he moved about the open corridor above the huge, square room. His form was powerful in the darkness. He walked with the ease of a black warrior on a hunt, a man who should be holding a bow and arrow seeking his prey. Catherine shivered at the raw sexual awareness that streaked through her as fast as lightning and as unexpected as falling off a cliff.

Jarrod wore a short paisley robe that stopped at mid-thigh. Strong legs that should belong to a basketball player extended from the hem of the garment. Catherine stared at them as he came down the staircase and eventually stood in front of her.

"I thought you would be asleep at this hour. You've had a very long day," he said. "It's not our argument, is it?"

Their first argument as a married couple. Why did television glorify that? Catherine experienced no glory from fighting with Jarrod. She felt bad after the encounter. It had disturbed her sleep, but she had the feeling she'd be awake on this night under any circumstances.

"We've never really argued before, at least not over anything important."

"I know. I feel bad that we did. It's just that I wouldn't want you to lock yourself away in some mental convent over a man who didn't deserve you in the first place."

The comment sent a warmth through her that was unexpected. Jarrod seemed to be surprising her a lot since his return.

"I should be tired," she said. "I suppose it was the stress of the day, the trip here and not sleeping in my own bed."

Jarrod immediately sat down next to her. "We should have waited until tomorrow to come."

Catherine put her hand on his arm. "I'm fine, Jarrod. Don't worry about me." Then, realizing he was also up when he should be asleep, she asked, "Why are you awake at this hour?"

He smiled. "The same reason."

"You miss your bed too?"

"Just my pillow." They laughed. "And I want to apologize for saying what I did."

"I suppose there is a grain of truth in what you said. The breakup was angry. I don't suppose a person can go through any emotional experience and not have it effect some part of her, how she views the world or acts in the future."

Then the room quieted. Only the crackle of the fire and an occasional popping of burning logs created sound.

"You said you weren't in love with him."

"At the time I thought I loved him, but it was an illusion." Jarrod shifted in his seat. Catherine wondered if it was relief she felt in him. "Life was different in New York, something happening all the time. I loved the rush of it, the fast pace, the nonstop rhythm. It was moving so fast, I didn't see the reality of it."

"And what about loving the sea, the smell of the wood in the building yard?"

"I love that too." She smiled.

"Would you want to go back?"

"To New York?"

He nodded.

"I wouldn't mind." She had liked her job in the news department. It was frenzied and hurried and she was always running to get a tape to the floor or finish a flash that had just happened somewhere in the world. She was constantly on the phone with reporters the world over or passing out pages that needed facts checked. Would she do it again? Yeah, she would.

"You know what you haven't told me?"

She only stared, waiting for him to tell her.

"You haven't told me what you'd lose."

"Who I am," she answered. She waited again for him to comment. When he didn't she went on. "I know it doesn't sound like it could happen, even that I'd let it happen, but if I don't fight for me, no one else will ever know I was here."

"I'll always know," Jarrod told her.

After that they sat quietly, listening to the silence. Catherine tried to think of something to say, but her mind kept going to his legs and the robe. She watched as the satiny fabric slipped over his body. Was he wearing anything under it? Arousal fired inside her at the thought. She had to stop this. Jarrod was her friend. He'd agreed to help her fool her sister and her mother. She had no right to think of sex with him. She'd ruled sex out. But she couldn't stop thinking of it. Sex with Jarrod.

"What are you thinking?" Jarrod asked.

Catherine nearly jumped, as if he knew what her thoughts had been. Could he see it on her face? He could often read her like a book. Was this also open to him?

"That you must be cold," she said finally

"I am," he said. "Share your blanket with me." It wasn't a question. He grabbed the end of the afghan and pulled it over himself, moving closer to her.

Catherine went hot immediately. She tried to move away, but that pulled the blanket. Compensating, Jarrod slipped closer until his leg aligned with hers. Catherine could feel his hard, naked muscles against the sheer fabric of her gown.

He rested comfortably against the back of the sofa. Catherine sat stiffly next to him. "What did you think of the ceremony?" he asked, seemingly indifferent to her discomfort.

The wedding was a safe subject. She relaxed slightly, although her rising temperature was vying for her concentration. "It was longer than I thought it would be."

"Did you like it?"

"Like it?"

"Did you listen to the words the minister said?"

She nodded.

Jarrod raised his arm and slid it behind her neck. Her back went as straight as if she had a pole in place of her spinal cord.

"I listened," she said. Even though a tremor made her voice a note or two higher than normal, she kept her reply noncommital.

"And—" he prompted.

"I thought Audrey did a wonderful job on such short notice."

"I'm not talking about Audrey. Tell me why your hands were ice cold when we joined hands."

Catherine cleared her throat. "I've never been married before. I was nervous."

"Why? You knew what kind of marriage we'd have."

"It was all those words." She hadn't intended to say that.

"The minister's words. The vows."

Catherine leaned forward. "Jarrod, why are you giving me the second degree?"

He pulled her back, but not to the place where she had been on the sofa. He pulled her into the crook of the arm he draped over her as he repositioned the afghan. Catherine felt the heat again, but she liked it. She let it wash over her as she leaned against Jarrod. She'd stay here for only a moment. Then she'd resume her own position. It wouldn't hurt anything if she warmed herself with his heat for a moment.

Catherine didn't know how long she lay there. Her eyes closed and she listened to his heart beat. The sound comforted her. Jarrod's arm slipped from the back of the sofa and across her shoulders. He gathered her closer. Catherine let his arm pull her. Her arm slipped across the silky fabric of the paisley robe and rested at his waist.

"Cathy, you're driving me crazy." Jarrod's voice was a raspy groan, as if it were painful for him to speak. She raised her head and looked at him. He was closer than she thought. She could see his eyes clearly. The mischievousness she expected to find had been replaced by something deep, sincere. Catherine was caught in some kind of net—an invisible web that held the two of them. She wasn't afraid. Not even when Jarrod's head descended toward hers. His mouth dropped to hers. It was at once fierce, raw, wet and demanding. She shifted, turning into the kiss. Sensation raced through her, heat consumed the air like a flash fire. The all-consuming blaze robbed her of sensibility.

They were married. It was all right. Catherine heard the chant over and over in her head as Jarrod pressed her backward. The sofa became a mattress under her. Jarrod's mouth never left hers. Conflicting sensations warred inside her. Her body wanted his, yearned for him, cried out to unleash the pent-up need inside her and take the blessed release. Her mind told her to be cautious, to remember that this was an unreal situation, that neither she nor Jarrod was forging a lasting relationship. Neither she nor Jarrod was ready to commit to each other. But they wanted each other, and there was something in them exorcizing the need they had for each other.

His mouth was magic, taking her from the great room to the greater wonder and spangle of the night. Stars formed in her mind as his tongue mated with hers, asked for more, and she gave it without thought, pure need supplying an equal need.

He continued the wizardry. They slid from the sofa to the padded rug that ran in front of the glowing fire. The heat and color of the flames matched the raging inferno inside her.

"Cathy, I can't stand this much longer."

She heard his words. His body covered hers. She felt his hardness pressing against her and knew only the robe separated her from his naked skin. She ran her hands over the fabric, feeling the heat under her hands.

Jarrod's hands caught the hem of her gown. She felt the sizzle of heat when he touched her hips. Catherine didn't sleep in underwear. There was no barrier between the two of them. Jarrod pushed her gown upward, his hands going all the way to her breasts. Catherine couldn't stop the catch in her throat that bubbled out when his fingers reached her nipples. Sensation rioted through her body. Without volition her legs spread, accommodating him.

Jarrod groaned. He pulled her body up from the floor and yanked the gown over her head. His own robe was discarded and his body, red in the glow of the firelight, mixed with the lighter chocolate turned reddish-brown of her own. They stared into each other's eyes. Catherine's hands moved to his chest. She ran her hands over him, feeling the taut skin and rapid beat of his heart. Jarrod took her hand and pulled her back into his arms, his mouth aimed for hers. He pushed her down, threading his fingers through her hair.

"This is what our wedding night is supposed to be like," he whispered against her mouth.

The fire snapped.

Catherine jumped, pushing against him. "Jarrod, we can't."

"What?"

"We can't," she repeated.

"Cathy, we had blood tests for the wedding. We

made sure they checked for all diseases. We both know everything came back negative."

She pushed him away, trying to get out from under him. He held her.

"I'm not thinking of disease." She looked directly in his eyes. "I could get pregnant."

Chapter 6

The sun pierced his eyes when Jarrod finally woke. Rafael Patterson loved wide open spaces, the ability to bring the outside in, and since only the mountains had a view of the cabin he saw no need to shroud the windows with coverings. Jarrod's years in England, where every square of space contained something historic and there was very little available open space, left him a man welcoming curtains to block out the blinding light and the memory of Catherine in his arms that sprang to his mind the moment he became aware of the day.

He rolled away from the sun, a groan going with him. Last night had been a disaster. He'd heard Catherine's footsteps along the wooden floor. The clatter and snap of the slippers and the cadence of her walk when she left her room. He'd been awake, telling himself it was their argument, the room, the bed, the wedding and all its details keeping him awake. When the truth was, he was obsessing on Catherine. When he didn't hear her return in a reasonable amount of time, he went to the door. The fire burned bright as she stared into it. He'd wished he could see her face. She stared so blindly into the flames, he wondered what she was thinking. Then he called her name, and surprise registered on her face as she looked up at him. Her expression was one of being caught. Had her thoughts been the same as his? Was she dreaming of a real wedding night?

Jarrod swung his feet to the floor and stopped his wayward thoughts. His body was already hard just thinking of Catherine. He stood up and went to the shower. Thirty minutes later he was dressed and hungry.

He heard the music first when he opened his door. Looking over the railing, he saw everything was in place. The afghan he'd shared with Catherine was folded and lying across the back of the sofa. The smell of firewood mingled with flavored coffee permeated the warm air that rose from below. He could see the fire, not banked and dying but alive and leaping, as if it was being regularly tended.

Catherine, he thought. His gut wrenched and he grabbed the railing harder. He didn't know how to approach her, but she was down there, probably in the kitchen, if the coffee and music were any indication. Taking the steps slowly, he went to the kitchen door.

Pushing it inward, he found her. At the stove, her back was to him. Every cabinet in the room stood open. The center counter was covered with copper pots, bowls, measuring cups and various ingredients, including butter, milk, sugar, salt and baking powder.

The entire conglomeration was covered with a light coating of flour. Catherine had an apron tied around her waist as she bent over to open the oven.

She extracted a metal tray and turned around. She stopped abruptly when she saw him. Then she smiled, but her eyes were weary. "Good morning," she said. "I hope I didn't wake you. I tried to play the music only in this room, but it took a while to get used to the system."

She was nervous, Jarrod thought.

"I need to put this down," she said, moving to the cluttered counter and setting the tray on top of a pot.

"It smells good," Jarrod said. "What are you making?"

"I'm trying croissants," she answered. "Would you like some coffee?"

"I'll get it." Jarrod glanced at the coffeemaker. The pot was full, and in front of it stood a cream-colored mug with GOOD MORNING printed on it in five languages. He filled it and took a drink. He liked coffee. In England he drank tea with his colleagues, but at his home he savored the American coffee his mother sent him every couple of months. He leaned against the counter. Catherine's coffee tasted every bit as good as his own.

"I didn't know you could cook."

She swung around to stare at him as if his comment was a challenge. "I meant it," he said defensively.

"I can't cook," she told him. "I can do breakfast, spaghetti and any number of sandwiches."

"And croissants."

She glanced at the cookbook. "Your friend must

like French cooking. Most of the cookbooks specialize in some form of French food.''

"Can I try one?" He indicated the croissants.

"Do you dare?"

They were golden brown and a little lopsided. Some of them were completely round like biscuits, but they smelled good. Catherine looked around the room in several directions before deciding on a specific path. She went to a cabinet next to him and pulled down a saucer. Lifting a croissant from the tray she'd retrieved from the oven, she set it on the table. Jarrod sat down.

"Aren't you going to have one?" he asked as she turned away.

She nodded and picked up her own mug of coffee, which matched his. She sat across from him and bit into the misshapen piece of bread.

Jarrod tried his. "It doesn't look good, but it tastes fine."

"It's a little greasy." Catherine frowned. She reached for the marmalade and lathered a thin film on the delicate bun.

"Catherine," Jarrod began. "Last night—"

"Jarrod, I'm sorry." She cut him off. "I'm not a tease. I never intended . . . I mean, things just sort of got out of hand."

Jarrod put his hand on hers. She stopped talking.

"I don't want an apology," he said. "I don't want us to be uncomfortable with each other either. We've always been friends. Even through our jokes, we never lost sight of our friendship. I want to preserve that."

She pulled her hand free and picked up her mug. "You think we can be friends?"

Jarrod nodded. In his heart Catherine had taken

up a position greater than friendship, but friendship was all he could offer her and all that she would accept. From their conversation last night, before their aborted lovemaking episode, Jarrod knew she feared marriage. He didn't totally understand her fear of a long-term relationship, but he knew if he offered more she'd turn away from him.

"You weren't the only one on the floor last night."

Her eyelids dropped, concealing her expression. She'd pulled her hair into a ponytail with curls that dropped down her back. Jarrod was sure she'd made sure no errant strands could come loose and dangle at her throat for him to touch and set off the chain reaction that had had them naked and in each other's arms. Jarrod knew she was replaying that scene in her mind. It crowded into his consciousness with all the fire and color of the hearth as it had glowed in the early morning hours of their wedding night.

It took two days for the awkwardness to go away. Despite their agreement, being around each other, knowing that they had come so close to making love, had stolen most of their comfort with each other, but eventually Catherine relaxed and began to talk to Jarrod the way they had before anything happened. The two spent little time in the cabin. It seemed to be the one setting that made them most aware of each other. In the cabin they were alone, the mountains their only chaperones.

"This is it," Jarrod said. Catherine looked around. She sat astride her horse, the early morning light and the clear, fresh air of the mountains, green and lush on one side, brown and golden on the other, surrounding her. Jarrod dismounted and came to help her down. She went into his arms without hesitation and he lifted her to the ground. Immediately he released her, stepping back.

"Where is here?" she asked.

"This is what I wanted you to see."

Catherine walked in front of the horses, which Jarrod tethered to a low branch. The scenery was better than anything that could be captured on movie film. The display of colors couldn't be translated. It had to be seen, firsthand, with the naked eye. Catherine turned, taking in the full panorama of the scene.

"It's beautiful," she said, breathing in. He was quiet. Catherine glanced around. Jarrod smiled at her. "What?" she asked, seeing the Cheshire cat grin.

"Look over there." He pointed to a place on his left. Catherine followed the line of his hand. She saw only the mountain. Pine trees clustered about in groupings. "See anything interesting?"

Catherine glanced at the mountain and back to Jarrod. He was playing a joke, she thought. "Is this a trick question?"

He shook his head and came to stand behind her. Catherine immediately stiffened. He hadn't come anywhere near her in days.

"You can only see it twice a day. It's nearly time."

"See what?" She scanned the hillsides and the valley below.

"Just a second," Jarrod whispered. Then he put his hands on her shoulders. Catherine steadied herself. Heat poured into her face. Jarrod turned her slightly toward the west. "Look now." Again he whispered. Catherine felt his breath on her ear. She closed her eyes a moment to find her bearings. Then she opened them and she saw it.

"The cabin!" she said, as if she'd never seen it before. "Where did it come from?" Immediately realizing she'd made a stupid comment, she continued, "I mean, why couldn't I see it before?"

"It's a trick of the light and masterful engineering," Jarrod explained. "Rafe did it on purpose. He wanted to preserve the mountain, so he designed the cabin using its own material. In some cases, the sides are carved directly out of the rock. When the light hits it the right way, it appears and disappears when the light goes. If you don't stand exactly in the right place, you can't see it at all."

Catherine took a step to the side. He was right. The cabin disappeared. "It's like Brigadoon," she said, stepping back to the place where she could see the house.

"Exactly," Jarrod agreed.

"How long is it visible?"

"An hour."

"Brigadoon got a whole day."

"But it only showed up every hundred years. At least you can see the cabin twice a day."

"When is the next time?"

"It changes due to the seasons and the amount of daylight. On cloudy days you can't see it at all. When the light hits that ridge over there"—she had to turn around to see the place where he pointed—"light bounces off that rock and reflects backward toward the cabin. For an hour you can see it. Then it's gone until morning."

"You must enjoy being an architect, seeing your dreams come to life." She turned back, realizing her statement could turn into another discussion of dreams.

"It's restoring too. My years in England involved total restoration of some buildings. And what about your ships? You get to see them being built day by day."

"It's not the same as doing it yourself."

"Like those croissants."

She laughed. "I got a lot of satisfaction from baking those," she said, again revealing more of herself than she wanted. "If I keep at it, I could probably get the shapes right. It's the dough that's the hardest, according to the cookbook, and I managed to do that all right."

Jarrod sat down on a large boulder and took her hands. He pulled her forward and put his arms around her waist. "As long as you don't stay up all night making them, I'm willing to eat them." Catherine swallowed hard. She wanted to relax in his arms, but she knew better. This was the first time he'd made physical contact with her in days, and her body screamed for her to move into his embrace. His hands moved slightly at her waist, then stopped, as if he remembered they weren't supposed to do that. He pushed her back and looked up into her face.

"How would you like to go to a dance tonight?"

"Dance? Where?"

"When Rafe's caretaker delivered the horses he said there was a dance in town and we were expected."

"Expected?"

"Yep." Jarrod made the sound as if he were imitating the man. "There'll be barbeque to eat and the dance is in a barn."

"A square dance?" She hadn't been to a square

dance since ... She stopped. Square dancing reminded her of Jeff. He loved going to places where they did western dancing. Catherine had become really good at it.

"I didn't say that." Jarrod interrupted her thoughts.

"I'd love to go," she said. "Square dancing is something I can do. At least I'm as good at that as baking."

"I would never have thought it."

"You're mixing me up with Audrey. She's the one—"

The tone of his voice stopped her from speaking. "I would never mix you up with anyone."

If Catherine had wanted to say anything, the lump in her throat wouldn't have let her. What was going on here? What was going on in her head? Why couldn't she even think about Jarrod without her mind and body going on point? When he said things like that the hairs on the back of her neck stood up. She read everything and nothing into his words. She knew she made him nervous. She knew he was attracted to her. That night on the floor was one indication, but the first day in the gazebo at Audrey's house should have been a warning.

Why had she ignored it? She didn't want entanglements. That had been a prerequisite to this course. Neither of them wanted to be married. So why was she finding her thoughts focusing on Jarrod every moment of the day? They only had another two days before they would return to their lives in Newport. Her house wasn't as large as the structure across the other side of the mountain, but it was big enough for them not to get in each other's way for the next six months.

They only needed to play public parts. When the doors closed behind them, they could become the individuals they had been before Jarrod returned from England. Catherine squinted. She told herself it was due to the sun, but reality insisted it was something else entirely.

"Catherine, if we don't leave now, we're going to be late," Jarrod called from the bottom of the stairs.

Catherine rushed out of her room and raced along the corridor. "I'm ready," she said. "Almost." The last she whispered. "Are you going to be this persistent for the next six months?"

"Absolutely," he replied, a wide smile showing on his dark face.

Skipping down the stairs, she took in Jarrod's appearance. He wore jeans and a blue short-sleeved shirt with an open collar. The shirt was tucked in at the waist, and he had on a golden belt buckle. Catherine's jeans skirt was the same color as his pants and her western shirt had red pockets and fringe on the back. She wore matching boots with red tassels and carried her jacket over her arm.

"I can see this isn't your first barn dance." His appraisal made her heart flutter.

"Do you think I look like a drugstore cowboy?"

"You could never look like a boy. Come on."

He grabbed a jacket from the sofa and headed for the door.

"Wait a minute. I have something in the kitchen." She turned.

"You didn't make—"

Catherine stopped. The look she gave him cut his

speech. Going to the large room, Catherine picked up the silver disposable pan covered with aluminum foil and containing a generous portion of baked beans. She found a box top that was nearly the same size. Setting it in that, she headed for the front door.

Jarrod opened it and she swept through and down the front stairs. He opened the back door and she put the box on the floor of the Jeep.

"What's in that?" he asked.

"Baked beans."

"I thought you said you couldn't cook."

Catherine got in the cab. "I can't," she agreed. "I cheated."

"You did?"

She tried not to laugh, but she couldn't hold it in. "I called Audrey. She walked me through it until it was done."

Jarrod's laughter was deep. He started the engine. "You'll never be able to live this one down for the rest of your life." He put the Jeep in gear and it rolled down the driveway.

An hour later they arrived at the barn. It was on the property of August and Opal Corcoran. They owned a cattle ranch, and this was the final event before the cold weather was to set in. Catherine was greeted with hugs and best wishes and offers of assistance if she needed anything. She felt as if the people she met were going out of their way to welcome her and make her feel comfortable.

Opal Corcoran had taken the baked beans and placed them in the oven to reheat them. Jarrod took Catherine's arm and introduced her to the Belles, the Cranfords, the Smithsons, the Bufords and the Armstrongs. The others he did not know. Names whirled in her head as the music of fiddles and banjos reached to the top of the barn and bounced off the walls.

Catherine and Jarrod lined up with three other couples for the first square dance. Jarrod had two left feet, but he tried. Catherine's previous years of practice made her steps sure and her movements fluid. Often Jarrod was tangled, going in the wrong direction or turned back when everyone else faced front. The dance ended with her thoroughly laughing.

"Are you going to be this critical for the next six months?" he whispered.

"Absolutely," she said.

The music started up again, and Mr. Corcoran asked Catherine to be his partner. She accepted and spent the next hour dancing with more partners than she thought had names. But she was having fun. Her eyes sought Jarrod frequently. He danced with a number of partners. Catherine wasn't jealous, she told herself, but she longed to be swung around in his arms instead of the other women who crowded around him.

Catherine should be used to this. When he came back from England and she discovered him at Audrey's party, he was surrounded by some of her friends. Here was no different. Jarrod attracted women as the huge Montana sky attracted stars.

"Tell me, do you like Montana?" Tom, the man she'd just finished dancing with, asked her. Catherine turned back to him.

"I've only seen some of it."

"Yes," he said. "You're on your honeymoon."

"Montana is a big state. You couldn't see it in a week anyway."

"You must go to—"

"Catherine." A shiver ran through her. She turned. Jarrod stood before them. "Would you like to dance?"

She'd been waiting all night for him. The other men paled in his presence. Catherine wanted only Jarrod. She wanted to be in his arms again. She nodded, unable to speak. Tom excused himself, saving her the need to use her voice. The small band didn't play another square dance, but a country western song. The guitar cried out. Jarrod took her into his arms and folded her against him.

Catherine stared into his eyes as they began to move. His were dark. She thought they were darker than she remembered them. His hands on her waist were like hot irons. Catherine swayed to the music. Her arms closed around his neck. She closed her eyes and leaned against him. The smell of hay in the barn receded next to the cologne Jarrod wore. The faintly musky smell was warmed by his skin.

"Are you having a good time?" he asked, keeping her close.

"Yes," she breathed. She was having a wonderful time in his arms. "They are very nice people. How did you meet them all?"

He didn't release her to look in her eyes. He held her closer, and Catherine felt his arms cradle her with tenderness. His breath stirred her hair, and she felt it warm on her neck, expelled with a controlled slowness. "When Rafe built the house I came out." She felt his voice against her stomach. "We met then. They treated me as if I were family."

"I feel that way too," Catherine said, her voice difficult to get out. She relaxed her cheek against his,

going up on her toes to reach it. Pressing her body
to the contours of Jarrod's, she lost herself in the
song. He didn't speak again. For Catherine the room
did not exist; the people around her had disappeared.
Only the feel of Jarrod's arms holding her and the
sway of his body against hers made any sense, yet it
made no sense at all. She freed her mind to think of
nothing but the moment, being in his arms, feeling
as if they were the only two souls on earth. For the
three or four minutes of the song, she would stay in
this fantasy, where she felt loved and where she could
love.

Then the music ended.

By the time Jarrod pulled the Jeep into the circular
drive of the cabin, Catherine had been asleep for
nearly the entire hour's drive. She lay against his
shoulder and he didn't want to disturb her. He cut
the engine and the lights. Darkness swallowed them
as quickly as if someone had snuffed out the sun.
Jarrod listened to her breathing. Brushing his hand
over her hair, he reveled in the softness of it. He
wanted to wake her, gently urge her away from sleep,
have her look at him and want him as much as he
wanted her.

Softly he kissed her temple. Moving her with the
care he'd show if a doctor handed him a newborn,
he eased her back against the seat. He released his
seat belt and opened the door. The interior light
shone on her. She shifted but didn't wake. Jarrod got
out. The air was cold. He took a deep, restoring
breath. Walking around the hood, he went to Catherine's side. Quietly he opened the door and released

her seat belt. Then he leveled her toward him. Her eyes opened but didn't focus. Jarrod shifted her into his arms. She put her arms around his neck and settled her head against him.

"Oh, God," Jarrod breathed, adjusting her tighter. He stood still a moment. He couldn't move, not due to her weight, but rather to the weakness that threatened to buckle his knees when her mouth accidentally brushed his neck.

He went into the house and kicked the door closed. The sound woke Catherine.

"Don't do that," he said when she squirmed in his arms.

"Don't I have legs?" she asked, her voice groggy, almost child like. Jarrod thought she was fully awake, but maybe she was dreaming.

"You have legs."

"Can I walk?"

"No," he told her.

"Why not?"

"They don't reach the floor." Jarrod played her game. "And no one can walk if their legs don't reach the floor." He'd reached the stairs and began the ascent.

"Would you carry me?" She tightened her arms around his neck.

"It would be my pleasure."

"No, it's my pleasure. I get to see the stars." Jarrod stopped at the float point, the place on the stairs where he felt they were suspended. "It's beautiful."

"Catherine, how much did you drink?"

She sat up. "You think I'm drunk?"

She wasn't drunk. She was playing. He could smell

nothing on her breath except barbeque sauce and baked beans.

"I know you're not drunk." He continued up the stairs.

"Where are we going?" She turned to look down over the banister and into the room below.

"You're going to bed."

"Alone?" she asked. Jarrod stopped and stared into her eyes. "Aren't you going to bed too?"

"Yes." He resumed walking.

At her door Jarrod stopped. Catherine reached down and turned the handle. "You can put me down now," she said.

Jarrod didn't argue. He lowered her legs to the hardwood floor, holding her against him. For a charged moment they stared into each other's eyes. Jarrod brought his hands to her face. He cupped her cheeks and pulled her forward. His mouth touched her forehead in a soft kiss.

"Good night," he whispered. Then he stepped back and went to his own room.

He didn't look back. He knew she was standing in front of her door, waiting, staring at him as he walked away. He didn't know what Catherine was thinking. He hadn't known what he planned to do when he lifted her out of the Jeep, but for some reason he knew he couldn't look back, couldn't turn around and let her see how much he'd wanted to enter her room, how much he'd wanted to move his lips from her forehead to the soft, kissable mouth that had touched his neck and taken the strength from knees that could heft small logs or bound pipes or hold the weight of one beautiful woman. He reached his door, opened it.

"Jarrod."

He froze. He didn't breathe. His hand crushed the clear glass knob with a force that should turn it to powder. Catherine had called his name, stopped him. He'd hoped she'd do it, but he never thought she would. In the dark hall her voice was low and sexy and did things to his heart. He turned back. The only light came from a lamp farther down the hall. She stood in the darkness, almost silhouetted. Jarrod outlined her form with his eyes.

"I enjoyed the dance." Her voice was a murmur, but she meant it. He could tell from the tone of wonder and fulfilled dreams. She was Alice exploring all the gardens of Wonderland or Dorothy as she gazed upon the Emerald City for the first time. "Our dance," she finished.

Jarrod's heart leapt to his throat. She meant their dance, being in his arms, not the entire night of dancing, but the time the two of them had spent together. He could feel the room sway, exactly as it had before.

"Would you like to dance?" He paused. "One more time?"

"We have no music."

Jarrod walked back to her. He placed his hands at her waist. She turned easily into his arms.

"We both have legs," he said.

Chapter 7

The honeymoon was over. Catherine hoped the friendship was intact. Two nights ago they had danced in the hall. Both bedroom doors stood open, but when the dancing ended, they sat on the floor and talked until the sun tinged the sky. Catherine had sat against the wall outside her door while Jarrod stretched his legs in front of him and leaned his back on the carved railing. She didn't remember changing positions to lie down or crawling into Jarrod's arms, but that's where she woke in the morning. She was still wearing her skirt and blouse, and her boots stood together near her feet, out of reach. Jarrod's shirt had been pulled free of his jeans. His belt, with the huge gold buckle, and lay near her boots, and her arms were around his waist as if her hands were guilty of the removal.

Catherine couldn't move. Jarrod pillowed her head

on his shoulder. His arm ran down her back and rested on her hip. She looked at him for a long time. Then she closed her eyes and curled herself closer to him.

Catherine remembered that morning as the limousine negotiated the narrow streets of Newport. If she and Jarrod had wanted to return to Newport unnoticed, their plan was aborted by good ol' Audrey. A limousine awaited them at the airport. It stopped in front of Catherine's house. Jarrod took her hand as the driver opened the door.

It looked different, Catherine thought, getting out of the car. When she left the weathered, cedar-shake structure it had appeared huge and roomy; now it looked smaller. She shook off the notion, telling herself the memory of the size of the cabin and the vastness of the Rocky Mountains was still foremost in her memory.

Catherine's front door opened, and Jenny stood there. "Welcome back, Mrs. Greene." She turned to Jarrod. "Mr. Greene."

Catherine was confused. "Thank you, Jenny." Jenny was one of Audrey's maids. "What are you doing here?"

"Ms. Audrey sent me over to get you settled. She said all brides need help."

The limousine driver opened the trunk and set their suitcases on the ground. Jenny's husband Christian appeared behind her. He took the suitcases and went inside with a nod and a smile.

"A couple," Jarrod whispered. Catherine squeezed his hand, which she was still holding.

"This . . . this is a small house, Jenny." She didn't intend to stammer. "Jarrod and I want to be alone."

Jarrod took advantage of the situation and put his arm around her waist.

"Ms. Audrey knows that. You won't even know Christian and I are around. We'll be here during the day. You'll have the place totally to yourselves at night." She smiled sweetly. "Come on in. I've got a meal waiting for you."

Catherine looked to Jarrod for help. She would swear there was a smile on his face. Without warning, he bent down and swept her off her feet.

A slight scream escaped her. "What are you doing?"

"I'm carrying my bride over the threshold." He took her inside and set her on the floor. "It's traditional for the groom to kiss his wife in their first home."

Catherine stepped back as if he might do it. The thought caught her off guard. She remembered where his kisses had landed them the last time. It was better to keep away from things like that unless necessary.

"Don't worry, I've carried you in. I can wait for the kiss."

"Jarrod," she started, but found she had nothing to say. "The dining room is this way."

Catherine found the wedding gifts stacked against the wall in a room made for formal dining that she had used only three times since she'd returned from her time in New York City. Obviously Jenny and Christian had not arrived for the first time today. The room was dust-free and spotless. Even the windows gleamed from a fresh cleaning. The table was set for two, and Jarrod held her chair as she sat down. In front of her plate was a silver tray with an envelope on it. Catherine recognized her sister's hurried scrawl.

"What now?" she muttered picking up the cream-colored envelope. The flap wasn't sealed. She slipped it open and withdrew the single sheet of paper. "Welcome home," she read silently. "The first year is the hardest and we know you like living simply. To help ease your transition, here's one final wedding present. You may have the loan of Jenny and Christian for one year. They will alleviate the mundane tasks of daily living and give you time to yourselves." It was signed, "Love, Audrey and Dwayne."

Catherine handed the paper to Jarrod, who scanned it quickly and tried to hide the smile that curved his mouth.

"I'm glad you find this funny."

"Catherine, you're the only woman in the world who would balk at having a maid."

"Jarrod . . ." She looked over her shoulder to make sure Jenny wasn't hovering nearby. "We can't have them in the house with us."

"They said they'd only be here during the day."

"I know, but it means they'll expect us to use one room."

"One bedroom," he corrected, leaning his arms on the table and whispering the words as if they were co-conspirators.

"I can't share a bedroom with you. That wasn't part of the plan."

"You slept with me just two nights ago," he reminded her.

"I did not."

"Correct me, but what would you call that position of unconsciousness where you had your arms around my waist and your head on my shoulder?"

"Jarrod, you know that was different."

"Maybe, but when you woke up you didn't move your arms. And you stared at me for a full half hour before curling those long legs around me and going back to sleep."

Catherine gasped. "You were awake!" Her ears burned with embarrassment.

He said nothing.

"Why didn't you say something?"

"From where I *lay*, words were totally unnecessary."

"Jarrod, you know what happened was unintentional. And we're home now. We cannot stay together here."

Catherine needed to forget that morning in Montana. She was warm with feelings she had no right to even think about, let alone know and understand. She'd let her defenses down for that short period. She'd looked at Jarrod as a woman who could fall in love. She never dreamed he was aware of her.

"Why not?"

"Think about it, Jarrod. Where do we put your clothes, in the guest room? Then every morning you can get up, make the bed and come to my room before Jenny and Christian arrive to cook us breakfast."

"Isn't it usually the other way around?"

"This is serious, Jarrod."

"Catherine, it's not the end of the world. What are the consequences if we don't share a room?" Jarrod startled her.

"Audrey will know." Why wasn't he taking this seriously? "Jenny will mention it to someone and Audrey will find out. She'll tell my mother. The two of them will think we're arguing, and it's too soon for that."

"Then you'll have to tell them this is all a pretense

and we'll need to return all those gifts." He indicated the stack that flanked the wall and extended out until there was little room to negotiate around them. "And all of Newport will know about our scam."

His sarcasm irritated Catherine. "You're not going to try and help me, are you?"

"In sickness and in health, darling. In sickness and in health . . ." He dangled the vow at her.

Jenny came in then with their meals. She set plates in front of them with succulent London Broil under a light gravy, parsley potatoes and asparagus arranged for both visual appreciation and ease of hunger. The aroma caught Catherine's attention and her stomach growled in anticipation. She didn't know if Jenny had felt the tension in the room before she left. It was the first time Catherine actually felt that Jarrod was truly trying to work against her. And she had no idea why.

They ate in silence. The food was every bit as good as it looked. Unfortunately, it didn't solve their problem.

"We'll work it out, Catherine," he said when they finished eating.

"Would you like coffee?" Jenny reentered.

"I'll have it in the den," Jarrod answered immediately. "I have to make some phone calls."

"None for me," Catherine said.

Jenny left again, and they both stood to leave the room. Catherine walked a few steps in front of Jarrod.

"How?" she asked, turning back. "How can we work this out?"

"We could fire them," Jarrod suggested. Catherine's head snapped up to look at Jarrod. His expression belied his words. "Or we could sleep in the same room." He dropped a kiss on her surprised mouth and left her.

Catherine stopped as she walked across the hall. Why had he done that? Said that? She looked toward the den. She couldn't see it from here. She should go there and—what? she asked herself. He was only trying to shock her. She'd engineered this farce. Jarrod was telling her it was her problem. She could solve it herself.

Anger seized her. Catherine wanted to throw something. She settled for stamping her foot and heading up the stairs. Jenny snapped her suitcase closed as she walked into the room.

"Oh," Catherine said, surprised. "I was going to do that."

Jenny smiled, as if Catherine should know unpacking was no longer her job. "Ms. Audrey instructed me to move your winter things to the attic and make room for Mr. Greene." She picked up a card from the dresser and handed it to Catherine. On it, again in her sister's handwriting, only this time meticulously printed, was an apparent diagram of the dressers and closets. Where Jenny should hang clothes or place things like lingerie, socks, Jarrod's shirts and her panty hose.

"Thank you, Jenny." Catherine dismissed her.

Alone, she steamed. The nerve. The gall of her sister to go so far as to organize her underwear.

"My mother says hello." Jarrod startled her. Catherine hadn't realized she was standing in the middle of the room. She had no recollection of how long she had stood there.

"How is she?"

"She invited us to lunch tomorrow."

"Oh," she said, distracted.

"Catherine?" Jarrod must have noticed her absent-mindedness. "Are you all right?"

"I've made up the guest room." She sounded as if she was beginning a conversation in the middle. "You can sleep there. It was where I always intended."

Jarrod came into the room. She stopped talking at his approach. She wanted to move. For some reason she wanted to run, but something wouldn't let her. Jarrod wouldn't let her. He was holding her in place as surely as if he touched her.

"You sleep here?" Jarrod looked around the room. Catherine resisted following his gaze. Behind her was the bed, and she didn't want to look at it.

She nodded.

"And you never want to be married. For-real married?"

She shook her head.

"Why such a big bed, then?"

She had to look around. Her bed was king-sized, with a padded headboard. It had a green-and-white comforter covering the mattresses that matched the wallpaper on one wall, the curtains and the tablecloth on a circular table that sat in front of a window. The room had a fireplace with a fantail screen covering it. The dark cherry dresser and armoire left plenty of room to move around, but Catherine felt as if the air was being pumped out of it.

"I need plenty of room when I sleep," she answered, then remembered their earlier conversation. Jarrod thankfully let her comment pass.

"What time will they come in the morning?" He changed the subject to Jenny and Christian.

"I don't know."

"Well good night, wife. I'll see you in the morning." He walked to the door. "Early morning."

She was going to have to get used to his parting comments. It seemed Jarrod was back to his teasing ways. He'd always done it, but she'd forgotten that in the last few weeks. Returning home tonight, it was as if their time in Montana was lost forever. They were home, and at home this was how they acted. For a moment she was lost in the Montana sky, with the stars hanging overhead and Jarrod cradling her on the landing.

She pulled a drawer open to get a nightgown. Jarrod's underwear lay where her gowns used to. Catherine stared at the garments. They weren't cotton boxers, BVDs or Fruit of the Loom underwear. They were bikini briefs in leopard-skin silk, bright red, navy blue and midnight black. She picked them up, feeling like a voyeur sneaking into someone's private world, but the excitement that aroused her took control over everything else in her mind.

Put them back, Catherine told herself. She should close the drawer and consult the card to find out where her gowns were, but she was fascinated by Jarrod's choices. She admitted she'd never thought of him in underwear. If she thought of him under his clothing, her mind went straight to his naked skin. She understood now why men got aroused over women's underwear. This was more than erotic. It was downright sinful. Thoughts of Jarrod wearing this flimsy fabric made her nipples harden.

"I think you'd better give those to me."

Catherine jumped as if she'd been caught stealing. Jarrod stood in the doorway.

"I came for my razor and toothbrush, but I think I'd better take that too."

"Jarrod, do you wear these?" She didn't intend to say that. "I'm sorry. I—"

"Yes," he interrupted with a single nod.

Catherine didn't move, but Jarrod came in and took the garment she was holding. She didn't let go. The two of them each kept a piece, like a bond between them.

"My gowns," she started. "They're ... Jenny unpacked ... she moved ... I didn't mean to ..."

Jarrod didn't say anything. His eyes searched her face. Catherine stopped babbling and remained standing under his gaze. Her throat went dry, but she didn't swallow. She was afraid to move. She felt as if there was some invisible casing around them, something so fragile and light that even a breath could destroy it.

She looked into Jarrod's eyes. There was no anger there, no humor or confusion. Something else looked back at her, something soft and dark and mysteriously inviting. She knew exactly what it was. They'd been avoiding it since he returned to Rhode Island. It sparked in the gazebo. On their honeymoon it was the kiss in front of the fire and the long night of holding each other in the hall. Now they were home, alone and together. Showdown, Catherine thought.

The space between them shortened of its own volition, or maybe she moved toward him. She couldn't tell. She only knew Jarrod moved his hand, the one holding hers. He twisted it around her back, circling her waist and pulling her against him. She felt the warmth through her clothes. Her breath came slower. She was conscious of it, dragging it into her lungs to keep from suffocating.

His free hand touched her face and his mouth lingered over hers for a moment. Catherine stared at him. She couldn't take her eyes away. She didn't want to. She wanted nothing more than to remain here, with his arm around her and his body pressed to hers. He didn't kiss her, but dropped his mouth to within a centimeter of touching her. Only a moment passed before he moved back. He didn't move away, only deviated an inch. The lingering scent of his aftershave clung to him. It was an exotic fragrance to her senses, potent on its own. She felt it take her senses, her defenses, and weave them in a tantalizing smoke that curled about her, drawing her nearer to him as if it were a rope coiling about them in ever-closing circles.

Jarrod continued his teasing dance while she stared into his eyes and leaned into his kiss just as he moved away. The cat-and-mouse action made her want to end the game. Then his lips touched hers. Her eyes closed and fire exploded in her head. It traveled the full length of her, running down her neck and passing into her chest, flooding through her arms, into her stomach and through both legs until it warmed even her toes. She swayed in his arms, turning into the kiss.

Letting go of the silky bikinis, Catherine didn't see them flutter to the floor. Her arms wound around Jarrod's neck and shudders raced through her. Every one of the things she remembered about Jarrod rushed into her mind as his tongue filled her mouth. The way he looked at her as they sat on the beach during the summers before he left. The smile he offered her when they'd run into each other jogging. Why had she never seen the truth in his eyes? Why had she refused to acknowledge the playfulness for what it was—a disguise for true feelings?

Catherine felt his whole body pressing into hers. Jarrod overtopped her by six inches, yet she fit perfectly into every contour of his body. His hands banded her back, gathering her as close to him as he could get her without squeezing the life out of her. They slid over her features, down her torso and over her hips. She felt her body burn in the path made by his hands. Then they were under her sweater, on her skin. She sighed at the pleasure that fissured through her when warm skin met warmer skin.

Her knees grew weak. Jarrod supported her with his arms. She felt as if her clothes would either melt or spontaneously combust. Jarrod raised his hands under her sweater until they brushed over her breasts. Catherine bit her lip, trying to remain solid. Her body wanted to liquify. He pulled the garment over her head. It and her hair fell at the same time. The sweater dropped to the floor while her hair cascaded over her shoulders and hung down her back.

"Cathy," Jarrod said on a guttural breath. Then, as he had when they entered the house, he lifted her and carried her to the threshold of the bed. Slowly he lowered her onto the coverlet and sat with her. He kept his arms around her waist. Her arms remained around his neck. "I want you, Cathy, more than I thought possible."

His kiss wasn't sweet this time, but hungry, potent, demanding. Catherine met it with her own need. Her heart raced, blood rocketed through her body like out of control lightning. Jarrod slipped the hooks of her bra free, unlocking the lace cloth that held her breasts from him. Slipping the straps down her arms, he followed the offending fabric until his mouth closed over her nipple. She clung to him for support and to continue the wonderful sensation that spread through her. He pressed her back and removed her jeans. In a flash he took off his own clothes and joined her on the bed. Catherine thought of nothing except the present, the here and now, the raging emotion that came over her when he joined with her.

It had been a long time since any man had touched her, and she felt as if it were the first time. Jarrod's body was hard, muscular. She smoothed her palms over his arms, his back, down his legs, the moon-shaped curve of his buttocks. She felt the snap in him, the eddy of control that tried to contain the whirlpool of passion that matched the storm raging inside her.

With one fluid movement he spread her legs and entered her. Catherine bit her lip to keep from crying out. Rapture as bright and electric as any thunderstorm sent shockwaves through her.

"Jarrod!" she cried, unable to contain the word. Jarrod sank completely into her. Catherine called his name again. His body filled her, her legs moving to increase the pleasure. Jarrod's mouth covered hers as his hands lifted her, keeping her close to him, joined to him in the most intimate way, in the ways of man and woman since the first man met the first woman. Catherine was first. She felt first, felt as if she and Jarrod were the only ones to walk this path, the only ones to know each other, know the experience of giving and taking pleasure, reveling in rapture, intimate with the knowledge of the fathers and the mothers, the only ones to taste the sweet waters of life and understand its meaning.

Catherine writhed back and forth, lost in the realm of time that suspended Jarrod and herself. She met Jarrod, taking his body into hers and loving the feel, accepting the hardness of his legs, the powerful thrust of his body as it met hers, joined hers, annexed, bridged, associated, cemented, intertwined with hers as if the two of them were the only perfect fit in the whole universe. Millions upon millions of combinations of couples on earth, and the two of them had been lucky enough to discover each other, discover the secret of coming together, the secret of being made one.

Catherine's body convulsed. She clung tighter to him, unable to control herself, digging deeper into herself, accepting the pleasure-giving sacrifice Jarrod offered, taking what she needed, wanting what he gave. Jarrod found the chord in her, the central core that, if touched, would drive her to a burning river of need. Jarrod knew where it resided, knew that he alone had the ability to take her to the heights of desire, suspend her over the abyss of explosion that rose like a colossal wave and shattered into a spangle of lights simultaneously pressed deeply onto all her pleasure points, overloading her with the supreme rapture that only he could elicit.

On a knife-edge between pleasure and pain, Catherine dangled, sure at any moment that her life would end. No one could stand this kind of torture, this enchantment that robbed her of everything except the dying vow that it wouldn't stop.

Catherine heard a scream she was surprised to realize was her own voice. Blessed release came. Jarrod collapsed on her. Her body was drenched in sweat and her arms were around him, crushing him to her and holding on to the feeling that shrouded her in its midst, a feeling that Jarrod had produced in her. One that only the two of them would ever know.

Jarrod woke reaching for Catherine. He didn't open his eyes. He didn't want to destroy the euphoria that overtook him at the memory of making love to her. His hand found her naked body and pulled her into his arms. He aligned his legs with hers, his body with hers. She was as warm as brandy and he was instantly aroused. Catherine took his hand and drew it to her breasts. Jarrod relaxed, smelling her hair, feeling the strong, steady beat of her heart.

It hadn't been like he expected. It was indescribably better than anything his mind could conceive, design or build. No experience equaled it or compared to what had happened to them when they made love. Catherine was incomparable. He could compare cement to natural rock, bridges to skyscrapers, lemon cake to lemon meringue, even Catherine's lopsided croissants to a three-tiered cake from any of Audrey's caterers, but for Catherine there was nothing in his repertoire that gave him an inkling of what being with her was going to be like.

At this moment Jarrod took back all the jokes he'd ever played on her, retracted all the awful things he'd ever said and thought about her. At this moment all he wanted to do was go on holding her for the rest of his life.

He wondered when it had happened. It wasn't in

the swing at Audrey's, although that was a catalyst that triggered the feelings he'd been hiding. He knew now there had always been something in him that wanted Catherine. It was the reason he teased her, joked with her. It was the reason he never tired of her presence in a room, and the reason he often found himself sitting with her when there was a storm brewing or they were alone without an audience. He wanted her attention, so he got it in the only way he knew how. He played jokes. The jokes were over now. There were hundreds of things he wanted to do with Catherine. Joking was only one of them, and this time he wanted to joke with her, not make her the butt of the amusement.

Jarrod moved his hand over her breast. Her nipple pebbled and she murmured a sleepy sound. He snuggled closer to her. Their combined heat made the rose scent stronger. *Roses in Winter.* He had a name for what she reminded him of. Under the covers, with the aftermath of love redolent in the air, glowing embers in the fireplace, and Catherine's body hot in his arms, Jarrod wished he could bottle the fragrance, open it at any time and bring this feeling, this Catherine coming to mind.

She stretched against him, her bottom against his belly, brushing his erection and causing his stomach to tighten. Jarrod ran his hand over her smooth, even skin, extending it down her shapely legs and back to repeat the procedure, feeling the shudder that passed through her.

"Are you awake?" he asked.

"How could anyone sleep with what you're doing to her?" Catherine turned over, her arm and leg crossing his, her body finding the juncture of his that threatened his sanity.

He pulled her into full contact. Sensation raced through him. His erection was quick and fast. She did that to him. "Do you know what time it is?"

She shook her head. "Ask me if I care." Her voice was sleepy. He loved the low growl of it, as if she were dragging it over silk and straight through his emotions.

Jarrod ran his hand over her hair, pushing it off her face, staring down into dark, dreamy eyes.

"How could I have ever thought of you as a sister?" He lifted her chin and lightly kissed her. Her hand ran down his back, tracing his spine with a single finger.

She held her breath. "I don't have a brotherly feeling in my body."

He kissed her again. Her mouth was sweet and wet and Jarrod wanted to feast on it, plunge his tongue inside and let go, but he forced himself to hold back. He kissed lightly over her cheeks, her pert nose, her intelligent forehead and sensuous mouth, listening to the dark sounds, the hushed vibrations that came from her throat and went intravenously into his body.

The night was clear. Moonlight streaked through the windows, slanting across the carpet on opposite sides of the immense bed. Jarrod could see the contrast of their skin against the sheets. He pushed them away, exposing her milk-chocolate color. He kissed her shoulder, moving across her luscious body, dropping tender kisses on her collarbone and the quivering depression between it and her neck. His fingers brushed over her breasts. She moaned thickly, arching against him, communicating her pleasure in timeless jungle sounds. Jarrod found it difficult, almost impossible, to hold himself in check. His body was tight, his erection extended and hard, his mind craving her.

Catherine was like fire in his arms—too hot to hold, but he couldn't let go. She commanded him, like some strange drug that overtook his mind and sensitized his nerves. Jarrod pushed her back onto the mattress and covered her with his body. His mouth covered hers. This time he wasn't as gentle. Sensation raced through him. Her hands wrapped around his head. He could feel each of her fingers individually, each separate pad making contact with his skin, heating it, sinking into him, taking a hold on his mind as well as his body.

She writhed, under him, each movement of her slim frame driving him farther and farther toward the edge. Jarrod kneed her legs apart. He gathered her hips in his two hands and lifted her. As he slipped inside her, he found heaven. Excitement as electric as lightning shot through his veins, streaking them with light, boiling his blood. He filled her with himself, hearing her moans of pleasure mingle with his own. His heart hammered as he slid farther into her. He rocked. She rocked with him. The pace quickened. He couldn't stop. He could feel the wave of pleasure overtaking him, raising the quotient they'd set impossibly high. His hands moved to hers, straightening her fingers, pushing her arms above her head as the two of them raced inside the rapture wheel, increasing the revolutions, burning the gauge that measured their passion as surely as the two of them were burning.

Jarrod was crazy. He had to be. It wasn't possible to be sane and feel this good. It wasn't possible to have a woman this wonderful in his arms and around his body, holding him, moving with him, making love to him.

Jarrod heard his own groans as his body throbbed into hers, thrusting hard time and time again, answering her need, her wanton invitation for more and still more. Jarrod had never made love like this. He'd never lost such complete control. He'd never thought this possible, yet Catherine was showing it to him, doing it to him, driving him over the edge.

He heard the cry, heard the shout, felt the surge in his loins burst with strength. Lights exploded in his head, flooded his chest, extended down his arms, through his fingers, into his legs, and with a huge cry to the heavens he emptied into Catherine.

Calendars! Why were there so many? Catherine couldn't turn in any direction without being confronted by the day and date. She whirled around in the study. Jarrod slept soundly upstairs. After showering and dressing she'd come downstairs in search of food, but the sun shining through the windows of the study caught her attention and she'd gone in there, turning her face up to look at the gorgeous day.

The windows were open and a soft fragrant breeze blew in, shifting the curtains and teasing the papers on the small bulletin board where she'd tacked several notes. There she saw the calendar. Jarrod, their wedding date, last night's love making crowded in on her like the heavy hand of logic squeezing her brain.

The calendars were everywhere. All of them staring at her as if they had eyes. They scared her like a fetish or phobia involving dates. Numbers loomed at her, mocking her with their curls and symbols. Smiley faces, full moons, half moons, red letter days, they all looked at her with malevolence, as if they knew a secret she could only guess at.

Today's date jumped out at her as if the thirty-one squares all had the same number in them. Catherine blinked, clearing her head and banishing the confusion. She was scared though. Her hands were suddenly cold and her heart pounded.

Closing her eyes she took a deep breath and pulled herself together. She was all right, she told herself. Everything was all right. Her last menstrual period had come a week before the wedding. There was no red mark on the calendar. She'd long since passed the point of needing to make small red hearts on her calendar to keep track of the wretched blood-flow days. Her cycle was as regular as the phases of the moon.

A week away from home, she calculated, and last night—"Oh, God!" Catherine jumped, saying the words out loud. The truth hit her. It couldn't be right. Quickly she grabbed the desk calendar, dragging it forward. She started counting. As if playing Monopoly, her fingertip ended on the GO TO JAIL square.

She was pregnant!

At least there was a strong possibility she could be. She counted again. No matter what, she hit fourteen or fifteen days from the start of her menstrual cycle. "Ovulation is at its peak on these days." Catherine could almost hear her health teacher repeating it over and over. "Girls need to be prepared, and knowledge is the best way," she used to say. Catherine had the knowledge, but what good was it? She hadn't used it. She and Jarrod had made love—twice. No matter how she counted, both their lovemaking and her ovulation came together on night fifteen.

He wore no condom and she took no birth control. Birth control hadn't been necessary, she thought. There was no man in her life since she'd split with Jeff, and they'd always used condoms. And she wasn't going to have sex with Jarrod—But she had. And now she could be pregnant.

Maybe she should go to the drugstore and get a home pregnancy kit. Was it possible to tell this fast? She pushed the calendar away as if it had metamorphorsed into a snake, ready to strike.

She didn't want to know. If it was true—it wasn't true, she denied. She couldn't be pregnant. She couldn't be tied to Jarrod for the rest of her life. He wanted children. He'd told her. She'd never thought of actually being someone's mother. The idea frightened her. It was impossible.

Why had she let him touch her? Why didn't her mind warn her of the consequences? In Montana she'd managed to maintain her sanity, but last night, in her own home, where had her sanity been?

That was it, she thought. She hadn't been sane. It was no excuse, she knew that. Sane or not, she could still be pregnant now.

Catherine had to know. Her body had all the signs of ovulation. Her breasts were tender. She'd thought that was due to Jarrod and the tantalizing way he'd rubbed her nipples, then lathed them with his tongue. She started to tingle, finding him in an erotic memory zone she hadn't guessed was there. Immediately she sat up straight in her chair and stopped her thoughts. She could rationalize the tenderness in her breasts, but what about the accompanying feeling that she weighed a ton, and the overwhelming need, an almost hysterical craving, for a chocolate sundae? She didn't need any further clues. She was ovulating, the only time during the twenty-eight day cycle when pregnancy could occur. And they'd made love on that night.

Catherine *was* rationalizing if she didn't think more than just lovemaking had happened last night. She knew these feelings, knew them as monthly reminders of what was to come. Would they arrive on time this month or was a more permanent reminder in store nine months from last night?

Jarrod knew he was alone. His arms closed over air as he sought Catherine. Opening his eyes, he searched the bed. She was gone. The room was too quiet for her to be in it. The bathroom door stood open and he could smell the faint scent of roses permeating the air. He couldn't determine how long she'd been gone.

Turning on his back, Jarrod stared at the ceiling. Last night replayed in his mind like a movie in slow motion. He smiled, thinking of how dark Catherine's eyes were when she was aroused. Her skin glowed in the golden light of the lamp they hadn't bothered to turn off until sleep claimed them. He remembered her aggressiveness. He felt his own arousal at the memory of how she felt against him.

Where was she? Jarrod asked himself, throwing the comforter aside and sitting up. He didn't like waking up without her next to him. Her soft, warm body pressed into his was as natural as breathing. He wanted to hold her, feel her come awake next to him and turn her into his arms. He wanted to make love to her again.

His stomach clenched when he thought of them making love. Jarrod had no memory of anything that affected him more than Catherine had last night. His world seemed to have begun with her.

Pushing himself up, Jarrod headed for the shower. His bikini briefs lay on the floor where Catherine had dropped them. Jarrod whistled as he scooped them up. Today was a perfect day for leopard skin, he thought.

And growled.

For more years than anyone alive could remember, the waters had come in against the rocks of the island. Catherine ran along the jagged coast. She'd changed into her jogging clothes after work and left the office. She needed to work off some of the steam that she'd awakened with. Throughout the day it had increased until she felt as if she were in a giant pressure cooker, its gauges dipping into the danger zone.

She'd endured the office teasing about a honeymoon full of constant and incredible sex. If Catherine included the previous night, it was only one night, but it had been incredible. She'd never imagined making love could be mind-blowing. She'd read about it in novels, movies portrayed it, but Catherine knew how orchestrated those scenes were. They looked perfect on the screen, but they weren't real. Last night had been real. She'd never had anything comparable happen to her.

And it couldn't happen again!

There were rules. They'd agreed to them—she and Jarrod. She couldn't totally fault Jarrod. She'd been more than a willing participant in the sexual dance. And it had begun over a pair of leopard skin briefs.

Her feet pounded harder, keeping tempo with her heart as she ran. What had happened? Why hadn't she just let go when Jarrod reached for them? And now ... The houses along the route disappeared, taking on the aspect of pages of a calendar. Now she could be pregnant. Why didn't Jarrod have a condom? If they were going to make love, why didn't one of them think of the consequences?

Catherine stopped. She knew why they didn't think of it. Her muscles seemed weak, as weak as they had been the night before, when he looked at her with eyes that were so dark and sexy and tinged with a spark of something fathomless and mesmerizing. She couldn't look away, not even if she wanted to, and at that moment she hadn't.

Catherine started running again, pushing herself, forcing her feet to move. Her jog turned into a run. The run went faster, as if it were a race. She was racing herself or running away from herself, running from the truth.

What was the truth? That she felt more for Jarrod than she'd admitted? That she'd wanted him to make love to her last night? And not only last night, but nights before that. That if the two of them continued in this farce of a marriage she would be the one to lose. Her defenses were already weakening. She wondered what Jarrod was feeling. Did he have defenses too that she had breached in some way?

The thought made her run faster. Her breath dried in her throat. By the time she stopped, the gates leading to Audrey's house loomed before her. The black iron gates had been recently painted. Gold fleur-de-lis gleamed at the top in the waning light. Subconsciously she had probably been heading here from the beginning. She was tired and thirsty. The small sign indicating PRIVATE PROPERTY stood by the driveway entrance. Catherine passed it unheeded. The permanent residents of the island all had signs to tell the tourist this was not one of the Preservation Authority houses on the public tour.

Catherine was drenched in sweat when she rang the doorbell. Audrey saw her through the ornate ironwork and heavy glass door. Her sister rushed over, a huge smile on her face.

"Welcome home!" Gung-ho Audrey pulled her into her arms as she let go of the door. Catherine's arms hung at her sides, stiff like a doll's. Audrey pushed her away and searched her eyes. "What's wrong? You and Jarrod haven't had a fight already, have you?"

Catherine moved out of her sister's reach and walked farther into the room. "It's not Jarrod and me. It's *you* and me." She and Jarrod were a different story, and Catherine would have to deal with that later.

Audrey smiled. "You mean the maid. I knew you'd

be a little upset about me taking her to your house, but you have to admit she and Christian are godsends."

"Audrey, I don't want them."

Audrey's smile froze. "Come on in," she said, seeming to hear the concern Catherine felt. They went into the solarium. The windows were open to the ocean breeze. The cool air washed over Catherine. A slight shiver accompanied the sudden change in her body temperature. Passing a maid, Audrey ordered orange juice for them to drink. "Lots of it," she said.

Catherine calmed herself as she took a seat. "Audrey," she started, "it's not that I don't appreciate the gesture. It was really nice of you and Dwayne, but Jarrod and I need our privacy."

Audrey's smile was knowing. Catherine found her face turning warm. She hadn't meant that the way it sounded. She and Jarrod had made one mistake. They wouldn't make it again. But she didn't have time for that now. She had to deal with Audrey.

The maid returned with two glasses and a pitcher of orange juice. She poured the juice into the glasses and handed them to Catherine and her sister. The maid left them as Catherine drained her glass and poured herself another. She often jogged with a water bottle, but today she'd left the office and forgotten it. She needed to replace the sugar and salt her body had lost. And in the back of her mind health risks to an unborn child niggled at her.

"I'm sure Jenny and Christian won't be intrusive. They are very discreet."

"I know that." Catherine drank, taking the chance to formulate what she planned to say. "This is a big house, Audrey." She looked at the ceiling, indicating the vastness of the house. "Mine isn't nearly this size. We don't need a maid."

"Catherine, you have no idea how much adjustment is needed the first year."

"But—"

"Jenny and Christian will be able to do all the housework and shopping for you." She interrupted as if she weren't about to listen to Catherine. "You and Jarrod both work. With them helping you, you can spend time together instead of dusting furniture and washing clothes."

Audrey said it as if those were tasks she performed. Catherine would bet she hadn't seen a washing machine since Dwayne carried her across the threshold of this enormous house.

"I can do the work," Catherine said. "We both can. Maybe it will bring us closer together if we have to cook and do dishes."

"You hate doing dishes," Audrey reminded her. "And sending Jenny and Christian away will hurt their feelings. You wouldn't want to do that."

"Of course I wouldn't. They can return here and everything will be fine."

"No, it won't." Audrey stalled her. "I've already replaced them with a lovely couple who are here from Ethiopia. It was perfect timing. They'll be here for a year, and when I heard about them, I thought sending Jenny and Christian would be a wonderful surprise for you."

Audrey's enthusiasm was nauseating. Why couldn't she mind her own business? And why didn't she listen? Ever since they were children, Audrey was a control freak. She had to be in charge of something or she'd drive everyone mad. Even when she was in charge she drove people crazy. She was on the debate team, president of the creative writing club and head of the decoration committee for every dance the school had while she was there. In Catherine's junior year in high school she got a part in the school play. Audrey was the stage manager. Audrey would volunteer to sew costumes or paint scenery, anything as long as she had control of it.

Audrey should have joined the Navy, Catherine thought. Then she'd have a ship full of captive souls to order around. It was probably a good thing she didn't have children. Catherine chastised herself for the last thought. Audrey wanted children.

Catherine knew anything she said would be useless. Audrey rarely heard anything she didn't want to.

"They'll only be there during the day," Audrey continued. "After dinner the two of you will have the house to yourselves." She stood up. "And speaking of dinner," she went on, "I have to go check on ours. Would you like to stay?"

Catherine shook her head. She'd been gone long enough. She had one more confrontation tonight. She might as well get it over with. Hopefully, the outcome with the second would be better than the first.

"I'll call Christian to pick you up. You can't jog or walk home now."

Audrey left her. Catherine poured another glass of orange juice and drained it.

Christian arrived within minutes, as if he knew he would be needed.

Silently he drove through the streets of Newport. A light rain started. Catherine watched the droplets appear on the windows as the wipers quickly slapped them aside. Lamplights turned to glowing circles, reminding her of the superstitious blood moon, its precognition of future events. Through the hazy light she saw the words DRUGSTORE materialize like a ghost.

She asked Christian to stop.

Chapter 8

The shower was more refreshing than any Catherine had ever taken. She wrapped herself in the huge towel and used her hand to clear the condensation off a spot on the mirror. She took the comb and pulled it through her hair, pushing it all off her face.

She felt better. Jarrod hadn't been home when Christian opened the door for her and she got out of the car. She'd had time to move all his clothes to the guest room and to take a shower, wash her hair and blow it dry.

The heat from the blow dryer eased the pounding in her head, but it didn't take the tension away. On the counter lay the home pregnancy test package. In the store she'd surveyed the shelf of early warning products. She wondered why they called them *early warning* kits. The warning should have occurred before the need for the kit. Once this was opened and used, it wouldn't provide a warning, but a conclusion. Part of her life would be over, forever changed. Catherine put the package in the drawer. She couldn't use it yet. The directions said to wait at least a week; two would be better.

Coming out of the bathroom, Catherine stopped halfway across the room. Jarrod stood facing her, his expression stripping her of the towel that covered her. She'd forgotten him physically in the light of more pressing problems. She didn't understand how she could forget someone as dark and dangerous-looking as Jarrod, but she had. Earlier she had tried to regain some control of her life. She'd moved his things to the guest room. Doing something had felt good, but the effort hadn't accomplished much. With him in front of her, she could barely maintain the slender thread of control she clung to.

"Hello," he said. "I missed you."

The implication was clear. Catherine was at a disadvantage. Why hadn't she taken some clothes to the bathroom? Jarrod didn't know she'd removed his clothes, taken back her space. He probably assumed that last night— Why couldn't she think of last night without her knees buckling or her body going into fits of fiery crystals? Last night had been a revolution for them both, but today—tonight—would be different.

Jarrod took a step toward her. Catherine moved aside. She knew he was going to pull her into his arms. The thought was weakening, but she couldn't let it happen.

"I moved your clothes to the guest room," she told him.

Surprise registered on his face. "I thought you were concerned about Jenny discovering—"

"It doesn't matter what Jenny thinks."

"Last night—"

"Last night was a mistake," Catherine cut him off for the second time. "It shouldn't have happened." She wanted to turn away, but she couldn't. She had to say this to his face. "We agreed sleeping together wasn't part of the deal. Neither of us wants to be married. If we stick to the rules, then we won't end up with any . . . complications."

"It meant nothing to you?"

Catherine knew he meant last night. It had changed her life. She'd seen a future that held promise and wonder and a fascination to just be, but it was an illusion. It would wear off and she'd be left with—

"Nothing," she whispered.

Jarrod moved fast. He caught her, pinned her against him. Her towel slipped. Catherine stared down at her exposed flesh.

"Look at me and tell me it meant nothing," Jarrod commanded.

She didn't look up. She couldn't. She knew what she'd find in those eyes, and she wasn't sure she could say it if she did.

Jarrod grabbed her chin and pulled her head up so she had to stare into his eyes. "Say it." The anger staring back at her sizzled. Daggers, white hot and poised, pierced her body.

Catherine opened her mouth. Words failed her. She could do nothing, say nothing, only let him hold her. Her eyes welled up with tears.

"Say it." Jarrod didn't shout. His voice was surprisingly quiet, but Catherine felt the hard edge of it.

She tried to say something, but words still wouldn't
come. Then she threw her arms around his neck and
let go of the sob that choked her. Jarrod held her.
She felt the tightness of his arms ease. His squeeze
changed to a caress. Both arms circled her waist and
his cheek rested against hers. Catherine didn't know
how long they stood there. Shudders ran the length
of her. She wanted to say she was sorry. She wanted
to tell him what last night had really meant, how much
of herself she had given to him and what happened to
her when they made love, but she just held on, her
arms folded about his neck, her teeth biting her bottom lip. She clung as if her life depended on it.

Jarrod's head dropped, and she felt his mouth on
her shoulder. The fire of it sent ribbons of excitement
waving through her like a chorus of majorettes leading a parade. Her body heated, boiled, turned to
liquid. Jarrod continued to kiss her shoulders. She
lifted her head, giving him room. His mouth followed
the line of her throat to the soft hollow of her neck.
Catherine's towel slipped farther. She didn't try to
keep it up. She clung to him.

His hands smoothed over the towel, running over
her back and down her spine to the point where the
towel ended and her hips curved. Catherine dragged
breath into her lungs, heaving, shuddering, as sensation overwhelmed her. Jarrod moved his hand up
her throat to her chin, then her bottom lip. The
anticipation of him taking her mouth had her turning
toward it. Hands coursing over her naked hips pulled
her into him. She felt his erection and went up on
her toes to meet it. Her mouth searched for his,
burning for him, but he moved upward, past her lips

to her cheeks and eyes before starting his route back down.

Sliding his hands higher and higher under the towel, he pulled at it, all the while kissing one corner of her mouth, then the other. The towel fell to the floor as his mouth finally covered hers in possessive completeness. Catherine's world spun out of orbit. She sailed through the universe, flying over the planets, shooting stars and asteroids and seeing everything from a whole new perspective.

How could she be in his arms, with his wizard of a mouth doing things to her that no vampire could elicit by drinking the blood of his beloved? How could she even think of telling him last night meant nothing? It meant everything, drawing in her sails and respreading them, altering the course of her life. Nothing had changed her more, moved her more.

Suddenly she wanted to touch him. She wanted to feel the warm flesh of his body, run her hands over the mahogany paint of his skin and listen to the guttural moans he made when she touched a point that caused him the most erotic pleasure. Tugging at his shirt, she pulled it free of his pants. Warm skin met warm skin.

Catherine's hands went higher as Jarrod's kiss deepened. He bent her back as they traded one drugging kiss for another. Her mouth was hot. She was sure they would melt into each other and be irrevocably joined.

Catherine unbuttoned his shirt and pushed it over his arms. She went to the belt buckle at his waist, quickly opening it. Jarrod lifted her then, taking her to bed.

"This is a very big bed," he murmured in her ear.

He laid her on it. She looked up at him. He stared at her, but he didn't move, didn't proceed to undress. In a moment Catherine became aware that something had changed. As if putting her on the bed had somehow detached him from her.

"Jarrod?"

"This is as far as I go, Catherine. My bed is in the guest room." With that he turned and left.

Catherine sat up straight, her hands going to cover her breasts. Anger seized her.

"You bastard!" she shouted.

He was, Jarrod told himself. The guest room was at the end of the hall, on the side of the house that faced the backyard. Jarrod closed the door and leaned against it. He hadn't done anything like what he'd just done to Catherine in his entire life.

She tied him in knots in more ways than one. He should have understood her moving his things. They should never have been put in her room. They had agreed to an in-name-only marriage, but her do-good sister didn't know that.

But he'd agreed to the rules Catherine set. He knew where the boundaries were, yet in the past two days he'd broken them. He thought she wanted to break them. After last night there was no way he could think she wanted to live separately, sleep separately. They'd been together, seen the wonders they could create in each other's arms. How could she decide she wanted no part of him in her bed after that?

That had angered him. Jarrod wanted to teach her a lesson, but it hadn't worked. He didn't feel any better after what he had done. In fact, he felt like a heel, worse than any practical joke had ever made him feel.

He'd make it up to her. He'd apologize. He shook his head. Catherine wasn't in the mood to listen to anything he had to say, even if it was an apology. Maybe he could buy her something. Jewelry was supposed to work. He pictured her throwing it in his face. It didn't matter if it was diamonds or glass, Catherine would never be pacified with trinkets. Things were getting out of control. He needed to lighten the mood. She'd done it on their honeymoon, kept things from getting serious. He'd failed in the attempt to do the same, but he wasn't down yet.

An apology wouldn't be enough. Jarrod was going to have to do something outrageous.

The dining table was set for one. Jarrod glanced at the place setting. He didn't know if it was set for him or if it was a message that he should eat elsewhere.

"Jenny?" he silently questioned when she entered the room.

She smiled brightly as she followed his glance. "Oh, Mrs. Greene asked for a tray in her room."

"Is it ready?"

"In a moment, sir."

"When it's ready, I'll take it." She smiled and turned to leave the room. "Jenny, aren't you here a little late?"

"We'll be leaving right after the tray is ready, sir."

"Jarrod," he corrected her.

For a moment she looked perplexed. "Mr. Jarrod," she said. Her smile wavered for a moment before it became a sure grin.

He went to the den. Catherine had a full stereo system there, with a musician's collection of CDs. Jarrod remembered she'd once entertained the idea of music as her major. She'd played the violin, bought various recordings of piano concerts and made her own version of them with her as the major instrument. Jarrod couldn't remember what changed her mind. Music blended into something else and turned two or three more times before she entered college, where her major was communications.

She had worked for a large firm in New York, a television affiliate. She'd worked her way from writing press releases to writing the news. After a couple of years she abruptly quit and returned to the island. He knew it was due to the breakup with her former fiancé, and that the experience had sent her running to a safe sanctuary. She was hiding in this marriage more from herself than from the pressure of her mother and sister.

The den was a paneled room, its walls dark cherry wood. The desk was large, ornate and sparsely appointed. Bookcases lined one wall, with volumes ranging from decorating with fabric to the physics of *Star Trek*. But Jarrod was more interested in the CDs and the boombox. He scanned the titles, which were anally shelved in alphabetical order by artist. He pulled a Michael Jackson CD from the collection and checked the titles. He put it back. Michael was a dancer. His moves were precision ballet. They looked easy when Michael did them, but he practiced for days, even weeks, before walking in front of a camera and having them recorded for posterity.

Milli Vanilli was next. Jarrod laughed out loud. They had dread locks and wore spandex. They admitted lip syncing. Using them would be redundant. Michael Bolton redid everyone else's music, but the message in the lyrics was too revealing. Jarrod needed to find something appropriate to the situation. He went on selecting and rejecting. Catherine must have been collecting these CDs since she was fifteen years old. He'd say her taste was eclectic, but it only reflected the changing of time, the emergence of new artists and the retirement of others. Mostly it reflected the changes in Catherine.

Stevie Wonder and Luther Vandross. He held the plastic jewel boxes in each hand. These were his final choices. He looked at one, then the other. Finally, he slipped Luther Vandross onto the shelf and put the Stevie Wonder CD in the boombox. He took the box with him, returning to the kitchen to see if Catherine's tray was ready.

Jenny was placing a linen cloth over the plate when he walked in. "Just finishing up, sir," she said. She lifted the silver tray by the two handles and balanced it in the middle of Jarrod's single free hand. She smiled at the precarious way he leaned to one side to keep his center of gravity in place and prevent everything from toppling over. "We'll be leaving now."

"Good night, Jenny." Jarrod turned toward the door. Jenny rushed around him and opened it. The tray got heavy halfway up the stairs. Jarrod put the box down and repositioned the tray. Grasping it by the handles that Jenny had used, he took it to the top of the stairs and set it on the table in the center of the hall.

He retrieved the boombox and checked the CD. Then he knocked quietly on Catherine's door. He heard her soft voice say, "Come in." Jarrod knew she was expecting Jenny. He didn't hesitate. He pushed the door open and went inside. She was lying on the bed wearing a robe; not the one she'd had on during their honeymoon, but one that was older and worn, one that looked as if it were comfortable, something she could retreat to when she'd been hurt, her personal security blanket.

Hitting the PLAY button he set the box on the floor. Too bad he didn't have any sunglasses, Jarrod thought, going into a lip-synch routine of "Yester-Me, Yester-You, Yesterday." Stevie Wonder sang and Jarrod performed.

Catherine sat up, swinging her feet over the side of the bed. Jarrod paraded up and down the room, bobbing his head back and forth and stumbling like a blind man. He sneaked a look at her. Her mouth turned up in the slightest Mona Lisa smile. She looked down so he couldn't see her expression. Jarrod knew she was laughing. He'd laugh too if she did this to him. The song continued. Stevie's voice rose and he got into character, performing as if he were at a concert hall even if his audience consisted of this one member.

He was nearly at the end of the song. Catherine's shoulders were shaking. Finally she looked up. Her eyes were wet. Sound broke from her body as she laughed uproariously. Jarrod reached for her hand. She took it, and he pulled her up to dance. The song ended and with the precision of technology, Stevie's next cut began. "Signed, Sealed, Delivered, I'm Yours" summed up his feelings. He didn't say anything. He just swung her around the bedroom, the two of them acting like two teenagers on prom night. Jarrod didn't want the song to end.

"Do you forgive me?" he asked when the room was quiet.

"I suppose anyone who's willing to make a fool of himself like that"—she indicated the silent boombox—"deserves forgiveness."

Jarrod stepped forward to hug her but caught himself in time. "I almost forgot," he covered. "I brought your dinner."

Turning around, he left the room and returned with her tray. "Jenny was on her way home. I agreed to bring it." Catherine sat down at the small table in front of the fireplace. Jarrod placed the tray in front of her.

She lifted the cloth covering the plate. "It's set for two," she said. Jarrod tried to interpret the note in her voice.

"I didn't ask her to do that."

Catherine pointed toward the chair opposite her. He sat down. The silence between them was comfortable. He enjoyed the food. Then Catherine started to snicker. Jarrod looked at her. She was obviously thinking of the fool he'd made of himself a moment ago. From that she broke into a full laugh.

"I'm sorry," she apologized. "I keep seeing you prancing up and down the floor—"

"I did not prance," he protested.

"With your head bobbing." Catherine demonstrated. "I can't wait to tell Audrey."

"You do and I'll pull out a few secrets of my own," he asserted.

Catherine sobered immediately. "I'll deny everything."

Then the 1–800–WIFE line rang.

Catherine woke with a smile, then a giggle. She'd been so angry with Jarrod, but when he danced in her bedroom, she couldn't keep a straight face. She still laughed each time she pictured him strutting up and down the room, lip-synching to Stevie Wonder. Life had settled into a routine after that night two weeks ago. She pushed the covers back and got out of bed. Both she and Jarrod worked. They had to be out of the house each morning. They usually met at the breakfast table.

Heading for the shower, she thought of breakfast. What should she expect today? So far they'd kept things from getting serious. Since that first night they returned from Montana, they were getting back to being the friends they'd been in the past. Yet each day she found something from Jarrod, notes inviting her to dinner, small gift-wrapped packages containing nonsensical trivia, Cracker Jack prizes, marbles, McDonald's Happy Meal toys. Stepping under the water, she wondered what today's prize was.

She was enjoying this kind of marriage. She could do this for the next five months. In fact, if she were sure things could go on this way, she wouldn't mind being married. She liked being with him, especially in the evenings, when they talked or danced. The music they chose was upbeat tunes, fast tempos where their hands touched and occasionally Jarrod put his arms about her waist, but only for a moment.

Catherine shuddered under the hot water. She hadn't been prepared for the open fissure that ripped through her at the thought of being in his arms. She turned off the water. Montana memories filtered through her head; the kiss on their first night there in front of that mammoth fireplace. The return home and them making love in her bedroom. Catherine's breath came fast. She wrapped herself in a towel and left the confining shower. Sitting down on the chaise longue in her bedroom, she leaned forward, feeling as if she should put her head between her knees.

What was happening to her? How could she think things were light? Nothing was light. It was a charade. All she needed to do was think of Jarrod and her mind went off on unplanned vacations. Her body went into overdrive and she ended up hot and bothered.

Catherine searched for something else to think about. She latched onto her job. The new sailboat was near completion, but the cabin cruiser was only waiting for the final test and the owner to pick it up. She could go out on it for the final test. She loved sailing and didn't often get the chance to do much of it. It was also getting late in the season. There wouldn't be many more opportunities before spring. Catherine kept thinking about the office, what she had to do today, what ads she needed to compose, what she expected to come in today's mail. She steered clear of anything involving Jarrod until she was dressed and on her way to the dining room.

She smelled the coffee before she entered the room. Jarrod met her at the door.

"I heard you coming," he said.

Catherine took the cup in both hands and sipped. She tried to concentrate on the smell of the coffee, but Jarrod's cologne caught in her nostrils and she closed her eyes, savoring it while she forced her knees to lock. Jarrod looked better each time she saw him. This morning he had on a dark suit, white shirt and striped tie. Everything contrasted and conspired to unnerve her. The efforts she'd used in her bedroom were useless in his presence. She could only concentrate on him.

"Catherine, are you all right?" Jarrod looked at her.

"Oh, yes." She went to the table and put her coffee down. As she took a seat, Jenny showed up with her breakfast. At the same time the doorbell rang.

"I'll get it," Jarrod said as Jenny looked toward the door.

"Who's coming at this time of the morning?" Catherine asked, popping a piece of bacon in her mouth.

"I'll let you know."

Jarrod left the room. He came back moments later with a huge bouquet of roses. He set them down in front of her. "Happy Anniversary."

Catherine nearly choked. She'd never thought of an anniversary. They'd been married—

"Our three-week anniversary." Jarrod completed her thought.

Catherine got out of her chair and smelled the flowers. She pulled the card from the small plastic pick and opened it. *They say three's the charm, I say it's you.* She looked up, then threw herself into his arms. She hadn't thought about what she was doing. She was just there. Jarrod pressed her against him. The cologne again. It told her that she shouldn't be here, but she didn't listen. She let the skittering feeling work through her, the warmth of him enter into every cell in her body. He dropped a kiss on her cheek and pulled back. Catherine quivered at the sensations inside her. It was like an earthquake or violent subterranean reaction; she could do little more than stare at him.

Jarrod hesitated. She knew he was thinking of the rules. She thought of them too, but her mind was clouded. His mouth was enticing, too enticing. All she could concentrate on was the sensual lips above her own, the look in his eyes and the butterflies in her stomach.

"Cathy, stop me now," he whispered. There was almost a plea in his request.

Catherine didn't want to stop him. She knew this would happen. She couldn't be around Jarrod and not want him. Every fiber within her poured need and want like a narcotic into her bloodstream. Shivers raced up and down her spine. Her feet arched, pushing her up another two inches. Jarrod's mouth met hers. Like two war survivors, they clung to each other while they exploded in each other. Catherine stretched her arms around his neck, his circled her waist, pulling into full contact. She felt his arousal, knew he'd won, knew that the two of them were a fire waiting to spark. She understood they were on dangerous ground, that somehow the tectonic plates on which the earth balanced were dangerously tipping, that the volcanic flames of the underground reservoir were steering toward a volatile eruption. Yet flowing through Catherine were centuries of developing heat. It melted her defenses, reconstructed the walls she bore around her, eliminated the protective covering she maintained. It left her alone and vulnerable.

Jarrod lifted her off the floor, repositioning his mouth and devouring her with a kiss so drugging she couldn't think. She wanted to put her legs around him, but her skirt was too tight. Instead she threaded her fingers in his short hair and opened her mouth, further accepting the invasion of his tongue. Wet, hot, raw, powerful excitement coursed through her until the two of them were in a virtual battle. The kiss went on and on until they snapped apart in order to take air into their lungs.

Catherine's head fell onto his shoulder; her body sucked air into it, gasping for the life-giving oxygen that kept her alive. Her heart thundered, drowning out all other sound. She couldn't hear Jarrod. His voice reverberated against her body, but her mind was too hazy. She was too far over the edge to hear. Sound didn't travel in this dimension. She vibrated on some celestial plane where nothing moved but her. She floated there, clinging to Jarrod, holding him as only someone in love could. She knew it now, knew why she fought him so hard, why no one else had been able to touch her where Jarrod did. Her arms were rubber; her legs would be unable to support her if Jarrod let her slip to the floor.

"Cathy."

She finally heard Jarrod's voice. It was gravelly, as if he hadn't spoken in years and his vocal chords were unused to the vibration that produced sound. Yet in his last breath before dying he had to say her name.

"Cathy."

* * *

The streets of Newport were narrow, designed more for carriages than limousines. The summer tourists were gone, back to schools and jobs, leaving the small island unclogged. Catherine eased down Thames Street toward America's Cup Avenue. She turned left toward the water and parked in the lot of the Seagull Restaurant. From June through August she wouldn't think of trying to get into the Seagull for lunch. But it was nearly September, and the road was practically hers. Catherine got out of the car. She loved the way the sea smelled in September. The air was heavy and salt-thick. She lifted her face to it, almost able to feel the crystals smarting on her skin.

Elizabeth waited for her at a table by the window. Outside the water was dotted with sailboats. Several photographers had cameras on tripods facing the water, undoubtedly shooting postcards for the next season's batch of flybirds.

Catherine made her way to the table. A glass of iced tea sat before her. She took a sip.

"I ordered for you," Elizabeth said. Unlike their previous meeting, Elizabeth didn't have time for a long, leisurely lunch, and neither did Catherine. The waiter appeared almost as soon as she sat down and put a salad in front of each of them.

"How's it going?" Elizabeth asked as soon as he left them alone.

Heat flooded Catherine's face as if on cue. Other parts of her body stood at attention. After the way she had left the house that morning, she could only think of herself and Jarrod wrapped in each other's arms. The image played in her head as if some movie camera had circled around them, displaying the couple from all angles: front, back, top, bottom, around. Catherine was dizzy with the replay.

"I suppose you could say we're on some common ground."

"Hmmm." Elizabeth picked up her glass of iced tea. "That sounds interesting."

Elizabeth could always see through her lies. Catherine might as well tell her the truth.

"I didn't think it would be this hard," she blurted out.

"You mean living with Jarrod is more difficult than you thought? Having problems keeping your hands to yourself?"

"Elizabeth!" She acted surprised, but her friend obviously didn't need the customary three guesses. She'd discovered the truth on the first one. "I've never really lived with anyone before."

"Jarrod isn't *anyone*. He's your husband."

"In name only," Catherine added. She was surprised she could even say that. There was much more between them than a name.

"You mean you were alone with him for a week in Montana and another two weeks here and you're still in name only? Catherine, one of you is made of ice, and I don't think it's Jarrod."

"Neither of us is made of ice," she mumbled.

Elizabeth smiled.

"Stop it," Catherine said. "You don't have to look as if you knew this would happen all the time."

"I never said a word."

"I know you didn't. But you could have warned me."

"What fun would that be?" She reached across the

table and squeezed Catherine's hand. "What happens now?"

"I don't know. I suppose we continue as we have."

"How do you feel, Catherine?"

She didn't answer immediately. The thought had been trying to find its way to the surface of her mind for days, but Catherine had insistently pushed it to a hidden crevice of her brain. Now, with Elizabeth's question, it was at the forefront of her mind. She needed to admit the truth, even if it was only to herself. "I think I'm falling in love with him."

"That's wonderful."

Catherine didn't realize she'd said it out loud until Elizabeth responded.

"That's not wonderful. It's terrible. I can't fall in love with Jarrod."

"Why not? You're both married . . . to each other. It's a perfect arrangement."

"Elizabeth, you know my feelings on marriage."

"I do," she said. "I think they're old-fashioned and ought to be discarded with the next breath you take."

"Elizabeth, you've never said that before."

"It never mattered before. It matters now."

"What about your own marriage? It didn't turn out well."

"You can't compare mine to yours. You can't compare any two marriages. They're all different."

"They all have the same effect. Either they end in divorce or women are the losers."

"You've been married three weeks; what have you lost?"

"My . . ." She could think of nothing to say. "My house," she finished weakly.

Elizabeth rolled her eyes, letting Catherine know her choice was less than stellar.

She did enjoy having Jarrod around. Each night she rushed home to talk to him. That sense of humor he'd had since she could remember always made her smile. She liked sitting in the evening light and watching the sunset. She liked dancing and . . . She stopped thoughts of that morning, and another morning when she woke in his arms. She liked that too. She liked it too much.

"Since things are already changing for you, Catherine, why don't you just give them a chance? See what happens. You might find marriage is different than you thought it would be."

Catherine didn't remember eating the rest of her meal. She had a vague recollection of hugging Elizabeth in the parking lot and getting in her car. Elizabeth said something about her party next month, but Catherine's mind was reeling from what her friend had said about giving her marriage a chance.

Should she?

Should she change the way she viewed marriage? Could the relationship between herself and Jarrod really turn out differently than all the marriages around her? Marriage needed to be worked at fulltime. It was something both she and Jarrod would have to agree to. This was a drastic departure from the rules they'd set up, but things were drastically different already.

Catherine opened the car door and threw her shoulder bag on the passenger seat. It slid across the leather, spilling its contents as it landed on the floor of the car. Getting in, she leaned over, restoring the spilled objects to their rightful places. Then she saw the folded piece of paper. It was beige card stock with a lacy embossed pattern. It had been folded into an origami of a dancing couple. A hole had been punched in the top. A silky blue ribbon was threaded through it and tied in a love knot. Along the ribbon was writing, a crisp, clear print on the narrow fabric. She held it up, her head turned as she read the words along the curve. *Me—Fred, You—Ginger.*

There was no signature.

Chapter 9

The day at work was a useless waste of energy. The only positive thing Jarrod had done was call the phone company and have that phone line disconnected. 1–800–WIFE was a thing of the past. Catherine had a husband, even if he was only temporary.

Jarrod looked at the plans swimming before his eyes. His easel was spread with several projects in progress. He needed to visit the Ocean Avenue site, where they were constructing a house. He needed to continue the plans for the shopping center in Providence and the office building in Boston, but each time he looked down at his work he saw Catherine. Between the blue lines of the architectural paper he saw her face smiling up at him. Or her eyes glazed with need beckoning him to her. This morning was a colossal mistake. She'd done nothing other mornings but smile and say thank you to his gifts. This morning he hadn't anticipated the consequences. He should have remembered how small things made Catherine happy and how it was natural to hug someone for something special.

But he didn't let it go there. It had been two weeks since he'd touched her for more than dancing, always to songs that would keep them apart or only holding hands. For two weeks he had watched her when she wasn't looking, stared at her when she'd fallen asleep on the sofa, imagined her sitting across from him while he worked. She moved about the house with an easy grace that had his gaze following her around, imagining her as she had been that first night home, when they'd made love and slept in each other's arms.

Jarrod missed her in his bed. He wanted her there again, and this morning when she'd flung her arms around him it had all snapped, come rushing down on him like some ghost pushing him forward and forcing his hand, a hand that offered little resistance.

The phone rang, snapping his thoughts and bringing him back to the present. He picked it up on the second ring.

"Hello?"

"Jarrod, it's Catherine."

"Cathy." The object of his thoughts was on the other end of the line. She called often, or he called her. They spoke at least once a day on the phone, sometimes two or three times. Yet today he felt as if there was something wrong about this call.

Catherine hesitated. He could hear her breathing on the other end of the line. Had she guessed? Did she know he was thinking of her? He only called her Cathy when he was deep in a passionate state. And that was exactly how she had found him.

"Good morning," she said after a moment. "I forgot to remind you about Elizabeth's party on Halloween."

"The Westfield party? She's still putting that on?"

"It's traditional," she said. "She does it every year." He could hear the laughter in her voice. Jarrod loved hearing her talk; her low, sexy voice curled around him and he wanted nothing more than to rush to her office and drag her home to bed.

"I'll look forward to it," Jarrod said.

"What are you doing?"

"Right now?" he asked.

"This very minute."

He couldn't tell her what he was doing. "Why do you ask?"

"I just wondered if you were thinking about me."

Jarrod nearly dropped the phone. Her voice was full of innuendo. They'd never played this game before.

"I *was* thinking about you. I was having an erotic daydream about you." There, he'd said it. Now what would she say?

"Did it go any further than this morning?"

Jarrod's throat went dry. Where was this going? He thought of her this morning in his arms, her legs straining to get around him.

"If the phone had rung a second later . . ." He left the sentence open to her own interpretation.

When Catherine didn't come back with a response, Jarrod sat forward in his chair. He sensed something had happened other than their kiss at breakfast.

"Catherine, is everything all right?"

"I found the dance card."

It was his turn to hold his breath. He didn't know how she would react to the me-Jane, you-Tarzan par-

ody, but their dancing was part of breaking the ice
and he wanted to keep things light and easy.

"I enjoyed the dance."

"I liked the song better," she said. He could hear
the smile in her voice. He imagined her sitting in her
office, slumped back in her chair, dangling the folded
card in front of her.

"I haven't done much today. I need to go to Providence. Would you like to go with me?"

"I have a ton of things to do here." She sounded
disappointed.

"Can't they wait? The season is virtually over for
boat sales, isn't it?"

Another hesitation. Then, "Pick me up in fifteen
minutes," she said decisively.

It took Jarrod only a little time to clear up his desk
and tell his secretary where he was going and that he
wouldn't be back that day. Then he was heading to
pick up Catherine. Since morning their relationship
had changed. He could feel it, and he admitted he
liked the way things were going. She was discovering
that living under the same roof had its complications.
He felt she was getting used to him, even wanted him
around. But he had to take it slow. If he made the
wrong move at the wrong time, Catherine would bolt
as quickly as any two-year-old filly at her first race.

"Put this on." Jarrod handed her a hard hat. They'd
arrived in Providence at the site where a shopping
center was being constructed. She got out of the Jeep,
feeling out of place dressed in a navy blue business
suit with a white blouse and three-inch heels. All
around her were sand, red dirt, stacks of building

supplies and two-ton I-beams. She doubted the metal hat could protect her from the danger that seemed to lurk in this place.

Jarrod reached for her hand and she put it into his without hesitation.

"You should have brought me some shoes," she commented, taking a step.

"I did." He went back to the car and pulled a pair of tan work boots out of the backseat. "Sit down." She sat on the seat of the open door, and Jarrod carefully removed her heels. His fingers slid up her feet, tickling her and sending shivers from her toes up her legs. She yanked her foot back with a laugh. Jarrod looked up at her with a smile. He held her gaze for a charged moment. Then he took her foot and pushed the boot onto it.

"Whose are these?"

"My secretary's," he said. "The hat too."

Catherine stood up and walked a few steps. "Do you like my fashion statement?" She held her straight skirt as if it were a gown and she was about to curtsy. Then she put one foot out and cocked her head to the side.

"I like everything about you."

A tremor ran down her back. She stood up straight. Catherine told herself she had to stop reacting to Jarrod's comments this way. She was speechless, her throat as dry as the Sahara Desert, her body as hot as hell. If he got up and touched her, she'd dissolve. Had she always felt like this about Jarrod? Had their antics as teenagers been covering up their true feelings? Why had she picked him, over all the other men who called the 1-800 number? Why had Jarrod been the one she thought of as the best candidate?

Shirley Hailstock

Catherine waited as he stared, wondering now as he looked at her with something in his eyes that held her to the spot as surely as if she were tied to a stake, what was it about him that took her ability to think clearly away?

Jarrod got up from his crouched position. He took her hand and they turned toward the central area where construction was at its height. He spoke to many of the men, sometimes unrolling large pieces of paper with blue lines on it. There were notes on some of the pages. She could see Jarrod's handwriting and understand only a little of the jargon used exclusively by architects and builders. At the boat yard they had architects too, mostly men who'd been in the navy. Boats were also architecturally designed and plans had to be drawn for them. Catherine could interpret some of them, but these were much more complicated.

Jarrod introduced her to several of the men and the few women with whom he spoke. He kept close tabs on her if she wandered away from him. She presumed it was to keep her out of danger. She loved the fact that he looked at her often. Trucks drove in and out of the yard along rutted tracks in the ground. The constant beeping of backup horns indicated that people should take care. Cranes lifted steel beams into the air and men, balanced on surfaces the width of high-wires, guided them into place. She could hear the burst of battery-operated screwdrivers as they drove screws the size of her hand into the metal fittings. Behind her a dump truck left the yard. The wake of wind following it blew dust into her face, and she shaded her eyes with her hand. Her hat wobbled forward.

A shopping center didn't go up one store at a time, Catherine discovered. They built the structure first, much like an office building, a metal skeleton rising from the ground. What Catherine saw was an open framework that had a curvature to one side. She could tell the finished building would have several areas that were gargantuan arcs bound together and running the length of one side. At the end of them the beams would support straight walls. Girders soared into the air, and she had to hold her hat on her head as she looked up. It reminded her of being on the back side of a Hollywood set, where only support beams and anchor poles propped up a painted facade.

Men worked on all areas of the site. Catherine couldn't tell how large it would be. She could estimate the amount of warehouse space needed to construct a yacht, taking in the storage capacity for materials and waste to within three feet, but she couldn't determine the dimensions of this building standing in its own shadow.

Catherine kept moving, stepping and sidestepping one hazard after another, saying "Excuse me" over and over as people went about their duties. Jarrod saw her and came over. Putting his arm around her waist, he led her back to the group of men, as if she were a lamb being returned to the fold. Jarrod went back to the discussion, only removing his arm from her waist when he had to point out something on the blue and white plans. Then his arm was back around her waist.

He could be doing it for show, or to communicate possession. They had an audience of hard bodies who eyed her without shyness. She didn't care what

Jarrod's reasons were; she enjoyed being attached to him.

The meeting went on for several minutes. Finally, the men smiled, shook hands with Jarrod and nodded at her, then moved away, leaving the two of them alone. Jarrod rolled up his plans and stuffed them back in his leather case.

"You look like Alice," he said.

"I think I am." Catherine had left her sunglasses in her car. She squinted at the bright sun reflected off the skeletal structure. "This looks fascinating, like a huge erector set."

"You can't say you've never seen a building going up before."

She shook her head. "I've seen them, but often from a distance, while driving my car or sitting in another high-rise. I've never been this close to hundred-foot cranes, pneumatic drills, concrete by the pallet and *dynamite.*" Her voice rose on the last word and she took a step closer to Jarrod.

"Only designated people can handle that." They were looking at a truck with EXPLOSIVES written on the sides.

"Why do you need dynamite?"

"It doesn't take much time when you're digging to hit solid rock. We need to blast the stone to break it up and remove it."

"I see." She paused. "Why are you still involved? I thought an architect was done when the plans were accepted and a builder was hired."

They began walking back the way they had come.

"An architect's job isn't over until the building is done, all the electricity and plumbing are in place and the basic walls and floors have been finished."

Catherine stopped, staring up again, her hand on the crown of her hat. "You mean you're responsible until the place is leased?"

"Not to the stores that rent space. I'm responsible until the planned interior walls and floors are finished and everything is cleaned away, making the building ready for an interior decorator and the land ready for the landscape architect."

"You haven't been back that long." They started walking again. "Why is this project yours?"

"I inherited it when Mike Thomas left. It was already in progress. That isn't unusual."

Catherine knew Mike Thomas. He'd recently retired and moved to Arizona, where his daughter and his grandson lived.

"It takes about a year to eighteen months to complete a project of this size. Someone had to pick it up. I was the new guy on the block."

"You weren't new. You're a partner in that firm." She saw the smile on his face.

"I volunteered for this one. Mike did a great job on the blueprints, and I've worked with this builder before."

They'd nearly reached the car when someone called Jarrod's name. He turned back. A man waved him over, and Jarrod left her to see what he wanted. Catherine watched them, fascinated by the way Jarrod moved. He had always been athletic, and his years in England hadn't added an ounce of fat to him. They walked more in England, he'd told her, and he'd been fortunate enough to have a swimming pool at his disposal. The thought of his nearly naked body assaulted her nerves. She turned away, but not before heat flooded into her bloodstream.

She promised herself she would get some control. Yet she didn't seem to have the capacity to do it. Anything could have her imagining him naked, the two of them making love or the remembered feel of his heavy body on top of hers.

Catherine concentrated on controlling her thoughts. She didn't hear the sounds around her any longer. They blended together into a cacophony of white noise that disappeared as surely as the incessant pounding of the ocean and appeared soothing and safe. She didn't see the truck backing up in her path or hear the warning beeps. She didn't notice the truck coming forward from the opposite direction or the small incline that showed the deeper wear of tire marks. She didn't hear the shouts of the men on the rising building, hollering and waving for her to move. She heard nothing until Jarrod's voice penetrated the bubble that encased her. Then, like a deaf person who suddenly regains her hearing during the climax of a symphony, everything crashed into focus. Trucks from opposite directions bore down on her. Her brain told her feet to move, but it didn't seem as if she had time to get out of the way. Jarrod ran toward her, a slow-motion figure, his face contorted, cutting through air as thick as jelly.

Catherine looked at one truck, then the other. She turned to move. Jarrod launched himself toward her, crashing into her like a football player trying to stop a touchdown. His arms closed around her, lifting her off the ground. Together they were propelled through the liquid air. She landed on her back, her shoulder digging out a crater in the ground, Jarrod on top of her. Breath was forced out of her lungs. Catherine squeezed her eyes shut, clamping her teeth on her lower lip to hold in the scream accompanying the sudden impact. Pain shot through her shoulder. Her eyes filled with tears. She lay there holding herself stiffly, willing the pain to subside, waiting during the long, agonizing seconds that felt like hours for the burning pain to abate.

The crunch of metal from the two trucks colliding made her open her eyes and look up. Then she buried her head in Jarrod's shoulder.

"Are you all right?" he whispered, his voice parched and breathless.

"I think so," she responded, not wanting to tell him how badly her shoulder hurt. In seconds there was a crowd around them. Several voices asked questions. Catherine was embarrassed at so many prying eyes. She'd been thinking of Jarrod instead of paying attention. This was a building site. She worked at a place where they built boats. She knew the safety rules. She knew better than to lose track of her surroundings, especially with all the movement going on around her.

"Better get her to the infirmary," someone said.

"Can you stand up?" Jarrod asked. A paleness she wouldn't have thought possible underlined the mahogany color of his face. Catherine hugged him with her right arm. Her left was still pinned to the ground.

She nodded.

"I'm sorry, miss. I kept blowing the horn for you to move." This must be one of the truck drivers, she thought. "I thought for sure you'd hear it."

"It's not your fault," Catherine admitted.

Jarrod got to his feet. The crowd moved back a little. He took both her hands to help her up. The moment the extension reached her shoulder she screamed. A fresh batch of tears sprang to her eyes and spilled down her face. Jarrod was immediately beside her.

"Get a stretcher." Catherine recognized the voice as the builder's, whom Jarrod had spoken to earlier.

"What's wrong, Catherine?"

"I fell on my shoulder. It's a little sore. I'm all right, really." She tried to make light of it.

"We'll wait for the stretcher."

It was there almost before he finished the sentence. A petite blonde nurse in a white uniform who looked so out of place among these beefy men bent toward her. She didn't bother giving her name. The small identification tag on her uniform read IRENE.

With her fingers, she lifted Catherine's eyelids and looked in her eyes. She checked her pulse and her fingernails, and pressed her thumbs into Catherine's palms.

"Where are you hurt?"

"Her shoulder," Jarrod answered for her.

"The left one," Catherine supplied. The nurse moved to her side. Jarrod was forced to let her have room. Gingerly, she touched Catherine's shoulder. Catherine tried not to wince, but the pain was immediate. The concern on Jarrod's face alarmed her. He'd just told her that he was responsible for everything that happened here. That meant he was responsible for safety too. But this was *her* fault.

The nurse prodded and probed for several minutes, then said she should be lifted onto the stretcher and taken to the infirmary. Jarrod and the builder lifted her, taking care not to jar her shoulder. When the detail of men carrying her stretcher started across the yard, she heard the builder say, "Come on, you two. We've got plenty of paperwork to fill out."

"Jarrod, I'm so sorry," she told him.

He took her hand. "Don't worry about it. Just tell me you're all right."

They spent the afternoon in the emergency room of Providence Memorial Hospital. Jarrod refused to leave her side or to let go of her hand for anything except the X ray.

"She's going to be sore for a few days," the doctor told them when all the test results were in. "There's nothing broken, but there will be swelling and bruising, mainly from the fall. I've given her a prescription for the pain. She should be fine in a couple of days."

The emergency room doctor released her, telling her to see her regular doctor when she returned home. They left the hospital looking like two chimney sweeps, dirty and walking slowly, but all right. Some of the color was back in Jarrod's face, and his eyes, still filled with concern, no longer appeared forlorn.

"Do you want to lie down in the back?" Jarrod asked when they reached the car.

"I can sit. The medication is working. I'm not in nearly as much pain as I was when we fell."

Jarrod opened the door on the passenger side. She slid into the seat, moving gingerly. Jarrod took her good arm. "I should never have asked you to come. This wouldn't have happened."

"Jarrod, it was an accident. I wasn't paying attention, and I know better than to daydream at a construction site." She leaned forward and kissed his cheek. "Please don't blame anyone. It was an accident and nothing serious happened."

"Enough about this." He put his arm around her

waist. "Why don't we just get a room and spend the night here? We can head home in the morning when you're feeling better."

"That sounds good." Catherine shook her head as she spoke. She stopped when a twinge of pain reminded her of her fragile state. She would like nothing better than to go to a room and lie down for a while. "But Audrey invited us to dinner tonight. I told her I'd check with you, but she didn't give me a choice. You know my sister. I called to tell you." She paused, remembering their conversation, and the underlying lace of it, as if it were thin layers of fine chocolate ready to savor. "Things got complicated. We ended up here and I forgot." Her finish was weak in relation to the high-tension images that raced through her mind from their morning conversation.

"I rather enjoyed this morning too," he said, smiling for the first time in hours. Catherine knew he meant the phone call. It was playful and sexy. She liked it too.

Jarrod leaned forward and kissed her on the mouth. She gripped the car door tightly, ignoring any pain in her shoulder. Then he walked around the car and got in beside her.

"We'll call Audrey as soon as we're home and cancel dinner."

"No," Catherine said. Turning around was a problem, but she did it without wincing. "We'd have to explain why we weren't coming, and then Audrey would call my mother. My mother would call yours, and before we knew it the entire family and a myriad of friends would descend on us to make sure my sore shoulder was all right. We'll go but excuse ourselves early."

"We'll talk about this when we get home. It depends on how much pain you're in. If necessary, I'll stand guard at your door to keep them out."

Catherine's smile was wavery as she thought of Jarrod, the Viking, protecting her from Audrey and her family.

They barely had time to wash the dust away before it was time to leave. It was plain from the driveway that ran fifty feet from the street that this was not just a meal with Catherine's sister and her husband. The entire society of Newport appeared to have dropped in tonight. Jarrod recognized his parents' Lexus, his best friend Robert's Corvette and Catherine's parents' Lincoln. There were also BMWs, Jaguars, a Rolls and a vintage Lotus. This could be the lot for previously owned luxury cars or the house of the owners of castoffs from the rich. Or the parking lot of one of Robert's dealerships.

Jarrod parked his Jeep on the street. It was covered in red dust from the trip to the building site and didn't fit in with the parking lot of fine vehicles.

"It looks like this is a command performance," Jarrod said when he felt Catherine's trembling hand take his arm. He put his hand over hers. "Keep your chin up and smile."

She offered him one of her best.

"Well, Alice," he teased, as they started to cross the street, "you're a little battered, but I guess it's time for the Mad Hatter's tea party."

They went inside. The family waited in the reception room. In a normal-size house, Jarrod would have called this the family room, but in Audrey's house it was too large and held none of the computers, high-definition televisions and lounging chairs of a typical family. It had plenty of furniture arranged in small groupings. The inhabitants were mostly standing, talking to each other. They all seemed to quiet at once when Jarrod and Catherine walked in.

Jarrod had the feeling Audrey had asked everyone else to arrive half an hour earlier than she'd told Catherine. This way they'd made a grand entrance, and he felt like a cherry on a spit.

"Hello." Audrey came forward, her arms open wide.

He stepped in front of Catherine and hugged her.

"Thank you for the reception," Catherine murmured as Audrey hugged her too, though less fervently, since Jarrod had defused some of her strength. Catherine's voice was only loud enough for the three of them to hear.

"Oh, darling, we've all been dying to hear about your honeymoon. I hope you brought pictures."

She moved back. "Sorry, Sis," she said. "We thought we were here to eat, not be put on display."

In Audrey's usual fashion, she heard none of the censure in her sister's voice. She continued to smile and, taking both their hands, she pulled them to the center of the room. Seeing they had no choice, they went about greeting everyone, accepting a before-dinner drink and talking.

Jarrod kept an eye on Catherine. She showed only small outward signs that anything was wrong. Only someone looking for it could tell she had a bruise down the left side of her body that went from her shoulder to her thighs. He'd nearly lost his mind when he saw her between the two trucks. The noise in the yard caught his attention and he looked around. She was between the trucks and unaware of the danger. He shouted her name, everyone in the yard called, but Catherine hadn't heard any of them until it was nearly too late.

He wondered what she'd been thinking. What could arrest her attention so thoroughly that she didn't hear the racket in the yard? Then he'd tackled her. It was his fault she'd been hurt. She took the full brunt of his weight, but he'd had no choice. It was him or the trucks.

"Well, Jarrod, you already look like a changed man." Robert stood in front of him, a wineglass in his hand. Jarrod knew it held only sparkling water; Robert didn't drink. "I suppose marriage agrees with you?"

Jarrod glanced at Catherine again. She was talking to his mother. They were both laughing at something Catherine had said.

"So far, so good," Jarrod answered in a noncommittal manner.

"I suppose you have no need for that number anymore."

"What number?"

"1–800–WIFE."

"She's probably found a husband by now," Jarrod said. He knew she'd found a husband. He knew everything about that number, the woman who owned it, the man who'd married her and why.

Before Robert could respond dinner was announced. Jarrod found himself with Catherine after their being separated for most of the past half hour. "If she has throne chairs for us in there, it'll be the final straw," he whispered to Catherine.

"I agree," she said. "I wish we'd gone to that hotel in Providence and left Audrey holding the bag."

Thankfully they were spared the throne chairs. Catherine wasn't clothed in sequins. She wore a simple black dress with long sleeves and the necklace Jarrod had given her as a wedding gift. She knew that Audrey's dinners weren't come-as-you-are affairs, but she hadn't expected a large gathering. She was grateful she'd had time to bathe and change out of her soiled suit. Jenny had applied the salve and dressing to the raw areas of her back. The maid was upset at the bruises. She calmed down when Catherine told her the story of Jarrod's rescue. Catherine needed help getting into her dress and for the first time thanked Audrey for sending Jenny to her, even if she initially hadn't wanted the maid.

As Catherine circled the room, speaking to everyone and avoiding hugs if she could, no one noticed how stiff she appeared. The pain in her shoulder was temporarily eased. The medication took the sting away, but she found it hard to move both her neck and her arm. She wished she had listened to Jarrod and canceled, but it was too late now. It would be so much better to be home lying in bed, rather than about to eat a heavy meal in the open theater of family and friends.

She'd talked to all these people since she'd returned from Montana and constantly ran into them during her daily routine. Why Audrey thought to assemble them here had yet to be revealed.

Robert held her chair as Catherine sat down. He took the seat next to her. Elizabeth was sitting next to Jarrod on the opposite side of the table. Catherine looked down the row of beautifully appointed plates and fragrant centerpieces. She saw the makeup of chairs and guests. Audrey hadn't lined them up as they had been at the wedding, bridesmaids on one side, groomsmen on the other. She had dotted them in the boy/girl, boy/girl pattern, yet the line-up was unmistakable.

"Audrey, this is a first for me," Robert said when they were all seated and the staff of waiters, hired for the evening, began their dance of service to the queen.

"Dinner?" Elizabeth teased. "Robert, I'm sure I've seen you have dinner before."

He threw her a frigid look. Elizabeth took it without malice. The two of them had bantered back and forth for as long as Catherine and Jarrod had played jokes on each other.

"I don't mean dinner. I've been to wedding rehearsal dinners and after wedding breakfasts, but whoever heard of an after-the-honeymoon wedding-party party?"

"This is just a family dinner," Audrey protested. "The wedding was so fast. Jarrod had only been back from England a couple of months. Tonight is just to say hello and enjoy a little meal."

The first course was served on the tail end of Audrey's comment and promised to be anything but little. Conversation went in spurts; sometimes the entire table was engaged, other times only the couples sitting next to each other were involved. Catherine sat erect. Her shoulder didn't hurt so much as her back. She felt as if a hot poker had been placed directly next to her spine, and it was getting hotter as time went by. Jarrod eyed her for a sign that she needed to leave, but she continually shook her head. She didn't want to give anyone here reason to think she was ill.

"It would have to be someone who lives on the island." Robert was speaking when she came back to the conversation. She had no idea what he was talking about.

"Why do you say that?" Audrey asked.

"The tourists have returned to their homes, and they won't be back until Christmas, and the number still works."

Catherine's head snapped up, despite her stiffness. 1–800–WIFE? Were they talking about *her* number?

"You called it?" Jarrod asked.

"Sure," Robert answered. "I see the way you and Catherine look at each other; I thought I might be missing something in this marriage thing."

Without thinking, she looked at Jarrod. He did the same. What did Robert mean? Could other people see more than friendship in how she felt about Jarrod? Could *he*?

"But the message says—" Catherine started.

"I thought I heard somewhere that she was only looking for a temporary husband," Elizabeth interrupted Catherine, saving her from blurting out information she shouldn't know. That error would not be lost on the keen minds of most of the congregation.

"I might be able to convince her otherwise." Robert straightened his tie, a wide smile planted on a face that reminded her of a male peacock. "Or I might only want a temporary wife. In either case, I win."

"Robert," Elizabeth said, "I never realized how smug you are."

"Elizabeth, I'm not smug." He leaned closer to the table, his voice soft, as if the two of them were co-conspirators. "You can be my temporary wife any time."

"I wouldn't be your any kind of wife, temporary or otherwise," she snapped.

Suddenly the table was laughing. Everyone was looking at them. Catherine knew they liked each other much more than either would admit, publicly or privately, but they always bickered. For a moment Catherine scrutinized them both. She and Jarrod had always been at odds, yet it had been a cover-up. Could this be the same thing? Were Elizabeth and Robert hiding the way they really felt about each other, even from themselves?

"What's so funny?" Robert asked.

"That's exactly how it starts," Catherine's mother, who'd confined her conversation to the end of the table where she sat, explained. "We used to act just like you two." She looked at Catherine's father.

"And look what happened to us," her father finished. He reached over, picked up his wineglass and toasted his wife.

"Catherine, you're awfully quiet. Do you have a theory about 1–800–WIFE?" Robert asked, turning his attention away from his adversary.

"This is nonsense," Audrey intervened. "Anyone

who would advertise a phone number to find a husband must be really desperate.''

Catherine looked from Robert to Elizabeth to Jarrod and finally to her sister.

"I agree," Catherine answered.

Chapter 10

Half of Catherine felt like the Tin Man, while the other half was a rag doll. The right side of her body was flexible to the point of being floppy. Her left side had fused together during the night and movement was tantamount to wrenching metal apart.

She couldn't get out of bed.

She could hardly walk by the time she and Jarrod had left Audrey's the previous night. She'd taken a pain pill just before they left to go to dinner and couldn't take another one for four hours. Jarrod brought the Jeep as close to the front door as he could, with all the other cars blocking entry. She leaned heavily on him as they walked the last few feet.

Jenny hadn't been there when they got in and, against her protests, Jarrod helped her into her nightgown and carried her to the big bed. He hadn't closed her bedroom door, and now she could hear Jenny in the hall.

"Jenny," she called forcing the pain out of her voice.

The maid came quickly to the door. "I didn't know if you'd be awake yet."

"I need help."

Jenny took a step, then grabbed the door handle and pulled it. She didn't completely close it, and Catherine could hear her speaking to Jarrod.

"I'll help her, sir," she said.

"I want to know how she is."

"Mr. Greene." Jenny's voice was kind, but firm. "She needs a few minutes."

There was a moment of silence before Jarrod said, "I understand."

Then the door opened and Jenny slipped inside, closing it with a soft click. With all the efficiency of a trained nurse, she came to the bed and began asking her questions in a low, professional voice.

"Are you stiff?"

"Extremely. I can't get up."

"Your muscles are protesting the fall. You need to exercise them. I'll run you a bath."

She disappeared into the bathroom. Catherine heard the water running. Then she saw the rose on the pillow beside her. The pillow was slightly depressed. Jarrod must had lain there sometime during the night. The thought caught her off guard, shook her inside; then a kind of comfort settled over her. He'd stayed with her, making sure she was all right. Catherine reached for the flower. Around its stem was a woven piece of paper. *I'll kiss it and make it better,* it read.

"How sweet," she murmured aloud and kissed the delicate petals.

Jenny returned. Catherine slid the paper under Jarrod's pillow and laid the flower on top of it. With Jenny's help and guidance she slid her legs to the side and, using her good arm, braced around Jenny, she sat up. The effort made her dizzy. She waited a moment for it to pass.

"The worse of it is in the morning, Mrs. Greene," Jenny soothed her. "We'll get you to the bath and the water will loosen the muscles.

"Don't try to stand yet. Let me massage your neck." Jenny's fingers were magic. She climbed on the bed behind Catherine and gently cajoled her neck muscles into submission. After a minute, Catherine could turn her head from side to side.

"Catherine?" Jarrod called from outside the door.

"That husband of yours," the maid commented. "I swear, I wish we could hold on to that newlywed love." She climbed down and went to the door. "It'll be a moment, Mr. Greene. I want to get your wife into the bath." She didn't give Jarrod time to protest. The door closed. She went into the bathroom and turned off the water. Then she was back.

Wife, Catherine thought. She'd called her a wife. It caused a tiny wiggle in her insides. She didn't know how she felt about it. In Montana people had called her *Mrs*. Greene, emphasizing the *Mrs*. since they knew she and Jarrod were newly married. Jenny said it matter of factly, as if the two of them had been married for years and would continue to be so. She was someone's wife. Jarrod was her husband. Did he feel that way?

Catherine tried to stand. Her legs supported her and she walked to the small room.

"I'll give you some time alone," Jenny said.

Catherine felt a pang of guilt. Jenny was more than a godsend, she was an invalid's saint. As soon as she completed her toilet, Jenny helped her into the tub of warm water.

"How do the bruises look?" Catherine tried to see herself in the mirror. Her shoulder was dark purple under her brown skin. She couldn't swivel her neck around to see any more.

"They'll heal as expected," Jenny said diplomatically.

"Which means they look worse today than they did yesterday."

The water stung on the scrapes on her legs, but it felt good to descend into its warm depths. It covered her to her shoulders. Jenny had added rose-scented salts, and bubbles burst near her nose, reminding her of the flower lying on the bed and the man who had put it there.

"Catherine, I'm coming in." Jarrod's voice came from the bedroom. She was completely covered when he appeared at the door.

"I'll be back with your breakfast in a moment." Jenny edged past Jarrod. "Call me if you need me," she said over her shoulder as she left them alone.

Jarrod was dressed in jeans and a sweater. He looked as if he'd just pulled in from a thousand-mile haul through rain, sleet and snow.

"Haven't you slept?" she asked.

"I got a couple of hours in. How do you feel?"

"Guilty. I'm feeling like a terrible person for telling Audrey I didn't need Jenny. She's wonderful."

"How do you *feel?*"

"I'm much better," she lied. She didn't want him thinking she couldn't be trusted, and that he needed to look after her wherever they went. "I enjoyed going to the site yesterday. I'd like to go again. Please don't let this accident keep you from bringing me."

He strolled into the tiny space and sat down on the side of the huge tub. Catherine had often thought the tub was large enough for two people to sit in it side by side.

"I won't." He smiled at her, but his eyes were tired. "I liked you being around too. And the guys were ogling you to no end."

"I didn't see a thing," she teased, knowing the words had double meaning. "I guess your clothes mean you're not working today."

"I'm staying here. I already called your office to let them know you won't be in."

She didn't protest. She was grateful. "Then you should get some sleep."

"I will," he told her. "As soon as I eat. I wouldn't want Jenny to go to so much trouble for nothing."

"You just like Jenny's cooking," she teased.

"I love it," he agreed. "You must be feeling better; you can joke."

Jarrod stared at her until Catherine felt uncomfortable. She was vulnerable in the tub, naked, but she felt safe with Jarrod. He would protect her, sacrifice himself trying to keep her safe. She'd seen it in his eyes yesterday. For the split second between the time she saw the trucks and him and tried to move, she knew he would push her out of the way and take the consequences of his actions. She was glad nothing serious had happened.

"Aren't you hurt, Jarrod? After that crash to the ground, you must have some aches and pains this morning."

"None to speak of."

"Let me see it?" she commanded. She wanted to see his arm, where he'd fallen.

"It's only a small scrape."

"Let me see it?"

He pushed his sweater up his right arm past his elbow. Several long scabbed lines ran down the side, no wider than scratches.

"I'll live," he said lightly, pulling the sweater down.

"So will I. Now get out of here so I can get out of this tub."

"Anything I can get you?" He stood up.

"Something to put on." She thought of the caftan in her closet, but she didn't think Jarrod would know what a caftan was. She needed something without much shape to it, something that would not restrict her movement. "There's a long pink and brown dress in my closet. It's hanging near the far end. If you could get that."

He left her, coming back a moment later with the caftan and some underwear. Maybe she'd underestimated him.

"You've done this before," Catherine stated as he laid the garments on the counter and hung the gown on the back of the door.

"Should I help you, or would you like me to call Jenny?"

"It's all right. I can get out." It was the truth. Jenny's massage and the hot water had done the trick. Movement was much easier than it had been before the bath.

"I'll only be a shout away." He left her, closing the door.

Jarrod hadn't answered her question. It pained her more than her shoulder did to think of him dressing and undressing other women. Catherine knew Jarrod had dated many women. Newport alone had women vying for him, and it was a small community. While he was in England she understood he hadn't lived like a monk, and theirs wasn't a real marriage. They'd had only one night together—two encounters if she counted him waking her in the middle of the night. Jarrod was a masterful lover. She slipped down into the water, thinking of their joining, her muscles relaxing from the thought more than any medication could force them to do. She hadn't thought of Jarrod being celibate for six months, although she'd proposed the rule. And he'd accepted it.

He was a virile man. Why had he married her and agreed to her rule? And now that she'd broken it once, and he'd broken it once, did either of them really want it to hold?

She stood up. Water sluiced down her arms and legs. Catherine got out of the huge tub much more easily than she'd gotten into it. She dried herself quickly—at least the parts she could reach—and dressed in the clothes Jarrod had provided. She took a few practice steps in the bathroom to make sure she could walk, then opened the door and went into the bedroom.

Jenny came through the open door at the same time. She carried one tray. Christian followed her with a second one. Jarrod sat propped against the pillows on the side of the bed, where he had obviously lain last night. He held the rose in his hand. The paper was propped against her pillow.

"Where would you like them?"

They had eaten on the small table before, but Jarrod indicated the bed. Three pairs of eyes looked at her, waiting for her to take her place.

"I'm not spending the day in bed," Catherine declared. She smoothed the covers in place and pushed her pillow against the headboard, removing the message Jarrod had left her earlier. She climbed up without help and settled herself. Jenny set the tray in front of her. Christian set his in front of Jarrod on the opposite side. Then the two of them left.

"They probably wonder why we sleep in separate rooms," Catherine said as the door closed.

"I wonder that myself."

"Jarrod!"

"Eat, Catherine. It was a joke."

She didn't think so. She poured her coffee and added jelly to her toast. Nothing about Jarrod was a joke anymore. She knew the tension between them was escalating. Each time they talked or stayed together for any period of time the need to be in each other's arms grew more and more intense. No matter how she tried to lighten the mood, he'd touch her in some way and all thought processes, logic synapses and convictions would be shot all to hell.

Jarrod ate silently. He drank his juice but didn't touch the coffee or eggs. He was asleep before he finished. Catherine moved her tray to the center of the bed. Then she got up and slid it to the side. Then set it on the floor. There was only a twinge in her shoulder. Going around to Jarrod's side, she took his tray and put it on the table where they'd eaten their first night home. She removed his shoes and loosened his clothing, even unsnapping his jeans, but went no further. Jarrod stirred, turning into his pillow. He was on top of the comforter.

Going back to her side, she climbed onto the bed again. She didn't intend to go to sleep. She was serious about not spending the day in bed, but watching him sleep seemed a good way to pass the time. Jarrod wondered why they didn't share a room, but it was really the bed he wanted to share. This was as close as she could come. She looked at his relaxed face. He'd been worried about her. He'd stayed awake all last night, checking on her.

She inched closer to him, putting her right arm around him and sliding down under the covers. They were sharing, she thought. As close as they could come to sharing.

Jarrod was dreaming. He knew he was dreaming. He could smell the rose fragrance from Catherine's bath. And he had her in his arms. She felt real and warm. He gathered her closer, burying his face in her hair. He had to be dreaming. He opened his eyes. Blinked. She *was* real. He'd fallen asleep in her bed. And he had his arms around her.

"Jarrod?" Catherine looked up at him. "You fell asleep."

Her voice was the sexy, bedroom voice that woke the blood inside him, draining it from his brain and pooling it between his legs. Her eyes were dark. She licked her lips, making them wet and shiny and begging to be kissed.

Jarrod threaded his fingers through her hair,

smoothing it off her face. He heard her breath catch in her throat. Dark eyes, fringed with long lashes, stared up at him. He'd kissed her briefly at the construction site yesterday, but he hadn't touched her in weeks. It felt like months. He needed daily doses of her; he knew that now. He moved closer to her, shadowing her face with his own. Parts of her face blurred, but they were printed on his brain. He concentrated on her mouth. His eyes saw her lips, the small pouting movement as her head raised to meet his.

"Catherine, I know this is against the rules, but it'll take two jumbo jets to stop me."

He kissed her, tenderly gathering her closer to him, his arms completely around the part of her not covered by the blankets. Her one arm closed around him. She opened her mouth, and Jarrod's tongue mated with hers. He held her gently, as if she were precious. She *was* precious, more than she knew, more than he had ever told her. He was telling her now, holding her like a mountain flower, one that appears rarely and then recedes for decades. Catherine was his mountain flower, his beautiful, blooming bud. She needed his care to survive and he needed her to breathe, to go on living. He needed her softness to contrast the hardness in him. He needed her soothing bud of warmth to counter the winter in him. She was his opposite and his equal. Where he stopped she started. Where he ended she began.

Jarrod needed to stop. His body was hot and erect. He wanted Catherine, more than he'd ever wanted anyone. It wouldn't take much. He was already holding her. She was ready for him too. Her arms squeezed him, her body pressed against his, even through the covers. If he didn't stop soon, he'd pull those covers away from her and join his body with hers.

"Catherine," he breathed, biting at her lower lip. He could still call her Catherine. He wasn't over the hill yet, but he was almost to the top of it. "We need to stop."

Catherine groaned, continuing to kiss him. He heard the sounds in her throat. His body strained against his clothes. Then Catherine rolled over on top of him. The covers still separated them, but the pleasure that shot through him as her body settled onto his had him reeling. Jarrod reached up and cupped her face. He pushed her hair back and ran his hands over her shoulders.

He stopped. He remembered. Catherine hadn't shown any sign of pain, but Jarrod knew he could hurt her. He'd done it yesterday to save her life, but today it would be willful. Like falling suddenly into a cold lake, Jarrod stopped. He laid her down on the bed.

"Catherine, your shoulder."

"My shoulder is fine," she said. To prove it, she put her arms around his neck.

Jarrod wanted to pull her close. He wanted to bury himself inside her, find the release that only she could provide, but the outcome would be further hurt, both physical and mental. He wouldn't do it again.

He pulled her hands from his neck and leveled himself off the bed.

"I want you, Catherine; I can't tell you how much. But you're hurt and it's my hand that caused it."

"Jarrod—"

"However unintentional." He cut her off. "You need to heal first."

She stared at him. The dark promise in her eyes nearly killed him. For a long moment neither of them spoke. The room was noisy with silence. Electricity snapped as loudly as unspoken vows.

"Will you stay and hold me?" she asked.

It was impossible, Jarrod thought. She was asking the impossible. She stared at him with her hair falling over her shoulders, her eyes pleading, her body hot and her mouth swollen from shared kisses. Jarrod stifled a groan of surrender. He was a man, not a machine, and not a *god.* His stomach curled into knots, nerves screaming for release, his mind conjuring images of them joined, bewitched by sexual need, making love so fulfilling, so satisfying that he'd never experienced anything like it before. Yet he acted on none of these images.

He moved back to the bed, gathered Catherine to him and lay down. He put his arms around her and prayed for the strength of Superman.

Rain pelted the windows. It had showered off and on for the past hour. The sky was dark, and its gloom cast no shadows in the room. Catherine slept comfortably beside him. Jarrod listened to her breathing. The medication made her drowsy, and she'd fallen asleep shortly after she'd settled in his arms. Catherine had said she wasn't going to spend the day in bed, but that was exactly where she and Jarrod were, and although they were together, they really weren't together.

She stirred. Jarrod saw the pain on her face and knew the medication was wearing off. She was about to wake up. He got up and went into the bathroom to find the pills the doctor had given her. He didn't find them in the obvious place. The medicine cabinet had aspirin and cold tablets, but no prescription medicine. He opened one drawer on the right of the sink. Inside was a curling iron, hairpins and other paraphernalia for grooming the hair.

He opened the left-side drawer and his heart stopped, then started again with a thud. Catherine had a home pregnancy test kit. Why? He picked up the box and stared at it. His heart pounded, but he forced himself to calm down. She could have had the kit for months, he rationalized. Because he found it didn't mean she'd bought it recently. Looking down, he spied the slip of paper lying in the bottom of the drawer. It was a receipt. He looked at the date. She hadn't had it for months, only a few weeks. She'd bought it the day after they returned from Montana, the day after they'd made love. Was Catherine pregnant? Why hadn't she told him?

He heard something and turned around. Catherine stood in the doorway. She looked from his face to the box in his hand and back.

"Are you pregnant?" he asked. His voice was calm, controlled, in no way betraying the turmoil that raged inside him. She looked frightened.

"No."

The single word was all she offered. "But you thought you were?" He shoved the box toward her.

"Yes." She didn't look down, but bore his stare.

"Were you going to tell me?"

"I hadn't decided."

"What were you going to do? Have an abortion and keep everything to yourself?"

"I would never do that!" The anger flashing in her eyes was genuine.

"How would I know that?" he shouted. Yet Jarrod thanked God she wouldn't have aborted the pregnancy. He let out a sigh. Suddenly the small bathroom was too confining. He needed something large and open. Some place he could breathe.

He pushed the box into Catherine's hand as he passed her. "I'm going out," he said.

"Jarrod, we need to talk."

"Yes, we do, but we should have talked when you bought that kit. It's a little late now."

He slammed the bedroom door on his way out. Jarrod was angry, beyond angry. He had to leave the house to be alone, and he dared not drive. He left, walking east toward the end of the island, toward the Atlantic and England, six thousand miles away. If he could, he'd surely keep walking, past all the rock walls, through the sand, onto the cliffs and over the water until he was far enough away from Newport that his anger would subside. He estimated that would be somewhere over London's Tower Bridge.

He walked past the new homes on the point, places built with the same style and architecture of the other houses on the island. They appeared to have sat there since the first East India Company ship arrived from England in 1670. Yet they were as new as last year and those under construction, this year.

The rain coated his clothes, falling like a mist to shroud him and distort his view, but Jarrod kept walking. He knew this place well. He could identify it as a surveyor, knowing the line and tilt of the earth. The sky darkened, rolling over the blue areas of the heavens like a giant caterpillar leveling the earth. In seconds he was soaked to the skin. He didn't care. He pushed forward into the night, a ship taking no heed to the dangers of a rocky coast. Catherine thought she was pregnant and she hadn't mentioned it. In all the nights she'd sat curled in the chair across from him, she'd kept this secret to herself.

Jarrod could see the child in his mind. He walked faster, trying to outrun the image, but it moved with him, slowed when he slowed, ran when he ran.

That was his problem. He stopped, staring at the dark sky, not feeling the rain pound against his skin. He wanted a child.

With Catherine.

"Jarrod!" Catherine shouted. The wind took her voice. She saw him, but he wasn't looking at her. He walked across the grass, heading toward the ocean, head bowed and hands in the pockets of his jacket. The area was deserted and dark in the storm. She got out of the car. Rain drenched her.

"Jarrod." It was no good trying to call him over the wind and the ocean. Everything was against her. Not telling him was a mistake. She had been afraid, and she'd wanted to be sure. There was no reason to say anything before she knew the truth. Her reasons sounded like weak excuses now, as if she'd tried to cover up some terrible secret and, like all cover-ups, the disclosure pointed at much more guilt than was true or intended.

Catherine ran across the marshy grass, holding her dress, which had caught between her legs and tried to trip her. She called Jarrod's name, but he didn't hear her until she got close to him. "Jarrod, stop."

"What are you doing here?" He turned around to face her.

"I need to talk to you."

"It can wait, Catherine."

She caught his arm as he turned to walk away. "I don't understand why you're so angry." He stopped walking. "You should be glad. This marriage is temporary, remember? A baby would complicate our lives. And I haven't done anything that any wife wouldn't do, any *real* wife." He stared at her. She didn't know if he believed her, so she rushed on. "Every wife wants to make sure before she tells her husband." She took a deep breath. "Jarrod, I was so scared."

They stood as the rain drenched them further. Jarrod said nothing, but she thought she was reaching him.

"When did you find out you weren't pregnant?"

"Yesterday, in the hospital." Her shoulders dropped in defeat.

"But you told the nurse you weren't pregnant when she asked."

"I know. You were sitting right next to me. I was too afraid to tell her there was a possibility. When they took me to the X-ray room I told them. That's why the X ray took so long. We had to wait for the pregnancy test results."

Jarrod turned away from her. He took a few steps. Catherine thought he didn't believe her.

"Jarrod, it's the truth. You have to believe me."

"I do believe you." He turned back.

"Then why are you so angry?"

He grabbed her arms and looked her straight in the eye. "I'm angry, Catherine, because I'm in love with you."

Catherine backed out of his grasp. No, she thought. Her mind screamed it. He couldn't be.

"I see the feeling isn't mutual."

"Can we talk about this in the car, Jarrod? There's no need for us to catch pneumonia."

He came to her. Catherine stood her ground, even though she wanted to run. She couldn't run. She'd run out of the house after Jarrod left and she hadn't taken her pills. She could feel the pain in her shoulder returning, and the cold rain wasn't helping. Catherine turned toward the car. She'd only taken a few steps before Jarrod noticed her limping. It wasn't from the accident; a pebble had lodged in her shoe when she ran to catch up with him. He scooped her up in his arms. She buried her face in his neck and he tightened his arms around her.

Jarrod stood in the middle of the marsh, holding her. The rain beat at them, stinging like needles. He whispered something she couldn't hear, but she didn't need to understand him to recognize his mouth seeking hers. She turned her head and met his kiss. She could feel his desperation. This was nothing like the gentleness of that morning's kiss. Jarrod's mouth was fierce, hungry with need and raw with anger. He wanted her, and Catherine wanted him too. She embraced him, drawing him as close as she could get while he held her. He let her legs fall to the ground, but his arms kept her against him.

His hands went to her head, threading through the straight hair that plastered itself to her head, holding her mouth to his as he kissed her lips, her eyes, her cheeks and returned to the paradise of her mouth. Catherine had been kissed before, had kissed Jarrod before, but this was different; these were love kisses. Everything about them screamed *I love you.*

Catherine's heart pounded, above the sound of the rain, over the roar of the sea, hammering with a beat so strong that it drowned out all other sound except that of Jarrod's heart, which was beating the same drum as hers.

Jarrod raised his head and stared into her eyes. He said nothing. Words weren't necessary. Then he lowered his mouth and kissed her again. A sorcerer couldn't have summoned more magic than the drums beating through them, drums of their motherland, drums of their heritage, their past, the universal drums of life. The call came in all languages, in many tongues and over centuries. Yet Catherine heard it, felt it, understood it as only love could explain.

The wind howled about them, tearing at them, trying to separate them, as if the forces swirling in the heavens had gained intelligence, banded together to pull them apart. Catherine didn't know which of them moved first, but her hands were under Jarrod's soaked sweater. She felt his skin, hot even with the rain. She pushed her hands under the soggy garment, heavy with wetness, until she reached his back. Smooth, silky skin, subtle and warm. Her fingers tingled as she moved them across it. Jarrod groaned in her mouth when her fingers moved around to touch his nipples. She ran the tips over him, bringing the flat nipples to life and enjoying the way Jarrod moved back and forth against her.

He stepped back and ripped the sweater over his head as if it had just come fluffy and light from a drier and had none of the water weighing it down. Catherine gasped at the sheer virility of him. His muscles were defined, his chest carved in dark contours. The water sluiced over him, designating paths for her hands to follow.

"You're beautiful," she said, more to herself than to him.

"I love you, Catherine," Jarrod said. "I've loved you since you were sixteen years old."

He pulled her to him and kissed her again. She felt the zipper of her dress being dragged down, the coldness of the rain trickling down her back, along with Jarrod's fingers caressing her spinal column. She shuddered, not from the cold, but from anticipation. She wanted the dress gone. She wanted to feel Jarrod's naked skin against her own. He peeled the dress away from her body, defying the rain, which fought him for possession. It fell to her hips. He eased it down and dropped it. Jarrod kissed across her shoulder, holding her tenderly as he remembered her accident. Catherine wasn't thinking of her shoulder. She could only concentrate on the hot kisses Jarrod's open mouth rained over her skin.

She closed her eyes as ecstasy gained a foothold. Jarrod kissed the column of her neck and continued down until he came to the swell of her breasts. He reached around her and unhooked her bra. Immediately his mouth closed over her already sensitive nipple. Delight fissured through her at the sensations that rioted inside her. Like stars shooting through her, Catherine felt her body coming apart. She raked her fingers down his back until she reached his jeans. Moving around him, she fumbled for the fastening, then unsnapped it.

Jarrod shrugged out of them, forcing them over his wet skin. Catherine pushed her panties to the ground. The two stood naked in the dark day, with the wind whipping at them and the rain pelting them. Catherine stepped forward first. She clamped her mouth to Jarrod's and pulled him down to the ground. She didn't care that it was wet, that it was grassy, or that she was lying on her caftan, its colors bleeding a sea of pink and brown.

He covered her with his body, gently spreading her legs. Catherine should have remembered the sensations, remembered the burst of pleasure that shot through her when Jarrod entered her, but she didn't. It was as if they had never before made love. They hadn't, not like this, not with this new intensity. Jarrod's hands slid under her, lifting her slightly as he drove himself into her. Catherine felt each thrust with greater pleasure, each rise and fall with greater fury. The wind bellowed about them, tearing at them, unleashing the forces of nature but unable to match the gale-force frenzy with which they competed. Catherine's breath was ripped from her. She fought for more, dragging it into her lungs as Jarrod forced it out of her in powerful, measured strokes. She cried out with each virile thrust.

There was no lightning, no thunder opening the heavens. It was all inside her. She felt the raging storm, the electrical monster coiled and ready to spring, snapping and releasing its power over the land and sea. She felt the tear in her universe, knew the cry of rapture that gripped her, the long shudder of passion that burst open and shot into her as a final wave of uncontrollable emotion. Rapture flourished inside her; riptides overwhelmed her, lifting her to the eye of the internal storm and holding her there. Her body changed, morphed into a single unqualified pleasure vessel. She clung to the place, held on to Jarrod while suspended over the abyss. Balancing on the edge of forever, she felt the exhilaration of life, the onslaught of temptation, the fulfillment of fantasy and the explosion of ecstasy that burst inside her with a power so strong she couldn't contain it. The scream tore from her body, loud enough to reach the heavens, to cross the seas and to rival the storm that raged around them. The pleasure was uncontrollable, washing through her like the rushing waves that crashed against the cliffs. She crashed too. Jarrod came with her.

Together they fell back to earth, delirious, clinging to each other, knowing nothing except the past few minutes. They collapsed, and she finally felt the rain washing over them in delicious rivers of welcome coolness.

The bathtub *was* big enough for two. Jarrod had thought so earlier, when he saw Catherine in it. She'd looked pale and small then. Now she glowed. Even with his long frame and Catherine's shorter one they had plenty of room to luxuriate in the hot water. Catherine hugged him, her hand moving through the sudsy water to massage his chest.

They'd lain on the grass until they started shivering. Then Jarrod had gathered her and their clothes and hustled her back to the deserted car. He wrapped her in the car blanket and pulled on his wet jeans. The heat was on full as he drove back to the house on Ocean Drive. Jenny hadn't seen them running across the foyer and up the stairs, leaving wet footprints behind as they headed for her room.

Jarrod immediately ran water in the bathtub and rubbed Catherine's feet to warm them before they both got into the reviving water. He remembered her laughing as he tickled her feet. Jarrod had let some of the water out once and turned the faucet to heat it again. He held her, stroking her back, content for nearly an hour.

Catherine wore no makeup, her face completely clean, her hair wet and slicked back, yet she had never looked more beautiful.

Jarrod kissed the top of her head. "We can't go back, you know."

"I know," she said.

She didn't ask what he meant. Jarrod knew she understood. After their lovemaking on the grass, there was no way they could return to the rules. The rules no longer applied. The world no longer revolved around the same sun. Nothing was the same; not him, not Catherine, not the universe.

"What do you propose?" she asked.

Till death do us part was on the tip of his tongue, but he didn't say it. He'd told her he loved her. He'd said it twice, but Catherine had yet to say it. He knew she was afraid. He'd known her all her life, had discovered he'd loved her for years. She needed time to get used to the idea, but Jarrod wouldn't go back to the guest room. He needed her every day and wanted to be with her every night.

"One day at a time," he finally answered.

"What does that mean?"

"It means we give it a try."

"For the rest of the six months?"

Her hand continued to massage his chest. His stopped in the middle of her back. "You still plan to divorce me in February?"

Chapter 11

Catherine's period started the following morning. She wasn't pregnant. She stood in the bathroom, washing her hands. She looked at herself in the mirror. She didn't look much different, but she felt different. She looked at her stomach in the mirror. There was no child there. She touched herself just under her breasts. What was wrong with her? She didn't want a child. It was Jarrod. He'd mentioned it that day in the library, when he was drunk. And he'd been so angry when he found the pregnancy kit. So why did she feel depressed?

No strings, no complications for this temporary arrangement. She reminded herself of her convictions. A child would change her life, change both of their lives. A child would tie them together for eternity. It wasn't what they wanted, she told herself. But was it what Jarrod wanted? Had his anger been so strong, so uncontrollable because he did want a child? But with her? Catherine was too confused to think about it. Yet her thoughts kept returning to the possibility. She wanted to know if it would be a boy or a girl. Would it look like her or Jarrod?

She stopped her thoughts. She couldn't think like this. It was up to her to make sure a baby wasn't in their future. She and Jarrod were sharing space now, sleeping together, making love. She had to make sure they always used condoms, and tomorrow she'd make an appointment with her gynecologist for birth control pills.

Catherine had come to work today. No one protested her decision, not Jarrod and not Jenny. She supposed the determined look on her face told them both she would not be crossed this morning.

She went back to her desk, where papers and books were strewn in organized chaos. She was in her slow period. There were things to do, but nothing pressing. The season was over, but building would go on all winter. Sales would pick up during the boat shows in the spring. It was then she had to have everything done. All the brochures completed, the repair manuals updated and any information for previous customers approved and mailed.

This was the time for conferencing, for trips to warmer climates and learning about changes in motors, interior design and wind shirring. This was the time for ordering photographs or materials for the men working in the warehouses near the ocean. This was not the time to daydream at her desk, thinking of Jarrod and nothing else. But that was exactly what she was doing. He filled in the spaces of her life, spaces she hadn't known were open.

Jarrod had taken her news quite well. She *was* going to divorce him in February. It didn't matter that he could melt her with a touch. Or that she'd never made love with anyone who made her lose all her inhibitions, all her training and manners and her thoughts of moral acceptability. Between herself and Audrey, she was the wild one. Audrey did all the right things, while Catherine did them differently.

Maybe she should have been more like Audrey. Then Jarrod wouldn't be married to her and she wouldn't be in this mess. She'd be married to some nice, safe insurance salesman and have three children and a minivan. Somehow that life didn't suit her. She was more the . . . the what? The kind of person Jarrod Greene would fall in love with.

She didn't want his love. She hadn't asked for it. Why had he told her he loved her? Why had he made love to her? Why had he held her so tenderly in the bathtub yesterday? And why couldn't she forget the way their bodies fit so perfectly together or the way she felt when he put his arms around her, the way he smelled of musk and man? Catherine closed her eyes, pulling the smell in; even now when she was alone, even now when Jarrod was miles away at his own desk or out on one of his field visits, she could order his essence to fill the room.

"Oh my God."

Catherine jerked forward. She looked up to find Elizabeth coming into her office and closing the door. Catherine didn't want to see anyone, not even her best friend. She had a problem she couldn't talk about with anyone. It was between her and Jarrod. She couldn't tell even Elizabeth this one.

"Don't you have someplace else to be?"

"It's that bad, is it?" She closed the door and came in, sitting down in the chair in front of Catherine.

"Elizabeth, what are you doing here?"

"I ran into Jarrod. He looks almost as bad as you do. He said something about an accident at a construction site, but I'm sure your affliction is love." She paused for a long moment. "You're in love with him."

"I am not!"

"Protest," Elizabeth said. "That's a sure sign."

"It's a sign of nothing," she said more quietly. "Jarrod and I did have an accident." She attempted to change the subject. "But we're fine."

Elizabeth shook her head. "I can see that from looking at both of you." Elizabeth leaned forward, giving her the sarcastic face she'd come to know from years of friendship. "Catherine, it's not a crime to fall in love."

"I'm not in love."

"You're something."

Catherine got up and walked to the window. Her office looked down on both the construction yard and the marina. She looked out at the sea. The day was warm, but no sailboats were out in full sail. They were all moored to their docks. Catherine took in the scene as if it were an anchor.

"How do you feel about Jarrod?" Elizabeth asked.

"The way I've always felt about him."

"You've always been in love with him?"

Catherine turned around and stared at Elizabeth. She sat in the same chair she had taken when she came in, but she'd turned around to face her friend.

"Catherine?" Elizabeth called her name. "Have you always been in love with Jarrod?"

"Yes." Tears rolled down her face. It was true. She'd been in love with him ever since she could remember. It was why she found it so easy to talk to him, why his jokes hurt her so badly, why everything they had ever done together was printed on her memory, while the actions of other men had no staying power. It was why making love with Jarrod had been so different. They weren't having sex together, they were truly making love. It made a difference, a tremendous difference to her when he took her in his arms.

Had this been fate? Had Jarrod arrived home just in the nick of time, or had she refused all other comers because she was waiting for him? Was he the reason Audrey's comments got under her skin to the point that she needed to protect herself from all other men, protect herself for Jarrod? Then Jarrod had arrived, and she'd talked him into marrying her. Now she was in love with him, and as of last night they were living together . . . as man and wife.

Jarrod fingered the single red rose in his hand. He leaned against the hood of the Jeep, his legs crossed at the ankles. The Jeep was clean and his suit was pressed. He was waiting for Catherine to come out. He had a plan.

Their courtship had been short. Most couples dated for a longer time before they decided to marry. He and Catherine hadn't done that. Events after his return from England had been hurricane-fast. Changes were expected by any married couple, any engaged couple. It appeared there were too many changes going on in her life. She needed an adjustment period. And she hadn't had it. But she would.

Jarrod was willing to give her time to make up her mind. He knew her heart said one thing and her head another. She needed time for the two of them to synchronize. He'd allow the time, but he wasn't going to make it easy. He would date her, take her out to dinner, plays, concerts. He'd take her to construction sites and travel on business with her, and every night he'd make love to her.

They had five months before her planned divorce. If he couldn't make her fall in love with him in that time, then it wasn't meant to be. But he couldn't believe that the mast anchored to the deck of his heart wasn't meant to be connected to the wind that blew her sails. Tonight would be their first date.

Catherine came out of the building and headed for her car. She wore a red dress, the shade of the American beauty in his hand. The wind caught the hem and it swirled about her legs for a second, exposing the slender curve of her calf and the promise of her thigh above it. She waved to someone leaving at the same time. Jarrod pushed himself away from the Jeep. He was parked in the space next to Catherine's Intrepid, a sporty model that was low and fast and reminded him of a gentle tiger with a great roar on the inside. She stopped when she saw him, then started again. She was like her car, gentle to look at, soft to the touch, but she could roar, and she made him roar.

"Hi," he said and kissed her on the cheek. He offered her the rose.

"Thank you." She brought it to her nose and smelled. "I didn't expect you," she said. She was nervous. Things hadn't been very easy in the last day for either of them. She'd been on the same emotional roller coaster he'd ridden; in each other's arms one moment and clawing at each other the next.

"I thought I'd take you to dinner. I called Jenny and told her not to expect us."

"Oh."

"Did you have plans?"

"No, I just wasn't prepared."

"Do you feel all right?"

"I feel fine." She turned her head from side to side and lifted her shoulder, demonstrating the mobility in her joints. "I'm almost back to normal." Her voice was a little hesitant. Then she smiled. "I'd like to go."

Step one, Jarrod thought. She hadn't refused.

"Where did you have in mind?" she asked.

"How about that new place over in Portsmouth? Legacy's?"

She nodded. "I'll drop this in my car." Catherine put her briefcase in her car, and he opened the door of the Jeep and helped her inside. He was tempted to turn her into his arms and give her a real kiss, but this was their first date, even if she didn't know it.

"Robert tells me Legacy's has something for everyone. The food is good, and the music is terrific."

Catherine frowned. "Can we trust Robert?"

Jarrod laughed. "In this, probably."

They crossed the bridge and found the restaurant with little trouble. The parking lot was full, but they were shown to a table for two immediately. When the waiter left with their drink order Jarrod said, "You're nervous again."

She looked him directly in the eye. He knew she did this to hide her real feelings, to make him think there was no turmoil going on inside her, but these days he found it easier and easier to read her. Not in all things, but in some.

"I am nervous, Jarrod. I want to talk about yesterday, but I don't know what to say."

Yesterday didn't exist on first dates, but this part of their relationship was important. They couldn't go forward without settling it. Yet he'd rather postpone it until later. "We do need to talk about yesterday, but let's not do it now. Why don't you start by telling me how your day was?"

He smiled, and she did too. She seemed to relax a little. Jarrod was glad. He wanted her comfortable with him. He wanted her to trust him.

"I didn't get much done," she said. "Elizabeth came by to see me."

"She knows, doesn't she?"

Catherine had been twirling the rose stem between her fingers. She stopped. "How did you know?"

"The other night at Audrey's. She stopped you from giving yourself away. I was the only other person at the table who knew about the temporary marriage. It's not on the recording."

Catherine smelled the rose again. "She won't tell anyone."

"Why did she come to the office?"

"She'd run into you. She said you looked awful. Well, as awful as you can." She tried a smile.

Jarrod returned the gesture. She seemed a little less uncomfortable. Their drinks arrived, and the waiter took their dinner order.

"She wanted to know if I looked as bad."

He took her hands across the table and brought them to his lips. He didn't kiss them, only held them close. "And did you?"

"Yes." She nodded.

He laughed and she joined in. From then on the evening went well. They ate and talked about everything under the sun: tourists, the annual fund raiser at the local library, living other places. She told him about living in New York. He told her about England and Scotland.

"I loved Scotland," he said.

"The mountains," she finished for him. "It probably reminds you of Montana."

"I never thought of it like that."

"They're different from the mountains in Montana, but the air is clean and fresh, and there aren't many people around."

"Exactly," he agreed. "We'll have to go there some day." He said it before he realized he'd attached a longer future to their relationship than Catherine had planned. He wanted to travel with her, see the world through her eyes, be reminded of that Alice-in-Wonderland experience.

By the time they finished eating and having coffee they were back to being the old friends they'd been before marriage entered and altered their lives. A small band played soft music in a nearby room. The low strands of a bass violin and a saxophone drifted into the dining room.

"Why don't we dance for a while?" Jarrod asked. Catherine nodded and, leaving the dining room, they entered the bar and joined several couples on the small dance floor. When he took Catherine in his arms the music was haunting. He held her close, breathing in the scent of her perfume. The effect drugged his senses.

Together they danced about the floor, moving

together, in time and rhythm. Jarrod didn't want to let go of her. He wanted her now, but he restrained himself. After three dances they left for home. Arm in arm, he walked her to the Jeep and drove her back to her car.

Jarrod helped her down from the high seat and with his arm around her waist, he walked her to the door of her car as if it were her parents' porch. At the car he turned her toward him and kissed her tenderly, lightly. Catherine raised her arms around his neck and he crushed her to him, lifting her feet from the ground, giving her the good-night kiss he'd wanted to greet her with when she'd exited the building a few hours earlier. She was so soft. She felt so good in his arms. He wanted the kiss to go on forever, but he released her, setting her back on her feet. He opened the car door and she got inside.

"I'll see you at home," she said. He closed the door.

Their first date was officially over. Jarrod whistled.

Catherine didn't know what to expect anymore. Jarrod was consistent. She'd never been happier. She had always been decisive, coming up with a plan. Even though it might get her in trouble, she decided on it and put it to work. Yet lately she wavered, not understanding dilemmas that had her unsure of herself. The unexpectedness was inside her.

She sat at her dressing table repairing her makeup. Jarrod would be home soon. She'd taken to fixing her hair and her face each night before he arrived. He liked to play with her hair, and she often did it in ways she knew would tantalize him.

Tonight she pulled it up and used combs to hold it off her ears while curls cascaded down her back, and she thought about that rainy day. It was raining again, but the room was rosy and glowing. She and Jarrod hadn't talked any more about the uncontrolled lust that had overtaken them in the rain. Except for her telling him that she wasn't pregnant, they had silently agreed to drop the subject and go on. He hadn't pressured her into anything. They slept each night in the same bed and by morning were always entangled in each other's arms, as if some magnet drew them across the sheets until they were touching and holding each other.

Some nights Catherine woke to Jarrod's kisses, and other nights the kisses and lovemaking began before they got to bed.

He was killing her with kindness. And she was loving it. She found notes under her pillow in the morning, or he had flowers delivered to her desk. He'd arrive for an impromptu dinner or they'd take long, quiet walks along the coastline with only the wind and the gulls for company.

And the nights. The magnificent, magical, marvelous nights when they made love. She'd never known anything could be this wondrous, fantastic, extraordinary. Yet each night when they turned out the lights the amazement happened again.

Catherine looked down at the note in her hand. *I love the red dress. It's got all the right moves. Inside and out.* She'd found this note taped to the bathroom mirror the morning after their dinner at Legacy's. The tiny message said so much. She remembered Jarrod removing that red dress. He'd taken an excruciating amount of time to pull the zipper to its base, kissing her skin from neck to waist as each section of cloth revealed another square of skin. By the time he had it all the way down, she thought she'd burn up from re-entry into an unexpected atmosphere.

Catherine looked at herself in the mirror. The face staring back at her was vastly different from the one that had looked at her a month ago. The night they danced. The night Jarrod made everything right. Now Catherine longed to see him, wake to find him next to her, hold him in her sleep and laugh with him. She loved the laughter.

She heard Jarrod in the downstairs hall. Catherine returned the card to the box in her drawer where she kept all the cards and notes he'd left her, the origami couple and a pressed rose. She closed it. Her heart lifted and she left the bedroom almost at a run. He was later tonight than usual. Something was keeping him at the office, and he'd taken to bringing work home, but he didn't spend all his time working. She couldn't complain about his treatment of her. He'd promised her on their honeymoon that he would be attentive, and he was.

At the bottom of the steps he swept her into his arms and swung her around. "What's going on?" she asked, feeling the room spin.

"I have a wonderful idea."

He kissed her quickly as he did every night when he came in. Then, in a routine she'd come to expect, he kissed her again. This time with meaning and passion, pulling her against the full length of his body, threading his fingers into her hair and holding her like some precious object he cherished. It was a heady kiss, and she didn't fail to answer it with a frantic weakness that had her clinging to him.

"What's your wonderful idea?" Catherine asked on the breathless cloud where she floated when Jarrod lifted his head.

He loosened his tie as they headed for the kitchen. Jenny and Christian were gone and their meal was warm and waiting.

"I have to go to Maine tomorrow."

Catherine stopped in the middle of taking plates down.

"We've never been apart." She said it before she realized it. "Not overnight," she finished.

Jarrod took the plates from her and set them on the counter. She was still holding them in the air, as if she'd lost her ability to talk and work at the same time. He took silverware from the drawer.

"How long will you be gone?" She turned to get glasses, hoping he didn't hear the note of dismay in her voice.

"Three days, but—" He stopped, as if there should be a drumroll. "Come up Friday? We'll spend the weekend. Make it a mini-second honeymoon."

Today was Tuesday. He'd be gone Wednesday and Thursday night. She'd see him Friday. Two nights sounded like an eternity. She didn't want to be separated from him for that long. Yet Catherine smiled.

"I think it's a wonderful idea too."

Catherine tossed and turned Wednesday and Thursday nights. She missed Jarrod. The house felt strange without him. He'd only lived there for a little over a month, yet his presence was everywhere, especially in the huge bed they shared.

She took Friday off, wanting to leave early, but

had to keep her doctor's appointment. She saw the gynecologist, and in her purse was a prescription for birth control pills. She didn't have time to fill it.

Jarrod had driven the Jeep. She had only enough time to make the train. She would meet Jarrod at the hotel. A car waited for her at the train station in Portland and drove her away from the coast to the tiny town of Standish. Jarrod's things were there when she arrived, but he was still working. The hotel turned out to be a small country house he'd taken for the weekend.

The eighteenth-century building set behind a fence in the shadow of huge trees took on the charm of a Christmas card. It was made totally of stone, various shades of gray and white, and tucked into the setting as if some architect had designed it. She could see Jarrod in this scene. Humor aside, he saw the world for its beauty, a type that couldn't be formed with cement and bricks, but with time and care.

The house had two floors, three small bedrooms and no closets. The furnishings were replicas from the past, made more comfortable for guests. Warm fires burned in all the rooms, although the house had central heating. Catherine loved it.

She suddenly remembered when she was very small. She smelled bread, her grandmother's bread. They baked it from scratch, and her grandmother would let her help. Catherine could see herself, five years old, covered from neck to foot with a long apron and flour in her hair, on her cheeks and chin, her shoes, the floor and the apron. She sniffed, hoping she could really smell it and had an urge to bake.

She heard the front door open.

"Hey, Lucy. It's Ricky. I'm home."

Catherine didn't know where the tears came from, but they were in her eyes. Her feet moved of their own accord. She ran toward Jarrod, throwing herself at him, realizing how much she had missed him. He looked wonderful, better than wonderful. He lifted her off the floor and squeezed her tight.

"You missed me," he told her. She wouldn't have denied it if he'd asked. "Good."

His mouth settled on hers, his tongue mingling with the salt of happy tears spilling from her eyes. Catherine kissed him as if the last two days had been two centuries. She had missed him terribly, and she let her kiss tell him. She pushed his coat down his arms so she could feel the warmth of him, know that he was there, real, solid, and that she was holding him. She kissed him with the knowledge that something inside her had been pent up. Then, with a snap, the floodgates were torn from their hinges, and nothing short of a tsunami wave could reverse the emotion driving her.

"I was going to wait," Jarrod said, his voice dark as night. "I was going to take you to dinner," he breathed against her mouth. "Order champagne, buy you flowers." Each phrase traded kiss for kiss. "But I'll be damned if I can wait another moment."

In seconds he was hustling her out of the turtleneck sweater she wore and pulling her jeans down. There could be no waiting between them. They had been separated for two days and two long nights. Each second had taken hours to pass, each minute days.

Catherine was down to her lace panties and Jarrod to a skimpy pair of black silky briefs before they took in air.

"You wore those to work?" she asked.

"Yeah," he said. "And it was hell knowing you were going to be here when I got back."

He pulled her back into his arms. His aroused body pressed against hers. Catherine put her hands on his sides, under his arms, both to steady herself and to hold on to the sensation of raw sexuality that lit through her like a sudden fire-burst in the hearth. She ran her hand deliberately down Jarrod's side, feeling the tight muscles, until she came to the tops of the briefs. The fabric was slippery as water. She caressed his buttocks and felt his reaction pressed deeper into her body.

Jarrod's kiss deepened. The raw, feverish hunger in him pressed her back. Her fingers went inside the fabric, moving up to touch hot, scalding, naked skin. Her blood gushed through her. She pulled the fabric from the hem down, sliding her hands around his body. His hands gripped her shoulders. She felt his knees bend and heard the almost painful cry come from his throat.

Her hands continued around him, pulling as she went in a slow, determined pattern, as if they were on a road with only one entrance and no exit. There was no turning back. Her fingers closed over him, touching skin so rigid she could feel her own body flow in anticipation. Catherine rubbed her thumb over the tight skin of his penis. She looked at his eyes, saw them widen in rapturous pleasure, the pupils dilate to the size of saucers, saw the clear reflection of herself in his soul. The vision was like a narcotic, an instant high.

She took Jarrod's hand and they settled to the floor. The fire burned in the hearth and inside her. A hand-made quilt lay across the sofa back in case the room was too cold. Catherine wouldn't need it. Jarrod covered her body, and he was all the heat she would need. She lay down and he stretched out next to her, taking her in his arms and kissing her again. His hand worked a slow, zigzag line down her sides, across her breasts, over her stomach to the small bud between her legs.

"You're so hot," he said.

"I'm on fire," she answered him between kisses.

Jarrod moved quickly. He covered her. His body, huge and powerful in its wonder and excitement, drove smoothly and deeply into her. Catherine gasped at the pleasant torment of his entry. Her body contracted, holding him inside her, releasing a fraction to allow him to withdraw before grasping and taking him back in again. She was losing it. She knew she was, and she knew she had no control. Nor did she want control. The creature who lived inside her was out. That creature was aggressive, wanton, a hussy. Pushing Jarrod over, her hair flying out of its confines as she sat over him, her legs parallel to his, her body aligned with his. She gave, she took, she gave, she took.

Catherine thought of nothing but the man with her, giving him the pleasure he deserved, giving him what she had to give. Jarrod caught her waist and raised up with her to the rhythm she created. They danced through time, through the beat of blood drums, through the awesome tune of the mating dance, through the fever of attraction, need, arousal, satisfaction. In her blood was a new kind of power and in her arms was the only man who could call for it, speak to the drums, understand the language and answer it.

And Catherine heard the answer. She didn't know from which of them it came, but the scream reached the ceiling and she collapsed. Jarrod rolled her over, still joined in the most intimate way.

"I'm sorry it was so fast, Catherine. You don't know what you do to me."

"What I do to you? My God, Jarrod, what you do to me!" She took a breath. "I can't describe it. I wish I could make you understand." She buried her face in his chest, kissing him there.

"I understand," he groaned.

"With you it's like I'm . . . whole." It was the only word she could think of to explain how she felt. He completed her. He filled all the crevices in her that needed filling, even those she didn't know existed. Jarrod seemed to find them and complement them.

She was still thinking it half an hour later. Jarrod had dragged the quilt over them and fallen asleep. She watched him, wondering why she wasn't asleep too. After her previous two nights of tossing and turning she should be dead on her feet, but instead she was giddy with satisfaction. She wondered how and when it had happened. When had she stopped looking at Jarrod as the practical joker and started seeing him as a lover? Why were his kisses so powerful to her that the thought of them made her breasts point in his direction?

She didn't understand it. He'd spent five years in England and she'd only thought of him on his birthday and when something triggered the memory of one of his embarrassing jokes. Yet here she was, lying next to him, married to him, even if it was temporarily, and all she could think of was running her hands down his face, under the covers, down his chest, waking him and making love again.

Catherine knew better than to call it having sex. The room was filled with the electric smell of their lovemaking. That was what they had done. She'd had sex before, been engaged to someone else, but no one had made her feel as complete as Jarrod.

The kitchen in Stone House, the name Catherine had given it, was a mixture of ages and times. The old stove was a wood burner. There was a pantry filled with dry goods and a locker with churned butter and cured meats. The worktable looked as if it had been there since the stones were set. Its surface was deeply contoured from use by many working hands.

Catherine had never cooked on a wood stove. She'd only ever seen one in a movie. She had no idea how to regulate the oven, how much wood to use or even if adding more wood would produce more heat. She could start a fire in a fireplace and, if pressed, could start a campfire with only rocks and twigs. But this house made her think of baking bread, and she would master that. There was something about the rustic nature of the house that brought out the cook in her. At home Jenny cooked all her meals except lunch. She hadn't cooked in a long while. When she'd lived in New York she mainly ate out or picked up carry-out on her way back to her tiny apartment.

She and Jarrod had spent most of the day trying to make up for the time they had lost while apart. They'd made love more times than she could count. In the late afternoon they'd gone upstairs, where they'd made love in the eighteenth-century bed with its high headboard. Jarrod still slept soundly upstairs.

Catherine was downstairs finding something to eat when the thought of baking bread came back to her. She wasn't clever enough to compose the notes that Jarrod left on her pillow, and she had no roses for him to find when he woke. While cooking wasn't one of her talents, baking was something she enjoyed, thanks to the hours she'd spent in the kitchen with her grandmother.

Catherine was surprised to find she remembered the ingredients she needed to make bread and that they were all there, including yeast that was still fresh. An hour later the kitchen was warm and cozy and the bread was covered for the first rise. While she'd found a cookbook that dated back to her grandmother's teens and used it to supplement her memory, she had flour and wet spots all over the workstand.

Catherine cleaned her mess, feeling satisfied with the result. She made herself a cup of coffee, added logs to the fire in the main room of the house and the huge hearth in the kitchen. Embers snapped and exploded between her and the firewall, spangling the air with fiery stars. Across from the center table in the kitchen was an overstuffed sofa that changed the kitchen into a family room, a place for guests to sit and have coffee while they talked to the cook. Catherine curled up on the sofa with her coffee cup and looked out the window onto the snowy yard. This was the time for storytelling.

When her grandmother was alive and they got to this point in the baking process, they would make hot chocolate and talk. Her grandmother would tell her stories from her childhood on the island, before it was fully developed. Catherine would pour out her problems and ask her adolescent questions. Her grandmother always listened. She never laughed or made Catherine feel young and awkward.

She smiled at the memory of the ebony-skinned woman with her gray hair and a hug that could solve all the problems of the world. She wondered what her grandmother would make of her and Jarrod. Catherine sipped her coffee. A glow passed over her as if her grandmother had touched her, as if she approved of them.

Outside the yard was white. Snow covered the ground from the door to the small pond that ended the property. Catherine leaned closer to the window. A deer foraged near the pond. She froze as surely as if she were outside and had turned around to find herself lined up with the animal. She watched as another one joined the first. They came closer to the house, making footprints in the clean snow. Catherine watched them with the wonder of a five-year-old on her first trip to the zoo. She rarely saw deer where she lived. There were plenty of trees around her, but development, new houses and condominiums had forced the wildlife farther and farther into the woods.

Catherine was only six years old when she'd seen her first deer. Her grandmother was driving and she was in the backseat, barely able to see through the side window. Jarrod was nine and sat in the front passenger seat. He was tall for his age, although Catherine didn't know it then. He looked like a giant to her. And a mean giant at that. She smiled at the thought of him now. He was still a giant, but he could be gentle. She knew how gentle. She glanced up, taking her eyes away from the window and the deer outside, as if she could see Jarrod through the thick walls of Stone House.

It was winter then too. There had been snow, but it had been cleared to the side of the road. The sun was shining brightly, reflecting off the fields of white. She had to squint to keep her eyes open. Her grandmother had been taking them shopping. They were going to buy Christmas presents for their parents.

There weren't many houses along that road then, only a few here and there set back from the road. Now there was a development there, with all the same gray siding and covered chimneys to make them maintenance-free. She could see one house in the distance. It had been decorated with twinkling lights that outlined the entire structure. The lights were on even in the bright sun. Catherine remembered thinking it was Santa's house. In the yard was a sleigh. Her mind remembered it as life-sized. Sitting on the seat was a Santa Claus with a bag of brightly colored boxes.

They were almost past it when she saw the deer. They came running out of the woods, three of them. Catherine screamed, thinking they were Santa Claus's reindeer. They rounded the house and headed toward the sleigh. Her grandmother stopped the car. She watched them running around the yard until they disappeared into a different part of the woods. No matter how much Jarrod told her they weren't Dasher and Dancer and Comet, Catherine knew better.

She smiled at this memory of her youth. She remained still. The two deer in the yard could easily be part of Santa's herd. She watched them until they moved off and she could no longer see them.

The bread had risen by the time Catherine poured

her second cup of coffee. She punched it down, kneaded it and prepared rolls. Her grandmother could break off pieces of dough and form perfect rolls that were even and all the same size. Catherine had never been able to do that. Hers looked more like the croissants she'd tried on their honeymoon, missized and shapeless. She cheated by using a rolling pin and making perfect circles with a floured glass. She set them aside for the second rise.

By the time the first batch of fresh bread came out of the iron-stove oven, Jarrod walked into the kitchen. He wore a long-sleeved white shirt and gray slacks. The combination was striking in itself. Catherine immediately felt herself respond to his presence. They'd made love all afternoon, yet she still wanted him. She wondered if it would always be this way. It was a question she would like to ask her grandmother.

"It smells good in here."

"It must be my perfume," she said. "Oeau de yeast." Catherine stirred a pan on the stove.

"Definitely." He reached for one of the rolls and took a healthy bite. Then he lifted her mug and drank the remainder of her coffee.

"These are perfect," Jarrod said, obviously remembering her previous effort.

She ignored the implied insult, thankful that the kitchen was in order and the glass she'd used to make the rolls uniform had been cleaned and stored away in the cupboard.

"Those are for dinner, you know."

He turned her around and into his arms. "What's for dessert?" He kissed her soundly, bending her back until she was so off balance she had to cling to him or fall.

Catherine clung.

"We'd better eat," she said in a breathy, surrendering voice.

"I agree," Jarrod said, his voice in her hair, as ragged as hers. "I'm starving to death." His tone told her everything, and it had nothing to do with food.

She stepped back, out of his reach, and took a deep, calming breath. The kitchen was hot. He was making it hotter. "I'll get dinner."

Jarrod moved to the table, which was already set. He took the basket of rolls with him. Using a dish towel to protect her hand, Catherine opened the bottom drawer of the oven. It was heavy and fell down from the unaccustomed weight. She pulled the pan out and set the lamb steaks on the counter. The crushed rosemary and butter mingling with mushrooms and onions permeated the air, wafting up to combine with the baked bread smells. Quickly she turned them onto the plates, added piping hot potatoes, baked without the skins, and fried zucchini and set them on the table.

Jarrod got up and took apple butter from the refrigerator. He returned to the table.

Catherine sat down across from him.

She watched to see Jarrod's reaction as he dug into the tender lamb steak. He looked as if it was the best meal he'd ever eaten. She tried hers. It was surprisingly good. She'd never tried to cook this dish before.

"I thought you could only cook breakfast, spaghetti and sandwiches," he commented. "I see you've been practicing."

"And you've been sleeping the day away." She tried not to grin, but didn't do a good job of it.

"When I fell asleep I believe you were in my arms."

A flutter quaked through her at the memory of them in bed. "This is one of those places that makes me want to cook." She glanced around the country kitchen.

"You like it here."

"I love it, Jarrod. How did you find it?"

"I've been here before." He took another roll and lathered it liberally with the apple butter. "I never stayed here, but I've camped in the area. I wondered about this old house. I always wanted to see what the inside looked like."

"The whole setting reminds me of every Christmas I ever had. I was thinking about one when I was six and we saw the deer. Do you remember that?"

Jarrod nodded. "I remember your eyes were so big I didn't think they'd ever return to normal size."

"I *was* six," she defended herself.

They passed the rest of the meal and the cleanup as happy companions, reliving some of their memories. When Catherine returned the final dish to the cabinet and dried her hands Jarrod stood at the windows. She joined him. She didn't touch him or take his arm. The two stood looking out on the same scene she had stared at before. The light was fading, turning the pond water a dark gray. The leaves had turned to the golden yellows and reds of fall, incongruous to the snowy ground. The bleeding light that made them brilliantly alive earlier was nearly gone. Their fire had diminished, but they blended together in that post-card portrait of New England in autumn.

Without looking at her, Jarrod reached for her hand. She put hers in his larger one. They stood like that, watching the light fade into darkness.

Chapter 12

It was working, Jarrod thought the next morning. Catherine was falling in love with him.

She was still asleep when he left the bedroom and went downstairs. He walked in the cold morning air on his way back to the house from the village. Sometime during the night it had begun to rain. The snow of yesterday was gone, a memory to pull out and relive on another day. He hummed "Yesterday" as he walked, remembering all of what had happened yesterday. There was ice on the windshield of the Jeep in the front yard and the path leading back to the main road was slippery. He didn't mind. It was unlikely that he and Catherine would be marooned here, but he wouldn't care if they were. He'd welcome having her to himself night and day without the routine distractions of work and daily living to intrude on the idyllic world they had in this stone house.

He went through the gate, along the cobblestoned walkway and up to the front door. The fire in the living-room hearth burned bright and gave the room a homey smell. Jarrod went into the kitchen and put his packages down. He found a pan of uncooked rolls she'd made the day before and put it in the oven. The stove was hot and ready, as best he could determine. Catherine had cooked on it last night, and in their childhood he was sure she'd never seen a wood-burning cookstove. It was his turn today. The fire hadn't completely gone out, and he'd added wood before going into the village. The kitchen was comfortably warm.

Jarrod removed his coat and made coffee. In England tea was the drink of choice. He found the English had as many kinds of teapots as they had occasions to drink the substance. The old-fashioned one that percolated on the stove offered no challenge to his talents. When he'd filled it with water and a measured amount of ground coffee he wondered if Catherine was up yet. He thought of going to check on her, imagined her relaxed and asleep, her hair loose and calling to him as surely as if it could speak. She'd still been under the covers when he'd left her, naked and warm from their long night of lovemaking. He decided against it, although his body tortured him for the decision. Going to her now would mean their breakfast would have to wait for lunch.

He was sure Catherine was falling in love with him. Being without her for two days had been agonizing. He'd spent long hours at meetings, finalizing as much as he could so he could get away early to meet his wife. He thought of her as his wife now. And if their reunion in the stone house was any indication, she'd missed him just as much. They kept the banter light, but it was only a disguise of their true feelings. Jarrod could feel the changes in her. The intensity of their lovemaking and the way she settled so completely in his arms told him that she wanted to be there.

Catherine stretched in the bed. It was smaller than their bed at home, yet she and Jarrod fit so well in it. She smelled the coffee and the bread. He was downstairs. She grabbed his pillow, hugging it to her, remembering the night before and going weak with nostalgia. His smell lingered. She smiled, heady at the scent as she settled against her surrogate lover.

After a moment she got up and went into the bathroom. The card was propped up against her toothpaste. It was the size of an invitation and had an embossed replica of the Stone House on it. Catherine smiled, wondering what Jarrod had left her this time. She loved his humor and his thoughtfulness with the cards, the origami and the poetry.

She picked up the card. On the outside was a quote by Goethe, written in Jarrod's unmistakable handwriting. *Nothing should be more highly prized than the value of each day.* On the inside he'd added his own epilogue: *Yesterday was a masterpiece.*

Catherine's legs buckled. She grabbed the sink for support. The card dropped to the sink counter. Her face burned with the reminiscence of the previous day. They had stood at the kitchen window, not talking, not needing to talk, only holding hands. It was as if everything between them was mutual and understood. Later they had put on coats and boots and walked in the cold, along the paths the deer had taken when she watched them from the window. The sun set, leaving the day in a blaze of glory, but Catherine had not seen it as the dying of one moment, but the beginning of another.

When they returned to the house they had made love so exquisitely that she didn't believe she would survive the experience. But dying in Jarrod's arms would have been heaven.

She sat down on the closed toilet, taking long breaths until her heart calmed and her legs would allow her to stand.

They were married, Catherine thought. She picked up the card and read the quote one more time. Her reaction wasn't as violent the second time, but she felt the chords inside her pull tighter.

She took the card with her when she went downstairs dressed in slacks and a long sweater. Jarrod was in the kitchen. The table was set for two. A large vase of flowers stood in the center of it. Pink, yellow and red roses, baby's breath and green leaves filled the glass container.

"Where did you find flowers at this time of the morning?"

Jarrod turned. "I didn't know you were up."

Catherine came around the center counter. She stood on the side near the stove, near Jarrod. She went directly into his arms and he kissed her.

"I think the bread's ready," she whispered when they parted.

Jarrod turned quickly and took the pan of rolls out of the oven. They were golden brown and perfect.

"What would you like to do today?" Jarrod asked the question when they were seated at the table. Catherine flushed. She slid the card across the table with all its meaning in tact.

The next two days were idyllic. They spent time watching the rain, lying in front of the fire, walking in the woods and along the path to the small town of Standish. They talked for hours, held each other without speaking for hours and made love like honeymooners.

This had been their honeymoon, Catherine thought when they were back in the Newport house. It wasn't the planned time after the wedding, where nervousness was part of the package, but the close time where they got to know each other, when they talked and ate, made passionate love, spent hours watching each other sleep and, in her case, received lovenotes from her *husband*.

She had used the word many times before. She'd heard other people refer to Jarrod as her husband. She had referred to him using the same word, but she'd never thought of it having a meaning, a connection, a bond that identified them as a couple.

Catherine never expected to be part of a couple, a wife. She felt differently now. Jarrod was changing her, making her think differently, feel differently.

Catherine stopped in the middle of her bedroom. A shudder ran through her. She turned fully around, checking every corner, every shadow of the room, making sure it was still her room, that she, like all wives, had not been lost somewhere within the lace curtains and chintz comforter.

The same cold wind that had Jarrod and Catherine wrapped in each other's arms in Maine swept down onto Rhode Island and seemed to drive a wedge between them. Jarrod sat on the stone wall, looking out on the Atlantic. He'd come here a lot lately. Why, he didn't know. It was Catherine's spot, where she came to be alone and think through her problems. Maybe he thought he'd meet her here one day and find out what had happened, but in the two weeks since they'd returned from the stone house he was at a loss to understand what was going on.

There was nothing he could put his finger on; they still talked, still made love, but the closeness they'd achieved had been left there. He'd asked Catherine if anything was bothering her, and she said there was nothing, but he could feel the change. He thought they were growing closer, that the dates were achieving his purpose, but now he wasn't sure.

Was it just a case of them getting used to each other, adjusting to routine and waiting for time to pass? It was already Halloween, and he felt he wouldn't be any closer to convincing her to stay married to him in February than he was now.

Maybe it was his confession. *I love you* had burst from him on a storm of surprise. Catherine couldn't have been more shocked than he was when he'd told her. How often had his heart tried to tell him the truth and he'd ignored it? The storm raged that day, drowning out all other sound, making it possible for him to hear what his heart had been telling him for years.

Jarrod faced the ocean. It was dark and gray, stretching to the sky, which was streaked with shades of gray, blue and white. He listened to the sea, wanting it to institute a dialogue with him, offer him its secrets, gossip, even lecture him, as long as it told him everything it knew about his wife.

"Jarrod, what are you doing here?" Robert Wells hunched his shoulders against the ocean spray. "It's freezing out here."

Jarrod looked surprised to see his friend.

"I saw the Jeep," Robert explained. Jarrod had picked up the Jeep the day after he returned to the United States. "So what's wrong? Don't tell me there's trouble at home. You two are my ideal couple."

Jarrod knew his friend could be trusted. Most people thought of Robert as talkative and unable to keep a secret, while Jarrod knew he could tell him anything and it would remain with him and go no further. But he hadn't told him about Catherine. Maybe Catherine wasn't hiding anything when she said there really was nothing wrong. Maybe it was all in his imagination.

"Just working out some kinks," he finally said.

"You might have picked a warmer day for it." Robert sat down on the Rhode Island rock next to his friend. The most prevalent building material in New England was stone. Consequently, many of the eighteenth- and nineteenth-century builders used it to construct homes and factories. Throughout the area stone houses and fences stood as they had for two hundred years.

"Do you want to tell me about it?" Robert asked. "I've always known there was something strange about your quick marriage, but I didn't know what. Catherine isn't pregnant, is she?"

Jarrod shook his head. "She's not pregnant." The question returned his mind to the spot several feet from where they sat, where she'd followed him after he accused her of keeping it a secret that she might be carrying his child and the devastating disclosure that he was in love with her during their storm-whirling lovemaking.

"Then what?" Robert prompted.

Jarrod took a deep breath and plunged ahead. "I'm her 1–800–HUSBAND."

For a second his words didn't register. Then Robert gasped. "Her what?"

"Her 1–800–HUSBAND," he repeated.

"Catherine owns that number?" Robert was clearly amazed. "I should have guessed. It's exactly like something she would do, and I'll bet I could tell you why. It's so obvious, it's almost transparent." The smile that had been on his face disappeared. "I must be getting old, not to have known, and Elizabeth . . ." He stopped.

"Elizabeth knows."

"She never said a word," Robert muttered. Jarrod thought he was talking to himself.

"Other than Catherine and me, you two are the only ones who know."

Robert sobered. "So what is going wrong with the plan? Is it her falling in love with you or you falling in love with her?"

Jarrod stared at him. Robert was perceptive, and his job was reading people's emotions, but Jarrod didn't believe he could hit the mark on the first try.

"Don't look so surprised," Robert said. "I've known for years. I was wondering why you didn't figure it out."

"You've known what for years?"

"How you and Catherine feel about each other. At least how you feel."

Even with his best friend, a man he'd trust with his life, Jarrod still felt his defenses rise. "And how is that?"

Robert turned on the wall to face him fully. "All right, I'll spell it out. Her first date; you scrutinized the pimple-faced young man until he was so uncomfortable I thought he was going to throw up."

"I did not."

Robert ignored him. "When she swam in the lighted pool at night, who stood in his bedroom window watching her?"

"She was alone. I wanted to make sure she had a lifeguard in case she got a cramp or something."

Robert threw him a look that said he didn't believe that for a moment.

"Do you want me to go on?"

"No," he said. "Even though I have perfectly logical explanations for everything you can bring up, the truth is, I am in love with her."

"Then I gather she does not return your affection."

Jarrod honestly didn't know. He would swear on his life that she did when they were making love, but when they weren't he didn't know how to read her signals.

"I don't know," he answered.

"Have you asked her?"

"Not point-blank."

"Why don't you? If you catch her off guard she's bound to show it in the way she reacts."

Jarrod was quiet for a moment. The sea rolled in and the gulls cawed overhead. "If I ask the question," he began, "I have to be prepared for the answer. And I don't know if I'm ready to hear it yet."

Robert nodded in agreement. It was one thing to

wish and hope, but they both knew people often acted one way and thought another. He had stood watching Catherine swim. She was alone in the pool and he'd had lifeguard training. If she got into trouble, he would be there to help, but he also liked watching her move. And he didn't think anyone had ever seen him looking.

Together they walked back toward their cars. "I'll see you at Elizabeth's tonight?" Robert asked.

"I'm going home to dress now."

Jarrod heard the soft tone he used when he said Elizabeth's name. It was the second time he'd noticed it. Had it always been there and he not known it before? There was more going on with his friend than he had told him. Jarrod had his secrets too, things he couldn't, wouldn't talk to Robert about. It appeared the same thing was true of Robert.

"See you there," Robert said in farewell.

Jarrod got in the Jeep and headed home. Elizabeth Wakefield's masquerade ball was tonight, Halloween. While the children of Newport traipsed from house to house, calling "Trick or treat," the adults dressed and played similar games. The entire town would be at Elizabeth's.

It didn't take Jarrod long to shower and dress. Catherine waited for him in the living room.

"Ready?" Jarrod asked, coming into the room.

Catherine was looking through the windows into the dark. She couldn't see anything. Jarrod wondered what she was thinking.

"You look wonderful." She smiled. He remembered her telling him that he was beautiful when they were standing on the grass in the rain, naked and about to make love.

"You're going to be the most beautiful woman there," he said. "In fact, I think we should stay home."

Catherine walked up to him and kissed him lightly on the lips. "If Elizabeth wasn't my best friend, you'd have a date," she teased.

For a moment he thought of the old Catherine, the one he'd been with two weeks ago. He looked into her eyes and thought he saw something there, something that scared him. He thought about what Robert had said. He wanted to ask her the question, but the thread between them was too fragile. A sudden move could break it.

"Catherine, I know something is bothering you. Please tell me what it is."

She stared at him closely. There was concern in her eyes. "There is something," she admitted. "We'll talk about it tonight when we get back. It's time to go now."

She started to move past him. Jarrod tightened his grip. Catherine looked up at him. "You're going to have to fix your lipstick," he told her.

"Wha—"

She never finished the sentence. He cut her words off with his mouth. She stiffened for a moment, then relaxed. His arms went around her waist and he pulled her into his body. Catherine's arms hugged him and she returned his kiss with the power and need he gave her.

The old Catherine was back.

Chapter 13

Traditions, once begun, are hard to forget or forgo. No one remembers the first October Masquerade Bash given at the Westfields', but Elizabeth was obliged to repeat it annually on Halloween with a flair that outdid the previous ball and anything Audrey could put together. Rivalry also abounded in the small community that might account for the tradition. No matter its origin, it was an event not to be missed. Some people spent the entire year determining what to wear and who they planned to come as. The costumes were lavish, and the decorations tastefully covered the entire house with spectacular arrangements of black and orange.

Catherine was dressed as Nefertiti in her Queen of the Nile regalia. She wore a huge black wig with the traditional flat crown and eyeliner extending back to her hairline. Her dress was a slippery gold that poured like water when she moved. Jarrod chose to wear only a mask and the colorful robes of King Akhenaton, Nefertiti's husband. The mask was trimmed in satin and he discarded it before they got out of the car. He looked like a king, powerful, tall and commanding.

Catherine slipped her arm through Jarrod's as they ascended the three wide steps leading to the columned entrance of Elizabeth Westfield's family home. The sand-colored stone was bathed in a light that could be seen as far back as the entry gate.

"Are you going to wear this outfit in bed tonight?" she teased.

With lightning speed he tightened his grip and slipped his other hand under her arm, tickling her. Catherine broke into gales of laughter, trying to get away, shouting for him to stop. He did. She kept laughing anyway.

"Say that again and you'll get more than you bargained for."

"Promises, promises," she said, dancing a step away as he reached for her.

"This is our third party this week. Doesn't anyone do anything else around here?"

"Why, my lord," she drawled, doing an Elizabeth Taylor imitation that he'd taught her. "They're all doing this to honor your homecoming. You should be appreciative, sire."

"Funny," Jarrod said.

"We haven't had three parties this week. Those were dinners."

They went through the door. Elizabeth greeted them immediately. Traditionally, the host and hostess didn't dress in costume, but wore contemporary formal clothing. It made it easy to find them for greeting and saying good night at the end of the evening. Elizabeth followed tradition. Her dress was a regal purple strapless chiffon. She complemented it with a gold chain that had a diamond heart dangling off center and matching heart earrings. Her hair was up except for one tendril that curled down the side of her face to her neck.

"I see you two are fashionably late." She hugged Catherine and then Jarrod. "Everyone else is already here."

She hustled them into the room. The place was thick with noise and people. There was no theme other than masquerade. Obviously Audrey wasn't in charge, Catherine thought. Most people had opted for fictional characters this year. Several Laurels and Hardys skirted the room, at least three Denzel Washingtons dressed in the union uniform from the movie *Glory*. She recognized Carmen from Bizet's opera, a Dorothy Dandridge lookalike and three Oprah lookalikes, Star Trek's Georgi, complete with visor, and several versions of Tiger Woods.

As they passed through the room, greeting and smiling at friends along the way, they eventually made it to the dance floor. Jarrod slipped his arms around Catherine's watery-gold dress and pulled her into his arms. They gently swayed to the music of a band hired for the night, but Catherine didn't really need any music. When she was with Jarrod they made their own. She'd heard that before, read it in novels, but until she acknowledged to herself that she loved him, she never really knew it could be true.

Catherine hadn't told Jarrod her revelation and he hadn't pressured her with any declaration since that day a month earlier. He just seemed to cherish her.

He was always attentive, tender and loving. She couldn't remember the number of impromptu lunches they'd shared, or the weekends they had just picked up and gone somewhere. There was always a rose waiting for her at dinner, and often in the mornings she would find a cute little note somewhere.

Tonight he'd even tried his hand at haiku.

> Friendship, not enough
> Emotions like lava flow
> Lovers in the night

She found the Japanese-style poem folded between Nefertiti's robes. When she confronted him with it, he only said it was something he'd made up. But to her, it was the most wonderful seventeen syllables she'd ever read.

She wouldn't have believed it of him. Jarrod was such a man's man, virile, athletic, vigorous, even macho. Who would have thought he'd leave love notes for his wife? They weren't really love notes. They never said "I love you." In fact, they were never even signed.

No matter what Jarrod intended them to be, Catherine thought of them as love notes. She had a collection that she kept in her dresser drawer. Often she'd take them out and read them. They made her feel close to him when he wasn't there.

Robert danced by with Elizabeth just as the music ended.

"Looks like they made up," Jarrod spoke in Catherine's ear.

She nodded. "They aren't nearly the enemies they claim to be."

Jarrod looked over her head at his friend. He had to be blind if he didn't see their bickering was a coverup for how they really felt about each other.

"Hello, Jarrod." Julianna Stone and Ted Ward stopped in front of them. Ted was a local high school history teacher who also coached the basketball team.

Julianna had had her eye on Jarrod since they were in grade school. He even went out with her once. Julianna didn't know Catherine knew the details of that failed date. If she did, she might not stare at him as if she could eat him. Dressed as Bizet's Carmen, her cleavage threatened to spill over her top, and her short skirt had a slit higher than anything Dorothy Dandridge ever wore. "Catherine," she said as an afterthought.

"Julianna, you look . . ." Catherine trailed off. Julianna wasn't listening to her. She'd trained her attention on Jarrod, even to the exclusion of her date.

"Dance with me, Jarrod." The music began again, and Julianna stepped between Catherine and Jarrod. She put her arm through his and left Catherine and Ted standing alone.

"Would you like to dance?" Ted asked.

Catherine went into his arms. Ted's costume wasn't very original. He was dressed as Superman. She had to admit he had a great body: strong, muscular legs and broad shoulders. He worked with the team every day, and she knew he was very active outside of the school.

"I apologize for Julianna."

"You don't have to. I know how she feels about Jarrod."

"He doesn't return her feelings," Ted was quick to add.

"I know," Catherine said. She knew where Jarrod's sentiments lay. And she knew about Ted too, his feelings for Julianna. She wasn't one to give advice to the lovelorn, but it was time someone said something to Ted about how he allowed Julianna to walk over him. "When are you going to tell her, Ted?"

"Excuse me?"

"Ted, I've seen you when you coach. You're demanding, confident, able to leap tall buildings in a single bound." She raised her arm in a gesture.

"Well, only as high as the basketball net." He twirled her around, his red cape and her gold gown following them like the colors of a flag.

"The net's high enough. What happens to that confidence when Julianna walks in the room?" He looked embarrassed. It wasn't her intention to force him to share his feelings. "You've been trying to win Julianna for so long, you don't even see what's in front of you."

Ted almost stopped. Quickly he remembered and continued dancing. "What do you mean?"

"I mean look around. You might find someone who's just as interested in you as you are in Julianna."

The music ended. Catherine left him looking around the room at every female who was unmarried or unattached. She walked to the bar and ordered an orange juice. Elizabeth approached her.

"What did you do to the coach?"

"I did nothing to him, and his name is Ted. Don't call him 'the coach.' That makes him sound like an old man, and Ted is two years younger than we are."

"What did you say to him?" The music started, and

Ted asked Meredith Windsor to dance. She smiled like a thirteen-year-old as he led her to floor.

"I told him there might be someone with a crush on him."

"Who?"

Catherine hunched her shoulders and drank from her glass. "I have no idea, but he'll spend the winter trying to find out who."

"And that will make Ms. Julianna Stone sit up and take notice."

"Or Ted just might discover there really is someone out there who turns him on more than Julianna."

"Oooo, you are bad, Catherine." Elizabeth was shaking her head. "I am glad you're not matchmaking for me."

"Matchmaking is my sister's job. By the way, where is Audrey?"

"She called to say she'd be late. Something about her costume not being ready."

Catherine mocked a shudder. "Heads will roll." Both women laughed. Catherine caught Jarrod's glance. He was back on the floor. This time Emily Colter was his partner.

"Elizabeth."

They both turned as someone called her name. Elizabeth went off to play hostess to another African queen while Catherine circled the room, smiling and talking. She was truly enjoying herself. She hadn't thought she could relax enough with all the fast-paced things that were going on in her life.

"Catherine, that's a wonderful outfit." She smiled at Lois Brown and thanked her. Lois worked at the hospital and was dressed as a nurse. It wasn't much of a leap.

"Catherine." She heard her name called again. Audrey had arrived and was waving to her from the end of the room.

"That's my hat," Catherine said the moment she got close to Audrey."

"No, it's not."

"It is."

"Well, it's part of the costume." Her sister was dressed as Dolly Levi. With the wig and the hat, she stood several inches taller than her real height. Catherine glanced at Dwayne, who was standing at the bar. She could see he'd refused to complement his wife by coming as the pestered Horace Vandergelder. Dwayne wore a fake mustache and eyebrows. His coat was a black cutaway from the early 1900s. He reminded her of a dark version of Mark Twain, without the long white hair, but he was more probably W.E.B. Du Bois. Catherine knew Dwayne enjoyed Du Bois's writing immensely.

"Don't you think it looks nice?" Audrey turned in a circle, as if she were modeling, completely ignoring Catherine's anger over her pilfered hat.

"You should have asked me if you could wear it."

"Catherine, it's only a hat, and you left it on the swing."

She'd forgotten the hat. Her life had changed so much since that day on the swing. But Audrey had taken her things since they were children and assumed she could do with them what she wished. Catherine still hated it.

"And you built your entire costume around it."

"Forget the hat. I've got something much more important to tell you about."

Catherine waited. Audrey's smile was wide and

happy. She anticipated Audrey's news. She had to be pregnant.

"I'm opening my own business," she said.

"What?" Catherine was confused. She hadn't expected her to say that.

"Come on over here. I can't wait to tell you." She took her arm and dragged her to an empty seat at the edge of the room. It overlooked the back gardens and the sea in the distance. "Dwayne has been suggesting it for years," she said as they sat down. "But I'm doing this all on my own."

"Start at the beginning," Catherine said. Her sister was animated over this, much more jovial than usual.

"All right," she said, taking a deep breath. "You know how I love giving parties."

Catherine nodded.

"I'm opening a business as a wedding consultant. I'll plan everything for the bride: her ceremony, reception, party favors, cake, everything." She looked at Catherine. "It's such a stressful time for the couple. I can deal with all the details while they keep their heads, remain ecstatically in love and avoid the small details that can cause disasters during the actual event."

"Audrey, I'm so glad for you. This is wonderful, and you seem so excited about it." She would be good at this. Audrey took every detail seriously, and she was a good person to plan an event.

"Mother is going to help me. You know how good she is at selling. She can be the receptionist and talk to all the brides, while I come up with ideas for their affairs. We'll share the details for each event and cross-check each other. We're also going to do parties, proms, any kind of social event. You know there are hundreds of them around here, and I know every caterer, photographer, printer, tradesman in the area."

Catherine was astounded. "You've really thought about this."

"More than that. We ordered the stationery, and Dwayne pointed me toward a small office on Spring Street that is just perfect. We signed the lease this morning. I've talked to the phone company about installing phone lines, and we'll accept credit cards, and . . ."

"And I thought you were having trouble with the costume, while you were becoming Cornelia Vanderbilt." Catherine felt a tinge of guilt accompany her happiness for her sister. Audrey would love doing this and she was perfectly suited for it. Despite Catherine's dread at some of the affairs she'd been forced to attend because Audrey planned them, she was very good at what she did. She and their mother worked well together. She was living proof of that.

"You know me," Audrey said. "Once I get an idea, I'm off and running. And the costume needed a little bit of alteration. It's fine now." She paused. "We're going to have an open house around the first of the year, after all the holidays are over. Imagine the summer, with the tourists coming and all the events that they want to attend. We could—"

"Look at you two," Robert said, joining them. "I'd never guess you were sisters."

"Hello, Robert," Audrey said. Her face glowed with her news. Catherine was glad for her though a little surprised that she would take on a business. Audrey seemed to spend her full energy on her own parties and her house. This would take her into other areas, and Catherine knew her sister would master them.

"Audrey, I am so happy for you." She reached over and hugged her.

"Happy for what?" Robert asked.

"Audrey is starting her own business. She's going to be a wedding consultant."

"And you can be my first customer," she told him.

Catherine stared at her, then at Robert. "Is there something going on I should know about?" she asked.

They both waited for the other to explain. "Just an observation," Audrey finally said. "You have dealerships all over the area. Maybe I can plan an opening."

Robert let out a slow breath. Catherine didn't think her sister had been talking about a car party.

"You haven't danced with me," Robert said to Catherine. He offered her his hand.

"I would love to," Catherine said, rising.

"Excuse us, Audrey."

Audrey nodded.

"Save me a dance," Robert told her, and she smiled.

Robert took Catherine's hand and twirled her onto the dance floor. He was a really good dancer. They had once won a summer talent contest with a dance routine. Catherine loved dancing with Robert only slightly less than she liked dancing with Jarrod. In Robert's arms she could have fun. In Jarrod's she had fun and more.

Robert danced her around, spinning and twirling her as if they were back at that long-ago competition. The dance ended with a dramatic drop, where Robert bent down on one knee, she went through a series of turns around him and ended in a back bend over his knee, her head inches from the floor.

The execution was perfect and her crown stayed on, but as Robert helped her up they bumped into Julianna. The drink Julianna held spilled. Catherine jumped back, trying to avoid the liquid. The glass clattered to the floor and shattered. The liquid splattered the bottom of Catherine's gown and her shoes.

"Oops," Julianna said.

"Excuse me, Carl, but I need to borrow Jarrod." Elizabeth came to his rescue.

"Thank you," he said, walking away with her. Carl Wilson had been a chef on ocean liners for all of his adult life. Now in his sixties, he never tired of telling stories of his exploits at sea. Jarrod was sure the majority of them had only a nodding acquaintance with the truth.

"You looked as if one more story and we could use your eyes to glaze the ham."

They reached the dance floor and started to dance. "Carl means well, but his stories can sometimes be . . . hard to take."

"That's a polite way of saying he's a bore."

The two of them began to dance. Catherine had disappeared. She'd been dancing with Robert the last time he'd seen her. He looked around the room. She was missing.

"Do you think Robert is still calling that 1–800–WIFE?" Elizabeth asked matter-of-factly. Jarrod thought of what Catherine had said earlier and looked for his friend too. Robert stood at the bar. His expression was happy, expectant, optimistic.

"I hope not," Jarrod answered. "I disconnected it."
Elizabeth's eyebrows rose. "Don't look so surprised."
He mocked her with his own eyebrows. "Catherine
told me you know about the phone. And the marriage. Robert knows too."

Elizabeth smiled knowingly. She glanced at Robert
on the other side of the room. "I told Catherine her
scheme wouldn't work, but I guess I was wrong." Both
of them looked around. Neither saw Catherine.

"Ever thought of trying it yourself?"

"A husband?" She shook her head. "Been there,
done that; it didn't work."

Jarrod's step faltered. He'd heard that before, and
from his own wife. It was what she would tell her
parents when they finally dissolved this marriage.

"It might have some merit," she spoke softly, still
looking at Robert. Then she turned her gaze to
him and smiled. "Catherine's never looked more
radiant."

"She is beautiful."

"Being in love will do that to you."

Jarrod didn't falter this time. He stopped in the
middle of the floor. "What did you say?"

"She hasn't told you?"

"Told me what?"

Knowing she'd said too much, Elizabeth clammed
up as tightly as any crustacean fighting for survival,
but he wasn't willing to let her be. He glanced around
but still couldn't find Catherine.

"Tell me," Jarrod demanded.

"Jarrod, you should talk to Catherine."

"I will, but I want to know what she's told you."

Elizabeth took his hand. They left the dance floor
and headed for the hall. Every room they passed had

people in it. Elizabeth kept going until she was at the front door. She went through it and found the porch empty. The servants were taking care of the trick-or-treaters, but it was getting late for them.

It was cold outside, the wind stirring slightly, but the air had the teeth of winter deeply sunk into it.

"Promise me you'll keep this to yourself until Catherine tells you?"

"No," Jarrod stated. Elizabeth hugged her arms. He removed the huge robe of his outfit and slipped it around her, leaving him with only a shirt and trousers. He'd refused the headdress before they left home earlier in the evening.

"Are you in love with Catherine?" Elizabeth asked.

Jarrod didn't answer right away. He was in love with her, but he often hid it. For more than half his life he'd kept the secret. Now, looking at Elizabeth, he nodded.

"Do you think she's in love with you?"

"She's planning to divorce me in February," he answered. "But you already know that."

"When was the last time you looked at her, really looked at her?"

"I look at her everyday."

"But you don't see what's there."

He looked over her head, as if he had X-ray vision and could look through the heavy concrete wall into the house and see Catherine.

"Stop dancing around the story and tell me."

"She's in love with you."

Jarrod's hands reached out and took her arms. He pulled Elizabeth to within a foot of himself. "Did she tell you that?"

Elizabeth nodded.

Jarrod was gone in a flash. He left Elizabeth standing alone and returned to the house, bent on finding Catherine. He searched the dance floor but didn't find the gold dress that made her seem to float when she walked. He spotted Robert. "Where's Catherine?" he asked.

"She spilled something and went upstairs to clean it."

"Elizabeth is on the porch. Go keep her company."

"What's she doing out there?"

Jarrod didn't answer. He was already halfway to the stairs, which he took two at a time. Elizabeth's house was another one that they had played in and out of as children. He knew where Elizabeth had always slept, although she might have moved into the master suite since she was the sole owner of the house now.

"Catherine," he called. His heart hammered. He headed for Elizabeth's old room. "Catherine!"

"In here," she called back. Her voice was muffled, as if she was farther into the room than just beyond the door. He went into Elizabeth's room. It must be a guest room now. Jarrod closed the door. Catherine came out of the bathroom. She dropped the hem of her dress.

"It was just a tiny stain. I got it out."

"Are you in love with me?" he asked without preamble.

She stood rock-solid still, as if a lightning bolt had rooted her to the spot and she was now a life-size statue of Nefertiti in a dress of gold inlay. "Why do you ask?"

"Answer me." He came closer to her. She didn't move, but oh, she wanted to. He could see it in her eyes.

"I'm still divorcing you."

"I didn't ask if you were divorcing me." He stood directly in front of her, towering over her. He knew the effect he had on her. She got nervous quickly when things weren't comfortable between them, and this moment was not comfortable. "I asked if you were in love with me."

"That's not an easy question. I've known you—"

"It's very easy. Either you are or you aren't. So which is it?"

"Jarrod, this is not the place—"

"It will have to do. Now answer me." He put his hand under her chin and forced her to look into his eyes. "Catherine Melissa Carson Greene, are you in love with me?"

"Yes," she whispered.

Jarrod let his breath go. He swept her into his arms, holding her totally off the floor, his hand behind her neck, his head on her shoulder. He squeezed her to him, holding her, never wanting to put her down, never wanting to let her go. He wanted to stay here, suspended, for eternity. Knowing she loved him. It was too much. It was a hope, a dream, an impossible dream, but it was true.

This was what Robert had suggested he do only a couple of hours ago. Jarrod hadn't thought about it. If he had, he might not be holding her now. He might not have this knowledge.

"Jarrod, put me down."

He felt the change before his brain registered it. Catherine wasn't pliant, she wasn't holding on to him as a lover. She held on to him to keep her balance. He knew something was wrong. He let her slide to the floor. Immediately she stepped out of his reach.

"Catherine, what is it?"

"You know, Jarrod. You've known from the first. From the night in Montana when I explained everything."

"You mean you're in love with me and you're still going to go through with this asinine plan?"

"We agreed—" she started.

"To hell with what we agreed," he cut her off. "After the way we are together, the way lightning strikes every time we get near each other, the way we make love and even when you've told me you love me, you still want a divorce?" It was incredible. She couldn't mean it. It had to be a mistake, but when he looked at her face it was closed to everything. She loved him, but she wouldn't stay married to him because marriage, real marriage, scared her to death.

"Catherine, we don't have to wait until February. You can have your divorce tonight."

He turned and wrenched open the door. He was too angry, so angry that if he closed the door behind him, he'd slam it so hard the entire foundation of the Westfield house, which had stood for a hundred and fifty years, would crumble to powdered stone.

Life changed after she told Jarrod she was in love with him. The glass house they had been living in shattered to slivers. Jarrod didn't come home that night. She didn't know where he was. She waited all night for him to return. He didn't come home Sunday either.

He was there Monday afternoon when she got in from work. All his clothes had been moved back to the guest room. He barely spoke to her, and after dinner he excused himself and went to the den, where he worked until he was too tired to stay awake or she was already in bed.

Catherine missed being with him. She missed sleeping with him. She'd tossed and turned for three nights now. She turned over and hugged his pillow. It didn't smell like he smelled. She wanted Jarrod back and there was nothing she could do to regain anything. He wouldn't be her friend and she couldn't remain his wife.

Getting up, she didn't turn on any lights. It was after midnight. She'd try some tea. Maybe that would help her sleep. She headed for the kitchen. At the bottom of the stairs she saw the door to the den was open. No light came from any other room. Only a small amount spilled from the room where Jarrod worked. She approached the door. The room was warm with the glow of the fire.

Jarrod sat at his drafting table. The intensity light attached to the drafting table illuminated the paper on which he was writing. He didn't see her and she remained silhouetted in the stillness. It was amazing how well he fit into this room, into her life. A few months ago, this space contained only her books and music and an arrangement of comfortable furniture. Now it contained Jarrod's desk and drafting table, a computer hooked up to a special printer, the general clutter of work projects and most of all Jarrod.

Catherine moved like a cat, her satin nightgown making no sound as she sank into a large chair across the room from him. She watched, unobserved and quiet, looking at the man she loved. She could see only part of him and he could see none of her. He hummed ''Yesterday'' softly under his breath. She often heard him humming it unconsciously. It had become his signature song, although he would surely deny it if she called him on it. She wouldn't. She liked knowing he thought of her and the song was a subliminal method of bringing her to his mind.

"Trouble sleeping?" Jarrod's sudden question surprised her.

"I didn't think you knew I was here."

"Catherine, you can't walk into a room where I am and not have me know you're there." His voice was as sexy as his comment. It was the voice that had her heart doing somersaults. She got up and went to the table where he worked. She stood on the side facing him, hesitating, not knowing how to approach him. He hadn't really talked to her in days.

"What are you working on?"

"Come see."

He pushed the rolling stool back a foot or so and she walked in front of him. Blue lines and notes covered the paper. Arrows pointed to places with numbers written in. It was a confusion of color, but in it she could see the finished project.

"It's a roller coaster," she said.

"Not quite." Jarrod rolled the stool closer. It had a high seat, giving him the ability to work at the slanted table and read even the top of the paper. Catherine felt the warmth of him as his chest touched her back, pinning her between him and the drawing. He reached around her and pulled the paper aside. Under it were plans for another carnival ride.

She could hardly concentrate. He was so close. She felt the old weakness enter her legs and threaten to dissolve her knee joints. She wanted to lean back, sit on his lap and lean against him, have him cradle her in the safe haven of his arms.

But she didn't. She forced herself to stand and to concentrate on the design.

"A Ferris wheel," she said. When he pulled that page away and she saw the plans for a large mansion, she understood. "It's an amusement park." She turned to him. He was so close to her, his arms were completely around her.

"The Cantu Brothers are considering adding another theme park to their holdings. We're bidding on the project."

"I hope you win," she said. She paused for a moment. She raised her eyes to look at him. The light was behind her and she cast a shadow on him, obscuring his vision. "I'm glad you're talking to me again." He said nothing. Catherine thought maybe she'd been mistaken. "I thought you understood when we were in Montana that I didn't want to stay married."

Jarrod closed his arms around her. He felt so good. She went into his arms, putting her own around his neck. "Were you in love with me when we were in Montana?" he asked.

She was. She knew that now, but she didn't know how to answer his question. Now she knew she'd been in love with him a lot longer than Montana. He was the reason she took that 1-800 number. It wasn't Audrey or her mother. It was because she wasn't in love with anyone other than Jarrod. She didn't want to marry anyone but him. Yet she never thought she would. He wasn't even in the United States at the time.

Then suddenly he was there. He was holding her on the swing, much like he was holding her now.

"Catherine?"

She looked in his eyes. She nodded. She had been in love with him in Montana. She had to tell the truth. She didn't want to lie. She couldn't.

"Yet you think I'll take away from you the things you want to do in life."

"You won't mean to."

He stood up suddenly. His hands, which had been on her waist, went to her head. He finger combed through her hair. "People in love don't do that, Catherine. They make a life together, as a single union, not as two individuals on separate roads who happen to sleep in the same bed. They believe in the same things. We don't know what those things are because you won't let us find out."

She wanted to tell him that she did want to know. She wanted everything he wanted, but she said none of the things she knew he wanted to hear.

"There are several things I can do, Catherine." His mouth dropped and he kissed her. Her eyes closed, and the slow burn Jarrod had already kindled in her body cranked up her thermostat. "I could make love to you. Torture you with your own love." He kissed her again, his tongue dipping into her mouth, extracting a response that was immediate and overwhelming. He yanked her forward, slamming her body into him, allowing her to feel the entire length of him, the erection that pushed into her stomach, tantalizing her with what she wanted. Her feet lifted her to her toes, her body pressed into his, feeling his length, the hard strength of him as he held her. "It feels good, doesn't it, Catherine? You like it. I can tell. I can hear it in the sounds you make in your throat." He kissed her throat, then trailed his mouth across her shoulders, pushing the small straps of her gown aside. She felt the heaviness of her breasts release. Her body longed for him to touch her breasts, to touch her all over. "But I'm not going to do it, Catherine."

He pushed her out of reach. She felt the cold where his body had been.

"I'm going to let you torture yourself. I'll fulfill my part of the contract. I'll attend dinners and parties. I'll play the attentive husband, the doting newlywed, but once we're inside these doors, all bets are off."

He left her then. A moment later she winced as the front door slammed.

She'd really made a mess of this whole thing. Jarrod had been the first to tell her that she hadn't thought everything through. Now she'd hurt him immensely. She hadn't intended to, but she knew he wouldn't listen to an apology. She didn't know what to do except try and make him understand. It wasn't now that life would change. They were too much in love now. In time the fire between them would bank and the smoke would clear. Then she would be rid of her dreams of her need to be an individual. She would be Jarrod's wife and nothing more.

Catherine looked at Jarrod's drawings. She ran her fingers across the flat surface of the paper.

Was being his wife such a bad thing?

Jarrod's wife. Catherine paced up and down in the den after Jarrod left. They were always angry these days. Their emotions simmered just below the surface, and she seemed to set off some kind of bomb in him each time she got close. She wanted to be close. The idea of not having Jarrod around caused her physical pain. She'd become used to people smiling as they teasingly emphasized "Mrs. Greene" when they spoke to her.

She *was* Mrs. Greene. Catherine sat down on the stool where Jarrod's amusement park was taking shape. He was designing the plans. What about them? Could he design plans for marriage? Could she be married to him for always, for the death-do-us-part kind of forever? She tried to look forward to February, but all her mind did was race backward to the places they had been, the times they had laughed together, the silly, cute and loving things he did for her. He wanted her, actively pursued her and she ... she stopped him at every turn, invoking the divorce card like some carnival barker playing the badger game.

Catherine didn't want a divorce, not anymore. She wasn't sure now that she ever had. She wanted to change her life to keep him in it. She'd told him women changed their lives after marriage. She'd even explained how it happened. People did things for love and didn't even realize they were giving up something for that opportunity. They would look back and see all the things they'd wanted to do, but never had because somehow they had gotten lost in marriage. But life was full of those decisions, and marriage was no different. She could tell herself it was a compromise, but if that was true it was one she wanted to face. And she wanted to face it with Jarrod.

She looked at the desk, then went over and sat in his chair. On the side, next to the computer where he worked when he wasn't sitting at the drafting table, was a photograph of the two of them. It wasn't a wedding photo. It had been taken on their honeymoon, during the barn dance. She'd never seen it before. Catherine picked it up and stared at them. She touched the glass, running her finger over Jarrod as if she could touch him.

She wanted to be Jarrod's wife, with all its implications and complications. She wanted to fight with him, make love with him, talk, dance, read his poems and love notes. She wanted the changes in her life to remain a constant part of it. Jarrod's life had changed. He'd walked with her down a path she opened. He'd adjusted to her way of life. If anyone had lost some part of himself it was Jarrod.

Audrey came to mind, and her mother. They were opening a business and they were married. Audrey's husband was supporting her in her choice. He offered his advice when she asked and stood by her decisions when she voiced them. Their mother had raised two girls, but she wasn't old by today's standards, and it had been her decision to be a stay-at-home mom. She was making changes too, going into an endeavor with her daughter that would mean added stress and the promise of reward.

Catherine had wanted to make her own decisions. She didn't want family pressure or a husband tying her to a path. That was what she'd told Jarrod on their honeymoon. She knew he spoke for himself when she accused him of being the one man who was different, who would complement his wife instead of mold her into some unwanted role.

He *was* different. And she wanted him to remain that way. She wanted to tell him, rush out of the door and find him, let him know that nothing on earth was stronger than her feelings for him. That the two of them needed to talk, needed to redirect their lives and their marriage. That she was willing to work at the relationship, build it one day at a time, the way his plans were laid out. That her rigid ideas could be made flexible, and that she could adjust to the changes that life threw in her path, that she only wanted to walk that path if he walked with her.

But it was too late. She looked at the photo again, then hugged the frame to her chest.

Jarrod was gone.

Chapter 14

Catherine stared at the test kits. She didn't believe them. She'd been staring at them for hours, hoping they would change. Coming home tonight, she'd bought three more. All four of them showed the same result. She was pregnant!

Dry-eyed and stony, she sat on the bathtub rim and willed the results to change. But they didn't. The pink turned pink. The blue turned blue. The plus sign showed up bright and clear. Four tests couldn't lie.

What was she going to do? Jarrod and she? They were going to have a baby. She was going to be a mother. He a father. Where was he?

She hadn't thought about getting pregnant until it was too late. She knew exactly when it happened. At Stone House. She'd been so glad to see Jarrod that they had made love then and there, on the floor in front of the hearth. She hadn't filled her prescription in her haste to get to Maine. Neither of them thought of a condom or the consequences of their lovemaking, but here were the results. Four small packages hailing the beginning of life. She touched herself, smoothed her hand across her abdomen as if she could feel the small cells splitting, multiplying, growing larger with each hour, each day. She needed to talk to someone. She needed Jarrod. She wanted him. She wanted to crawl into his arms and have him whisper in her ear that it was all right, that everything would be all right. But she couldn't talk to him. He was either working or out of town. When he was home, he was in the den. Tonight she did not know where he was. He'd left a message with Jenny that he wouldn't be home for dinner, and it was past two o'clock in the morning now.

Catherine gathered all the tests and threw them in the trash. She dressed for bed, knowing sleep was not on the agenda tonight. As she got into bed she heard the doorbell. She glanced out the window and saw Jarrod's Jeep in the circular driveway. Grabbing her robe, she headed for the door. She couldn't think why he was ringing the doorbell. She was just glad he was home.

Pulling the door open, she was surprised to see Robert and Elizabeth. They had Jarrod's arms over their shoulders.

"What happened?" She swung the door wide and they brought him in.

"I got a call that he couldn't drive."

"Is he all right?"

"Sure, he'll be fine in the morning," Robert said.

"Maybe the afternoon," Elizabeth corrected.

Catherine closed the door. She came around to look at him. "He's drunk," she said.

"Where do you want him?" Robert asked.

"Can you take him upstairs?" The three of them got him to the second floor. Elizabeth got to the top of the stairs first. She went into the first bedroom, which Jarrod was no longer sharing. Catherine didn't say anything. She pulled his shoes off and Robert removed his tie. They pulled the blanket over him and the three of them left.

"What happened?" Catherine asked when they were downstairs.

"I don't know. He apparently drank too much at George's bar. George took the keys to the Jeep." He reached in his pocket. "I left them in the Jeep," he explained.

Catherine nodded. "I'll get them later."

"George knows we're friends, so he called me. Jarrod fell asleep on the drive here."

Catherine knew he meant he'd passed out and Robert was either saving her feelings or preserving Jarrod's dignity.

She wanted to run upstairs to Jarrod but remembered her manners. "Can I get you two something to drink?"

Elizabeth shook her head. "Robert was about to take me home." Elizabeth hugged her and Robert kissed her on the cheek. They went out and Catherine ran upstairs. Jarrod was sprawled across the bed, snoring.

Catherine climbed up next to him. She ran her hand down his chin. He needed a shave. He stirred but didn't awaken. He cleared his throat and the snoring stopped. Catherine knew it was only temporary. He'd snore again before long. She was glad he was home, glad he was back in her bed, although he would feel awful in the morning. She imagined it was feeling awful that drove him to the bar. It had to be her and her feelings about marriage that drove him away. He had been in love with her since she was sixteen years old, he'd said, and she was planning to divorce him.

Catherine pulled the covers back and unbuttoned his shirt. She took it off him and removed his pants and socks. He wore black silky underwear, the same ones he'd had on at Stone House. She wondered if he was wearing them for the same reason. Did he want her, and this was his way of keeping the memory of her close? He said he wouldn't torture her with his lovemaking. Was not making love torturing him as much as it was abusing her?

She covered him before she let her hands run over his body the way she wanted to. Then she got into bed. She moved close to him, and instinctively his arms wrapped around her, almost as if they could do nothing else. She felt content. Tonight she would sleep. She'd let tomorrow worry about itself. Tonight she would lie in Jarrod's arms even if it was for the last time. She closed her eyes and relaxed. She drifted off, lulled by the rhythmic nature of Jarrod's snore.

Suddenly her eyes snapped fully open. The pregnancy test, kits, cups, sticks and results were in the bathroom. Catherine eased out of bed as carefully as she had eased into it. She had at least one more mile to go before she slept.

* * *

Why wouldn't that ringing stop? It hurt, but it was insistent. Jarrod opened his eyes. The room spun. The light stabbed him. He lifted his head. It felt like someone had hit him with a sledgehammer. He fell back. The ringing continued. *It's the phone,* his mind told him. He reached for it, and his body nearly crushed Catherine's. What was she doing in his bed? How did he get to bed? The last thing he remembered . . . he didn't know the last thing he remembered. The phone rang again. He grabbed it and pulled it onto the bed. Catherine opened her eyes.

"Hullo." His voice was thick. His tongue felt like it was swollen and his mouth tasted foul. Then he remembered George's.

"Who is this?" Jarrod tried to make sense of the voice on the phone. The person was talking fast. "Slow down," he said, holding his head.

"Here, let me take it." Catherine took the phone. "Hello?" she said. Then listened. "Hello, Elizabeth."

Catherine looked at the clock. "Elizabeth, it's six o'clock in the morning. What's wrong?" Catherine pushed herself up in the bed. Jarrod pulled a pillow over his head. She was speaking too loud for his hangover.

"What?" Catherine shouted. Jarrod pulled the pillow back a little. It penetrated his brain that something was wrong. "Newspaper." Catherine's normally low voice was scaling up from a middle C.

She twisted around and hung up the phone. Jarrod felt her scrambling out of bed. "You talked to a reporter," Catherine shouted. He looked up.

"What?"

"How could you?"

She left the room, then. What was she talking about?

What had Elizabeth said? Jarrod turned over. He didn't care. His head was going to explode. He needed to keep it attached so he could hold his brains together.

"Jarrod." He heard the door slam closed and Catherine's high-pitched voice at the same time.

"Catherine, please be quiet."

She yanked the covers back. "I will not be quiet. How could you do this? Are you just trying to get back at me because I'm still planning to divorce you?" He stared at her as she paced the floor in front of the bed.

"What are you talking about?"

"Jarrod, this is low. I never thought you were this vindictive." She threw a newspaper at him. He brought his hands up in an instinctively protective gesture. "Now get out of my bed and out of my house."

Jarrod swung his legs over the side of the bed. Catherine left the room with a bang. He hung his head and fought back waves of nausea. When the room stopped moving and he felt he could focus, he picked up the paper. What was in it that could make her so angry?

He turned it over. Photos of himself and Catherine looked back at him. Sandwiched between them was the headline. HIS 1–800 WIFE jumped off the page in bold black letters in 90-point type. The words hit him squarely between the eyes. An arrow pointed from the word *his* to the photo of him. A corresponding one pointed from *wife* to Catherine.

"Bulldog," Jarrod said out loud. Last night at the bar. The man he was talking to. "I've got a bulldog to put to bed." That's what the man had said. At the time Jarrod thought he had a dog. He was a reporter. He didn't mean a dog. He was going to get his bulldog out, his bulldog *issue*, his newspaper.

"Oh, God," he groaned, wishing he could die right now.

Every detail was there. The phone number, the reason, the temporary nature of the marriage. Everything, including the fact that he was in love with Catherine.

He knew why she was angry. The next couple of days were going to be hell for her, and people would bring it up for years to come. He'd done her a terrible injustice, however unintentional. There was no way he could make it up to her; no amount of apology could retract the damning nature of the story. It wasn't on page one, but that didn't matter. In a town this size and with a community this small, word would be all over town by noon.

Jarrod stood too quickly. His head reminded him of the amount of alcohol he'd consumed the previous evening. If only he'd come home last night instead of stopping in George's. He hadn't. He couldn't take another night of being so close to Catherine and not being able to touch her, hold her. He told her that he wouldn't torture her, but he was the one in pain. Every time he looked at her, thought of her, he wanted her, and to be in the same house, knowing she was in bed only a few doors away, was too much. He'd stayed away and gone to George's.

He tried to walk. He had to find her, try to explain, to apologize.

Where were his clothes? He didn't know how he'd gotten into Catherine's bed, who had undressed him or where they had put his clothes. He went to his room and pulled on the first pair of jeans he saw. A shirt hung on the valet and he grabbed it. Barefoot, he padded down the stairs, pushing his arms into the shirt as he went. His head was throbbing. Jenny was in the kitchen.

"Is there coffee?" She poured him a cup, saying nothing. "Where's Catherine?"

"I don't know, sir."

If it hadn't been scalding hot, Jarrod would have upended the cup. He took a sip, hoping it would help his head and cursing himself for going to a bar.

"Catherine?" he called, leaving the kitchen. She didn't answer. "Catherine, where are you?" Jarrod looked in all the rooms on the first floor. He found her in the den, pacing back and forth like an angry cat. "Catherine, I'm sorry." She turned and looked at him with rage in her eyes.

"Jarrod, how could you? I trusted you."

"I didn't mean to. We were sitting at the bar, just talking. I had a drink."

"You had a lot to drink."

He nodded. "I did." His head still throbbed with the amount he'd drunk. "I'd never have said anything if I hadn't had too much to drink."

He stopped. He wanted to hang his head, get the ringing to stop. He sipped the coffee. It was cool enough to drink and he drained the cup. He wished he'd asked Jenny to bring him a pot.

"What can I say, Catherine?"

"I think you've already said enough."

"I've been tortured living here. I just can't go on like this."

"It's torture for me too, Jarrod. And as of this moment, you don't live here anymore."

She moved to pass him. He took her arms and restrained her.

"You don't mean that."

She wrenched herself free. Eyes the color of pitch glared at him.

"With every breath in my body."

She left the room, head high but shoulders in a defeated slant. The phone on the desk rang. He ignored it. There was no extension in the kitchen. The answering machine would get it. He couldn't talk to anyone right now.

He'd lost Catherine. No matter what he did, the wedge between them grew wider. His tactics, the dates, the stone house weekend, his resolution to torture her into submission, had all failed. And the paper, the damning evidence of too many drinks, stared at him where he'd dropped it.

Catherine would never love him now. She had, but he'd killed it with a bottle of Jack Daniels and the loose tongue of a drunk. Jarrod didn't drink often. After last night he never should again.

He was sorry, but sorry wasn't enough. The phone rang again. He left the room. His jacket lay over a chair near the door. He pulled it on and left the house. He realized he was barefoot when he stepped onto the cobblestoned driveway. The cold, uneven rocks bore into his feet, unbalancing him. Jarrod rejected the idea of returning for his shoes. He got into the Jeep and found the keys still in the ignition. Backing down the driveway, his anger hot and intact, he slammed into the plastic trash receptacle. It tipped and spilled plastic bags onto the pavement.

Jarrod sped away, never seeing Catherine staring at him from the upstairs window or the open bag of trash with the revealing contents of Catherine's four pregnancy tests.

Elizabeth's call was only the first. The phone started ringing and didn't stop. Jarrod was already gone. Catherine hadn't realized how many phones they had. They rang in the bedroom, in the den, the fax phone, the one in her office upstairs.

The first call was from her mother.

"Catherine, is this true?"

"The newspaper story?" She didn't need to confirm her mother's question, but she did anyway.

"Of course the newspaper report. Did you and Jarrod really marry as a way to keep me from hounding you?"

"Mom, the newspaper is exaggerating." She could hear the hurt in her mother's voice. She'd never intended to hurt anyone, especially the people she loved. The phone started to beep, alerting her that there was another call coming in. "Mom, please hold on a moment." Depressing the switch hook, she took the next call.

"Catherine," Audrey said, her voice already higher than normal.

"Audrey, I'll have to call you back. Mom is on the other line." Catherine didn't give Audrey time to say anything. She pressed the button to go back to her mother.

"I'm back," she told her.

"Then it isn't true?" There was hope in her mother's voice.

"Newspapers never tell the whole truth."

"Which part of it isn't true?"

Catherine sighed. "I haven't read it all yet," she hedged. She had read most of the half-page article. In newspaper terms that was an inordinate amount of space.

The beeping started again. She ignored it.

"If you weren't in love with Jarrod, there was no reason for you to feel you needed to marry anyone."

She said *anyone* as if Catherine had pulled the first man she saw off the street.

"It wasn't like that, Mom."

"Then tell me, Catherine, exactly how was it?"

"All right." She sighed again. She wished Jarrod were here. She needed someone to support her, and while this newspaper story was his doing, he was the only person who could possibly understand. The two of them had gone into this scheme together. It had been her plan, but he'd bought into it. And nothing had worked out the way she thought it would. She'd fallen in love with Jarrod. That wasn't supposed to happen. She'd fought with him, ordered him out of her house. Now he was gone and she wanted him back. And she was pregnant! She choked on the thought. She'd forgotten. How could she forget such a thing?

"We, Jarrod and I, thought we would get married for six months and then we'd get divorced."

"Why?"

She had to say this delicately. The newspaper reporter had already slanted it in the worst possible way. "We were invited to cozy dinners for four introducing us to eligible young men or women. We thought if we combined forces we could live like we wanted and no one would be hurt."

She couldn't tell her mother how that story ended up in the paper.

"Catherine—"

"Mom." They'd spoken at the same time. "Mom, I know you're upset. I love you and I would never do anything to intentionally hurt you. I just wanted to give you what you wanted."

"What I wanted? Catherine, you'd put yourself into a loveless marriage for my sake?"

It wasn't loveless, not anymore. It had never been that way.

"You and Jarrod have fought with each other since childhood. When you announced the engagement we all thought the hostility had only been hiding your true feelings."

"You were right. We don't dislike each other. We never have." *We love each other,* she finished silently.

More beeps sounded in her ear.

"Mom, I'm going to have to go. Audrey called earlier and I know she's trying to reach me."

"What do I tell everybody?"

"The truth," she said.

Audrey was trying to reach her. She went through the same conversation she'd had with her mother. Audrey was more affronted than their mother had been. She shouted at Catherine, telling her that she'd had no right to bring her into this awful mess. She'd had no right to marry for any reason other than love. She ranted on and on, and Catherine was forced to listen. She had to listen. She loved Audrey with all her faults, and this had happened because of something she had done. She owed her sister the right to chastise her. Catherine only got her off the phone by promising to come over and talk to her in person.

As soon as she hung up, Esther, Jarrod's mother, called. It wasn't even seven o'clock, and all the morning papers had been delivered. Catherine could almost see all of Newport opening to Section B of the paper and finding her photo with the huge headline exposing the truth. It would blow over in a few days, she told herself, but her family would be hurt for much longer than that.

"Jarrod isn't here."

"Is he at work?"

"I don't know. He left a few minutes ago." He'd walked out without anything. After their argument he'd left, wearing only the jeans and shirt he had on. He'd taken the jacket Robert had dropped near the front door when he and Elizabeth brought him home last night, but he had no shoes and no socks. She was worried that his feet would get cold.

"He didn't say where he was going?"

"He was angry," Catherine admitted.

"Over the newspaper article?"

"That too," Catherine said. "We had a fight."

"Catherine, what were you two thinking? Didn't you know this kind of thing would never work? That you could never keep it quiet?"

She thought they could. Only three people really knew about it. It was only happenstance that Jarrod went to a bar and sat down next to a reporter. The odds of that happening in Newport had to be astronomical.

"We thought it would help us and no one else would be affected." Catherine didn't want to go through the same conversation she'd just had with her mother, but there was no getting Mrs. Greene off the phone. Her voice didn't hurt her as much as her own mother's, but it still dug into her. She repeated several times that Catherine and Jarrod never should have married. Catherine understood. She could only agree with her. Mrs. Greene said nothing that Catherine hadn't already said to herself. And the beeping in her ear continued.

When she finally hung up Catherine decided she wouldn't answer any more phone calls. She instructed Jenny to tell everyone she was unavailable and unplugged the phone in the bedroom.

Catherine was tempted to crawl back into bed and remain there for the rest of the day. It was the cowardly thing to do, and she was a coward. She hadn't stood up to her family and their constant chorus of marriage songs. Then, when she thought of a solution, it was not of the love, honor and cherish variety. She couldn't get into bed. She had to make sure her face was seen everywhere until this died down. She went into the closet and looked for something to wear to work. She wouldn't explain herself to every acquaintance or stranger who stopped her on the street, but she was a target. There was no getting around that.

She chose the scarlet dress. She'd be easy to spot in it, especially for the people looking to point darts at her. This was as close as she could come to a bull's-eye.

It was the longest day in recorded history. Her office was a revolving door of curiosity seekers. Her phone calls were more from reporters or friends who wanted to confirm the story than from those with business interests. Catherine fielded them all. She only asked the secretaries to screen out the reporters. She took every other call. At lunch a contingent of reporters and photographers followed her to the restaurant where she ate and back. She refused to comment on anything they said.

Elizabeth and Robert showed up together after she returned.

"How's it going?" Elizabeth asked.

"Can't you tell?" Catherine sat back in her chair. "Didn't you just fight the lions to get in here? And what are you two doing here?"

"I went looking for Jarrod. I can't find him," Robert told her.

"We had a fight," Catherine admitted. "He left." She stood up, rubbing her arms as if she were cold. "He had no shoes," she said. "He just left, wearing only what he had on."

Elizabeth came to her and hugged her. "Is there anything I can do to help?"

Catherine shook her head. "Only if you can turn the clock back to July and erase all this."

"It's been bad." Elizabeth stated the obvious.

"Nothing I can't handle."

"You look tired," Elizabeth said.

She *was* tired. She hadn't slept well in days, since Elizabeth's party, when Jarrod had left her. Last night she'd been up until two, when they brought Jarrod home, and the phone had waken her at six this morning.

"Why don't you pack it in for today?" Robert said. "We'll drive you home."

Catherine shook her head. "This will be over in a few days, but until then I can't let it seem as if I'm hiding."

"Business as usual is a lot of garbage," Elizabeth told her. "You're not getting anything done here. You're only answering phone calls."

"If I don't answer, people will just keep calling, and what they can't find out, they'll make up."

"They're going to make it up anyway," Robert said. "You've never been one to care."

"I care about my family. I hurt them terribly. That article makes it seem as if my mother and Audrey are monsters." Catherine felt anger rise in her like a giant animal. She wanted to scream, but she pulled back, forced herself to relax. She returned to her chair and sat down. "Where did you look for Jarrod?" she asked Robert.

"I tried his office and a few places we used to frequent."

"Bars?"

"You know Jarrod isn't a drinker. He probably only had a couple of drinks last night."

"He smelled like a still."

"I went to George's. He hasn't been there. I looked at the wall."

"What wall?"

"The one by the sea. He goes there sometimes." Catherine remembered the morning he'd found her there. Was it the same place, she wondered, the place where they had made love on the grass in the rain? "I drove all around town to places I thought he might be, but I haven't found him."

Catherine got up and walked around the office. She stopped at the window overlooking the marina. "I told him to get out. This was all his fault. He'd promised me he wouldn't tell anyone and he talked to a reporter. He didn't take any clothes." Tears ran down her face. "He left with . . . no shoes." Her voice cracked.

Catherine sat down across from Elizabeth.

Elizabeth leaned forward in her chair. "That means he'll be back, Catherine." She said it softly, as if strong words would cause her to shatter. Catherine felt as if they might. She was wound tight. Lack of sleep, the inability to eat, people shouting questions at her and Jarrod missing left her on edge.

Robert took her hand and pulled her out of the chair. "Put this on," he said. It was her coat. She didn't argue. She slipped her arms into it. "You're going home."

Outside the reporters waited for them. Robert suggested she take the side door that led from the warehouse and go through the locked fence. He and Elizabeth went the way they had come and drove away without much interference. They picked Catherine up at the end of the small alley. Catherine actually smiled at eluding them. She didn't know how long it would be before they found out she was gone.

Instead of taking her home Robert drove to Elizabeth's. Her house sat behind gates that closed electronically. They went inside and the gates slid together like an interlocking fortress. The moment she was inside she called the Ocean Drive house to leave word with Jenny in case Jarrod returned.

"I won't hide in here," Catherine stated when Robert and Elizabeth tried to get her to take a nap and made references to a tray in bed.

"You're not hiding," Elizabeth said.

"I'm going out to dinner. Out in public, where all the wagging tongues are."

"You haven't had enough for one day?" Robert asked.

"When did you two become a couple?" Catherine asked.

"We're not a couple," Elizabeth said before Robert could answer. "And don't change the subject. Why do you want to subject yourself to that?"

"Elizabeth," Catherine said in a very soft voice, "I have to do it. If I hide, I'll have to do it from now on. If I'm lucky, this will all blow over in a couple of days, but if I hide it will never go away."

"I understand. It's just that there are so many vicious people out there. I don't want to see you hurt."

"They can't hurt me," she said. No one could hurt her any more than Jarrod had when he left the house this morning with no clothes and nothing on his feet.

"Where do you want to eat?"

"The busiest restaurant in town."

Robert and Elizabeth both left to make the reservation. Catherine rambled through Elizabeth's closet for something to wear. Thankfully they wore the same size, and Catherine's black shoes would complement anything.

Elizabeth convinced Catherine to take a short nap. She did, but slept fitfully, with dreams of Jarrod being stabbed at by a giant fountain pen that spilled rocks instead of ink.

An hour after she woke, she was overdressed for any Tuesday night dinner in Newport. She had on red again, not scarlet this time, but fire-engine red. The top of the two-piece outfit was freckled with beads. She could be seen by everyone, and if it was fire they wanted, this evening she was a psycho-arsonist.

Catherine paused at the dining room entrance, Elizabeth and Robert on either side of her like sentinels. She glanced at them.

"This is my show," she said. "I can handle it."

She took a breath and followed the maître d', a step ahead of her guards. Heads turned, forks full of cordon bleu, Cornish hens with glazed oranges and crème de menthe truffles stopped as if stuck halfway to gapping mouths. Conversations ceased or continued in whispered conspiracy as she angled between tables. Catherine played the room as she'd never done it before. She smiled, nodded, greeted the curious, the gawking and the uninformed. She made eye contact with everyone, waved occasionally as if she were a queen greeting her subjects after a prolonged illness from which she was not expected to recover.

Their table sat in the center of the room. Catherine wondered if it had been intended this way. She took her seat, accepted the menu and ordered orange juice to drink.

A low hum started as conversation went on. Catherine looked around, knowing everyone was talking about her. If anyone had failed to read the paper that morning, they were being filled in by the self-appointed reporters in the room. She smiled whenever any of them made eye contact with her. Some smiled back, others turned their heads as if they hadn't seen her.

Mrs. Jessie Melchoir had moved to Rhode Island when her husband retired forty years earlier. She was the oldest resident of the island and it wasn't often that she left her home. Catherine spotted her with three dinner guests at a table on the other side of the room. She looked as if she were celebrating something. Her dress was fancy and she took a while to stand up. Catherine thought she might be leaving. But using her cane and with the help of a man Catherine had never seen before, she slowly crossed the dining room and came directly to where Catherine sat.

She held her breath, wondering what the old woman, who had been one of her grandmother's friends, would have to say about the newspaper story. Catherine stood as she reached her. Robert and Elizabeth rose too.

"Catherine," she said. Her voice was raspy with age, but it could still be haughty and accusing. Catherine stiffened, ready to be chastised, reduced to a child whom her grandmother was ready to punish.

Mrs. Melchoir's eyes were gray with age, but there was still something behind them. "When I was your age," she began, "we couldn't afford a telephone. Newspaper ads were expensive too. I was a follow-the-rules child. I always did what people told me to do. I would never have taken a telephone number to find a husband. If I had, I probably wouldn't have married Mr. Melchoir. He was much too proud to call a number like yours." Catherine looked at the man with her. He raised his eyebrows but said nothing. Mrs. Melchoir looked from Catherine to Elizabeth and Robert. "But I approve."

Her comment wasn't lost on the room. It seemed everyone was observing what was happening at the center table. Mrs. Melchoir took Catherine's hand. Her fingers were thin and spiny on her flesh. She patted it. "Don't let them get to you," she said and turned to return to her table.

Mrs. Melchoir started the parade. As soon as her

cane tapped its way through the tables, the ice was broken.

"I love it, I just love it." Emily Colter came over. She hugged Catherine and plopped down in the empty seat at the table for four. "I wish I'd had the nerve to do it myself. And to catch a man like Jarrod . . . I certainly would forget the temporary thing the moment the ring was on my finger."

She chatted on and on. When she left the parade continued. A steady stream of friends joined her. The chair was never empty. Someone stood by it or sat in it, making Catherine ever mindful that Jarrod was among the missing, but also letting her know that she had friends.

Robert and Elizabeth had gone to the dance floor at Catherine's insistence that she was fine alone and didn't need them to protect her.

"Hello, Catherine." No voice was more distinctive than that of Julianna Stone. She slid into the chair that was momentarily empty. "It's amazing you came tonight."

"Why is that, Julianna? Is there something special about tonight? Anyone can make a reservation here. The dining room is open to the public."

Julianna's smile was venomous. "But the story is all over town. How can you show your face? I mean, advertising for a husband on the telephone."

"Isn't it just like me, Julianna? Isn't it something I would do? I'm surprised you didn't guess. You know how much I stray from the norm."

"This is even off the mark for you, Catherine."

Catherine leaned forward so only Julianna could hear her. "It worked, Julianna. I got Jarrod and you didn't."

She pursed her lips. "And where is the telephone-to-order groom tonight?"

"I'm right here." Jarrod spoke as if his cue had been given and he'd come on stage at exactly the right moment. "And I believe you're sitting in my seat, but don't get up."

Catherine was looking up at him. He put his hands on her shoulders and bent down. He kissed her long and hard. Catherine knew the drill. She'd initiated the show-and-tell. Jarrod was acting for their audience.

Julianna eased out of the chair. "I'd better get back to my party," she said.

"How did you know we were here?" Catherine asked when he sat down next to her.

"Robert left messages all over town; with Jenny, on my cell phone, at my office, even at George's, although he should have known I wouldn't be there. How's it been here?"

"Better than a picture show," Robert chimed in. "Elizabeth and I have been watching." They both resumed their seats.

"Except for Julianna, it's been better than I expected," Catherine told him. "She's in love with you, you know."

"Julianna's in love with herself."

"I'm glad you're here," Catherine said. Jarrod's smile was like a balm. "This morning—"

"Never happened," he cut in. "Come on, let's dance. They're here for a show. Let's give it to them."

Catherine got up. The smile on her face was wide. This was one of the things parents told their children about when they asked "How did you meet Daddy, Mommy?" She knew the two of them wouldn't be doing that, but she went into his arms. He held her close and they danced around the empty floor. She relaxed in his arms, her love shining through. Catherine didn't doubt he looked at her with love. No one there, including Julianna Stone, could doubt that, no matter how they were brought together, they were in love now.

Robert and Elizabeth joined them. A moment later Ted Ward led Meredith Windsor out on the floor. With her own life falling apart, Catherine had heard rumors that Ted was seeing other women. She didn't know if he'd told Julianna that the idea had come from her. From tonight's venom she was sure that somehow Julianna knew. Ted seemed to come alive when he started dating. He was often out with different women, and he looked a lot happier.

"Catherine." Jarrod regained her attention. She looked up into his eyes. "You know I'm in love with you?"

"The entire town knows. Newport County and parts of New Hampshire, Vermont and Massachusetts know you're in love with me."

His expression was serious. "All I want to know about is you. I know you—"

Catherine put her hand over his mouth. "It's time I said it. I love you."

Jarrod stopped dancing. Couples moved about them on the floor, some staring at them. "Are you serious?"

"Absolutely."

"Do you love me as in forever?"

"Jarrod, you won't mind being tied to me for the rest of your life?"

"I'd mind if I'm not."

Catherine went up on her toes to kiss him. Jarrod suddenly moved out of range. "There's just one rule," he said.

She hesitated, waiting. "Go on."

"No rules," he said. "We take it as it comes."

She nodded. "No rules."

He kissed her then, in the middle of the dance floor, in front of their friends, strangers, the country club crowd, the whole of Newport and anyone who cared to watch. Catherine didn't care. Jarrod didn't care. They only cared about each other and their new and shining love.

"Where did you go this morning?" Catherine asked. Jarrod pulled her closer to him in the huge bed. He loved having her in his arms, and she was likely to be there for the next sixty or seventy years.

"I went to Boston and I walked."

"Without shoes?" She sounded concerned, as if he'd walked all day barefoot.

He laughed. "I bought shoes. The clerk was surprised that I wanted them there and then."

"Where did you walk?"

"All over. I looked at all the architecture. I drew pictures, took photos, trying to get you out of my mind, but it didn't work. I could see your soft lines in all the straight ones. Everywhere I looked there was your image, not the one I was supposed to see. I had to come back. I had to make you love me."

Catherine turned over. She hugged him to her. "I'm sorry. I never meant to put you—"

"Shhh," he calmed her, stopping her with his finger on her lips. "It's all in the past. From now on, we go forward."

"I need to tell you. You once asked me why I was so afraid of marriage."

He nodded.

"I was afraid of losing myself like I said, but I was also afraid of loving you." He started to speak, but she stopped him. "There were always women around you, the Juliannas of the world."

"Cathy—"

"I didn't think I had a chance. You joked with me, so I joked with you. I didn't want you to know how I really felt about you. I didn't even want myself to know, so I did everything to keep you from finding out. Only Robert guessed."

"Robert? He never mentioned it."

"Robert can keep his mouth shut when it counts." She ran her hand over his chest. "Then you came back and there you were in the middle of the harem, looking every bit as if you enjoyed it." She pinched him.

"Ouch!" He grabbed her hand.

"I wanted to leave immediately, but you stopped me. I really thought I could handle being married to you for six months, but from the beginning nothing went according to plan."

Jarrod ran his hand through her hair. He turned her face toward his. "That's because of the third person."

Catherine frowned. "What third person?"

"The one who is created when the minds meld."

He'd told her that on their honeymoon. "The process doesn't have to take place on a conscious level. Apparently we created our own matchmaker in our minds. While we fought against our fears, somewhere we knew we wanted to be married."

He kissed her. She was warm and soft and sated from hours of lovemaking, but he wanted her again.

"Speaking of going forward . . ." she said when she could breathe. "We're going to need a good architect."

"Why?"

"This house is too small."

"It's not that small." He nuzzled her neck.

"It will be in nine months."

Jarrod froze. Then he moved back, pushing himself up on his elbows. "What are you saying?"

"I'm pregnant. It happened at Stone House."

"Stone House?"

"That beautiful house in the snow when we couldn't wait to make love."

"Are you sure, Catherine? This isn't a joke, is it?"

She nodded. "I'm sure."

Jarrod kicked the covers back and started to get up.

"Where are you going?" She grabbed his arm.

"I've got to get started. We don't have much time."

She stopped him. "We can at least wait until sunlight."

Jarrod turned back to her. She rolled into his arms and kissed him.

"I'm so glad I called that number," Jarrod said against her mouth. "I love you."

"I love you too," she said. "I'm glad you came

home when you did. Although I doubt I would have found anyone else suitable to marry. It was you or no one."

"So I really am your 1–800 HUSBAND?"

"1–800 . . . 1–900 . . . 1–ALWAYS . . ."

Epilogue

Elizabeth Audrey Greene weighed in at eight pounds even at 3:47 Eastern Time on June 27. Next to Catherine and Jarrod in the same hospital, Michael Winston Stokes and his twin sister, Michele Catherine, were born to Audrey and Dwayne five hours later. Both sisters left the hospital the same day.

Jarrod drove her past the construction site of their new home, which was supposed to be completed before Thanksgiving. It sat above the cliffs, behind the stone fence on the land where they'd made love. Jarrod had chosen the place and Catherine had agreed with his decision.

At home, he carried Beth inside, but had to quickly give her up to Elizabeth and Robert, who acted like they were surrogate parents. Jenny, who was too valuable to let go after a year, stayed with them, hovering over Beth as if the child were hers.

Catherine went up the stairs, and on the center of their bed was the trademark rose. Propped against it was a note. This one broke the rules of haiku, but he'd written it in the same form. Catherine read:

> Man, Woman
> Husband, Wife, Child
> Family, Forever

This one was signed, as none of the others had been. She rubbed her fingers across the strong writing. *I love you, Jarrod.*

Tears clouded Catherine's eyes. Life would never be the same, but she would live it with Jarrod. She loved him, and nothing could change that.

Dear Reader,

Change is inevitable in our lives. Catherine Carson in HIS 1–800 WIFE had a problem with change. To keep the status quo, she conceived a foolproof plan. Like all foolproof plans, something always goes wrong. When personal relationships are involved, they rarely follow the straight and narrow. Catherine and Jarrod found the truth of this, but they worked through it so life and love survived. I hope you enjoyed your time with them.

All my characters become personal friends. I'm glad Catherine took the phone number 1–800–WIFE and that it brought her the love of her life.

I receive many letters from the women and men who read my books. Thank you for your generous comments and words of encouragement. I love reading your letters as much as I enjoy writing the books.

If you'd like to hear more about HIS 1–800 WIFE and other books I've written, or upcoming releases, please send a business-size, self-addressed, stamped envelope to me at the following address:

Shirley Hailstock
P.O. Box 513
Plainsboro, NJ 08536

You can visit my Web page at the following address:
http://www.geocities.com/shailstock.

Sincerely yours,
Shirley Hailstock